The Qualities of Love

AND

The Love Season

The Qualities of Love

AND

The Love Season

I.M. FRESSON/PEGGY LOOSEMORE JONES

WORDSWORTH EDITIONS

The paper in this book is produced from pure wood pulp, without the use of chlorine or any other substance harmful to the environment. The energy used in its production consists almost entirely of hydroelectricity and heat generated from waste materials, thereby conserving fossil fuels and contributing little to the greenhouse effect.

First published by Robert Hale Limited

This edition published 1994 by
Wordsworth Editions Limited
Cumberland House, Crib Street, Ware,
Hertfordshire SG12 9ET

ISBN 1 85326 512 8

Printed and bound in Denmark by Nørhaven

The Qualities of Love

One

The funeral was over and Freya watched as her father crossed the lawn to where she was sitting. A tall handsome man as slim as a boy. A narrow band of white in the thick brown hair marked the line of the scar running across one side of his scalp and added distinction to his strong handsome face. The Rev Robin Marsdon, Rector of St Mary's, Upton St Clare, retired army chaplain.

He sighed as he took the chair beside Freya's.

'The end of an era.'

His voice was sad and Freya said at once, ''Yes, for both of us, but so much more for you. I know Mother meant a lot to you.'

'She was my life.' He smiled, adding without any embarrassment, 'I loved her very much.' He was simply stating a fact.

'And yet—' Freya stopped abruptly and, as if he knew what she had been going to say, he said mildly, 'We shared everything else, but that couldn't be shared or told because I don't know the answers myself. It didn't spoil our relationship.'

Freya frowned. 'Could she not have helped you?'

He shook his head. 'No. She helped me with everything else but no one could help me with that.' Touching his head, he added, 'It is in here. It must be and some day, pray God, I shall remember and then the nightmare will be over.'

'Something which happened in the Falklands war, wasn't it? During the air raid when you were wounded?' Hesitating, she added tentatively, 'It's so long ago now, is it so important that you remember something that happened then?'

'Yes, it is important, that is the one thing I am sure of, that and the fact that it should never have taken place.'

'Something connected with the bomb falling?'

'Yes – it has to be. Something terrible which happened.'

'But Dad, you were found unconscious – you couldn't have known what happened after the bomb exploded.'

He shook his head helplessly. 'It was there in my mind – something horrifying I saw before I blacked out.' His voice was positive and held the anxiety which had become so much a part of him since his recovery.

Freya said gently, 'Can't you let it go? It is so long ago. Surely it can't matter now?'

'Yes – it matters.' He passed a hand across his eyes. 'I feel guilty you see. My first conscious thought was guilt. Something important I should have done. Something I should have prevented.' He sighed then lapsed into silence.

Freya had been sixteen at the time of the Falklands war and as army chaplain, her father had volunteered for service there. She remembered very clearly the news of his head wound during a daylight raid and, later, his return home, pale and swathed in bandages, depressed and silent, very different from the father she had always known. It was many weeks before he recovered physically and by that time, he had been invalided out of the army and become rector of the lovely little church in his own village of Upton St Clare.

Ever since his homecoming, he had been haunted by his loss of memory, returning again and again to the conviction that he had witnessed something which had shattered him. The feeling of guilt was always on the edge of his mind. He looked at Freya sadly. 'I pray to God that I may remember, then perhaps, there might be something which I might be able to do even now.'

Freya said quietly, 'Dad, now that you will be alone, I will come home. I can let my flat and —'

For the first time, he smiled. 'No my dear. I have to get used to being without Louise and the sooner I do it, the better, but thank you just the same. Martha is here to look after me and, as you know, I am a survivor. Please stop worrying about me. I'll be all right.'

It was a long speech and Freya knew that he would not change his mind. She hated herself for the momentary relief which flooded her mind. Although she had always loved her father, she had found it difficult to live with him because of his strict religious beliefs. She said now, 'Promise to tell me if you change your mind.'

'Yes, but it wouldn't do, you know. We are better as we are.' Suddenly he laughed. 'And as you know, I am unlikely to be alone very much.'

'All your girl-friends in the village, you mean? I didn't think you knew that they are all after you in a big way,' Freya said teasingly and again, he smiled, putting up both hands in an attitude of defence.

'Oh yes, it is all very innocent but I have to go carefully. Sometimes it is a bit irritating, but they are lonely poor dears and it puts a bit of interest in life for them.' He stood up, adding with a sigh, 'Part of my good works you might say. I'm going over to the church now for a while.'

It was, Freya thought, typical of him that he was not

in the least flattered at the attentions of so many
women. He merely regarded it as part of his job. She
touched his hand as she looked up at him. 'You don't
have any doubts in your job, do you?'

Surprised, he said at once, 'No, no doubts. I couldn't
do this job if I had doubts.'

'But, don't you find it difficult?'

He nodded. 'Yes, quite often it is difficult. Life is so
complex. It is often impossible to see the wood for the
trees.'

'And you have no doubts even then?'

He shook his head as he reached the door. 'No,
because I have to accept the fact that God's reasoning is
on a totally different scale to mine – reasoning far
beyond my comprehension.'

'It must be wonderful to be so sure.'

'You could feel the same,' he said as he opened the
door to the house, as if that state was quite easy to
achieve. But she didn't attempt to answer as he
disappeared. It was unusual for them to discuss
religion, but it had been an unusual day, and during the
weeks of her mother's illness, she had seen facets of his
character that she had not known existed; he was a
self-contained man who, except for his intense love of
Louise, could not show his feelings, yet she knew that
his affection for herself was as deep as hers for him, but
as far as religion was concerned, they seemed to have
no touching point.

She went upstairs to finish packing her mother's
clothes, a task Robin had asked her to do. As she opened
the wardrobe door, the perfume Louise had used
wafted out towards her. As she lifted and folded dresses
and jackets they brought back memories. A navy and
white outfit, hardly worn. 'Your father never liked it,'
Louise had said, stating the obvious reason why it was

scarcely worn, a reason applied to many things in Louise's life, for if Robin didn't like something, for her, if possible, it ceased to exist.

The wardrobe empty, Freya was about to close the door when she noticed a pile of letters at the back. They were all in her father's hand. One came loose and the name Victor Warren made her pause. Victor had been killed in the Falklands and he was the son of Robin's closest friend, Colonel Warren, who lived a few miles away. Freya unfolded the letter and began to read.

You remember that Victor and I arrived out here at the same time and were able to see quite a lot of each other. It was a tremendous shock when I was told that he had been killed in the same raid when I was wounded. It was a terrible blow to Philip. It troubles me greatly that I cannot remember anything of that day. I am hounded by the conviction that something terrible happened just before I blacked out. Something that I should have been able to prevent. I feel this so strongly and that it was something terribly wrong. The doctors tell me that my memory may return. I only hope that they are right because not knowing is a torment to me.

I should be leaving hospital in about a week and the thought of coming home to you darling is very comforting.

Freya returned the letter to the packet and put it back in the wardrobe.

She and Victor had known each other nearly all their lives but had not met so often after he had joined the army. His mother had died just before the war and Victor's death so soon after was a crushing blow to the Colonel. He had asked Robin after his return home for details, but he could tell him nothing for he had no memory of that fateful day and the fact that he could not comfort his friend added to his own distress.

Freya was in the hall when Robin returned from the church. He looked white and strained as he stood in the doorway and as if he was undecided where to go next.

'Dad, go into the study and I'll bring you a whisky.'

He looked at her gratefully. 'Thank you my dear, I think that is exactly what I need.'

In a few minutes, Freya carried it through, setting it on a table beside him. Giving her a rueful smile, he said, 'You know, I've always tried to comfort anyone who has lost someone they loved.' He made a gesture with one hand. 'I know now that it is impossible, useless. It can't really help. You see, we know so little of what happens after death.'

Freya said quietly, 'You and mother were very – complete.'

He smiled at her hesitation over the word. 'Yes. Thank you for understanding.' After a moment, he added, 'If you are ever lucky enough to make a marriage as good as ours, you really *will* understand.'

He picked up his glass and sipped at it, saying, 'After I came home, Louise was so wonderful, so patient with all my nightmares and struggles to remember.'

'You never *have* remembered?'

'No, but I am still convinced that I witnessed something terrible that I should have been able to stop.'

'But you were wounded yourself.'

'Yes. I can remember the horror of not being able to move or speak, then I blacked out and there was nothing. The nightmares still come but not so often and I pray that one day I *shall* remember and know my part in it and perhaps be able to put that right.'

Two

Freya stopped the car at the end of the cul-de-sac, switched off the engine and climbed out, her key in her hand ready to open the front door. There were letters on the hall floor and the flat felt hot and stuffy after being shut up for two weeks and she went round opening windows. Small as it was, she was lucky to have found it, luckier to be able to afford it, and, luckiest of all to have the tenant above her.

Jill Tanner was a very young forty with a kind heart, a strong will and a nice sense of humour. Also, a very good friend.

Freya had nearly finished unpacking when she heard her door bell and knew that it would be Jill, who said as soon as the door was open, 'Don't mess about with supper, I've got plenty upstairs and I want to hear your news. I know it must have been rotten for you and Robin.'

'Yes, pretty awful, but Dad was marvellous – holding on tight when he ought to have been letting go, but that's his way and he's not likely to change now.'

'I suppose you offered to go home to look after him.' Jill was always direct.

'Wouldn't hear of it. Said that the sooner he got used to living wihout her the better.'

'So, you're staying on here?'

11

'Yes, but I must try to go down there more often.'

Over drinks upstairs in Jill's attractive sitting-room, they talked of all that had happened during the last weeks of Louise's life and Freya felt herself gradually relaxing, suddenly realizing that her father had not been the only one to hold on tight. Settling more comfortably in her chair, she asked, 'Now tell me what's been going on in the shop?'

'The little walnut desk has gone – to a delightful American who I'm sure will appreciate it. A very attractive man too.'

'A-ah.'

'What does that mean?' Jill asked innocently.

'Did he ask you out to dinner?'

Jill nodded, smiling. 'I went too.'

Freya looked at the woman sitting opposite her, thinking, as she usually did, how attractive she was with her deep chestnut hair curling neatly round her ears and the clear creamy skin to go with it. By no means classically beautiful, but with deeply set grey eyes and a mouth that smiled warmly Jill managed to come near to that description. Largely because she was so vividly alive.

'And, are you meeting again?'

'Possibly, but I'm not off to America if that's what you have in mind.'

'No. Don't you dare. What would I do without you within shouting distance?'

'You'd manage,' Jill said drily. 'Come on, let's eat, it's all ready.'

The dinner, like all Jill's dinners, was delicious and Freya appreciated the thoughtfulness of the invitation which had saved her from a lonely evening on her return home.

'Is Robin still chasing his memory?' Jill asked as she

made the coffee.

'Yes, as much as ever I'm afraid. It troubles him greatly, but I'm afraid that after so long, it won't return now.'

'Unless something out of the blue suddenly triggers it off.'

Freya shook her head. 'Pretty unlikely now I think. He would be a much happier man if it did happen. He has this fixed idea that he could have stopped something dreadful which happened. He says he feels guilty.'

'Poor man. How he must have suffered and whatever happened couldn't have been his fault.'

'No, but Dad's an idealist. There are no ifs and buts for him. Everything must be mentally tidy, like his own religion.'

Jill gave her a sharp glance. 'And, you don't feel the same way?'

Freya smiled. 'Oh no, he always regards my ideas as too much of a simplification. I remember one time when I was about eight, when I'd been walking on the Downs on a lovely day, I tried to tell him how I'd felt when I listened to a lark singing above me. I told him it had made me feel near to God.' Freya made an impatient gesture. 'He said quite kindly, "My dear, that's only just a childish idea". He didn't remotely understand what I was talking about.'

'No. He wouldn't. He needs the trappings of religion for his own beliefs.' Jill looked at Freya with affection. 'But you – I daresay that you still feel the same way today?'

Freya nodded. 'As a matter of fact, I do.'

'Your father's a really good man though.'

She offered the remark a trifle tentatively but Freya said at once, 'Oh yes, of course, I know that. He needs a formal approach – I don't.' She sat up straighter. 'I wish I could do more for him, understand him better. I know that he feels lost without mother and he worries so much about this memory thing.'

'I know that you are deeply fond of him, but you can't change either of those things for him.'

They sat silently for a short while, then Jill said with a complete change of subject, 'I've a few people coming for drinks on Saturday, will you come? I might want to borrow some glasses, if I may.'

'Yes, of course you may, and yes, I'd love to come. Anyone I know?'

'Oh yes, certainly, but I want you to meet my American who is bringing a friend who probably won't know anyone, so I can do with some help in that direction.'

On Saturday, Freya, discreetly spraying Opium on her wrists, looked at her reflection in the mirror. Her thick dark hair waved naturally and she wore it short. She had never considered herself pretty but knew that the widely set deep blue eyes inherited from her father were her best feature. For the rest, she thought her forehead too high, her nose too short and her mouth a trifle too wide. She smiled into the mirror as she summed up what she saw. At least she had good colouring which was natural and on balance, she allowed that the whole was quite attractive set off by the simple white wool dress she was wearing.

Upstairs, the party had already begun. The front door was ajar and Freya walked in, her gaze moving quickly round the room containing about eight guests. She knew everyone except for two men who had apparently just arrived. Jill beckoned her over to introduce her saying, 'This is Charles Bramber who is over from Cape Cod and this is Hazard who has just flown in from

Denmark.' Smiling at the two men she said, 'And this is Freya Marsdon who will show you where the drinks are, and please help yourselves while I greet some new arrivals.'

Leading them to the drinks table, the taller man said, 'First – what will you drink?' For a moment, she could not remember who was which but since he had no accent, she concluded that he must be the Englishman with the unlikely name. She settled for a gin and tonic, then turned to the American, asked him if he was pleased with his walnut desk.

'Oh, you know about that – yes, I am delighted with it. She has some lovely things in that shop of hers.'

They stood chatting and unobtrusively Freya studied the two men. Charles Bramber, the older by a few years, was powerfully built with light brown hair brushed straight back from a pleasantly handsome face with dark brown eyes and a humorous mouth. Hazard Denning, tall and rather elegant, craggy features adding a look of strength to a face boasting very green eyes topped by black hair with a deep kink in it.

Jill came back, whirling away again with the American to introduce him around, leaving Freya with Hazard Denning, indicating that she was to do the same for him. As she moved, he put his hand on her arm. 'Let's talk a bit first – do you mind?'

She shook her head with a smile. 'Not at all, but that's sure to lead to the inevitable question.'

He raised dark brows. 'The question being "what do you do?" ' She nodded and he said, 'It always amazes me why people want to know almost before you've met.' Looking across the room, he said with some amusement, 'Charles appears to have gone overboard for your friend Jill.' Following his gaze, Freya saw that the American had managed to corner Jill, his full attention on her, exclusive of anyone else.

'They've only just met,'' she pointed out mildly. 'Or is he always so easily smitten?'

'No. Far from it. His marriage broke down two years ago, and he has been very wary since.'

'Have you known each other long?'

'Since his first novel. It was an instant success here and I went over to America to interview him.'

'So – you are …?'

He smiled. 'Yes – we've come to the crunch question. I'm a freelance journalist.'

'So – I suppose you have to be pretty tough,' she said laughingly and saw his thin mouth tighten and the green eyes narrow as he said shortly, 'That's the general opinion I believe.'

Surprised, Freya said quickly, 'I'm sorry if I hit a sensitive spot. It was only a silly joke.'

He looked down at her then, saying abruptly, 'I've never seen navy-blue eyes before.' Adding before she could speak, 'Will you have dinner with me?'

'Thank you – yes, I'd like that, but I'll want to help Jill clear up after this is over.'

'Yes, of course – I can help too.' He said it as an old friend might have done and suddenly, they seemed to be on a different wavelength.

Freya said, 'Come on – I've not introduced you to anyone yet.'

Grinning at her he said, 'I can't say I've felt the necessity up to now.'

Three

Charles Bramber also stayed after the other guests had left and it was clear to Freya that Jill too, was being taken out to dinner, though neither man suggested making a foursome.

'What is Charles like?' Freya asked Hazard when they were in his car.

'Difficult to interview,' he answered, 'largely because he is a private sort of chap, I think, and perhaps because he is not yet over his marriage breaking up – a trifle on the defensive. I'd think that your friend Jill might be very good for him.'

'As long as she doesn't get hurt in the process.'

'I'd imagine she is well able to look after herself.'

'That sounds like the reporter speaking.'

He gave her a sharp glance. 'You seem to have rather a jaundiced view of journalists and reporters.'

Freya hesitated before saying quietly, 'All I mean is that you must have to be fairly tough to do the job.'

She heard him sigh before saying, 'Yes, perhaps, but it's not always easy to be as tough as one should be.' Then, abruptly changing the subject, he asked, 'What's your job?'

'I'm a photographer in an agency – botanical subjects.'

'Isn't that rather limiting, photographically I mean?'

'No, it's most interesting and it means travelling about quite a bit which I like and the difficulty of being able to photograph some of the subjects is also a challenge and part of the attraction for me.'

The car slowed, turning in through tall iron gates and continued up a long twisting drive until a lovely stone-built house came into view.

'Where are we?'

'On the borders of Surrey and Sussex. The house is called Huntley House and used to belong to my uncle. When he died recently, it was sold and is run as a small hotel with a very good restaurant.'

They chose a table overlooking the small lake and lovely garden which was full of colour.

'What a peaceful spot,' Freya said as she sat down. Smiling, Hazard said, 'I thought you might prefer this atmosphere to London. I know you've been going through a bad time.'

'Yes, worse for my father though because he and my mother were devoted.'

'Is he retired?'

'No. He became rector of our village church after he left the army.' She paused, then added, 'He was invalided out after being badly wounded.'

'Did he make a complete recovery?'

'Physically, except that he is slightly lame, but he has lost his memory of what happened that day and is haunted by the idea that he saw something terrible he should have been able to stop.'

She was very conscious of the green eyes watching her across the table as he asked quietly, 'Do you know what sort of thing he means?'

She shook her head. 'No, he can tell us so little about it but he is convinced that it happened just before he blacked out.'

The intenseness of the green stare was making her uncomfortable and, as if becoming conscious of it, Hazard leaned forward to pour more wine into her glass.

'Is there any chance of your father's memory returning?'

'The doctors are still hopeful. They say that it is possible that something may trigger it off, but it is so long now.'

A waiter brought their first course and the subject was not renewed.

She found that Hazard was easy to talk to. He seemed to have travelled half round the world and had an interesting way of describing his experiences, making many of them sound amusing. Freya found it pleasantly surprising to find him genuinely interested in her own work. He asked intelligent questions about what cameras she used and the types of assignment she specialized in. The dinner was delicious and it turned into a very relaxed evening. It was the first time she had really enjoyed being taken out to dinner since her mother's illness and she appreciated his thoughtful choice, which she found a little surprising. On the drive back, he told her that he was flying to Ireland the next day to do a piece on a young man who had just written his second successful novel.

'Do you only do that kind of interview?'

'No. I work freelance and my interests are pretty wide, but it's the sort of assignment I enjoy.'

'Do you find any of your work exciting – or sad?'

He negotiated a corner before replying. 'Sometimes, yes – both those things, but mostly it's rather run-of-the-mill stuff.'

'Do you ever find yourself becoming involved in any of it, or do you never allow it to become personal?'

In the light of a passing car, Freya saw the thin mouth tighten and his frown. 'Not often. Hardly ever in fact. You wouldn't last long if you allowed everything to get to you.' His voice had hardened and she felt that she had asked a silly question, that somehow, it had spoiled the flavour of the evening, and she was almost relieved to find that they were nearly home.

He stopped in front of the house and switched off the engine. As he came round to open her door, she asked a trifle tentatively, 'How about a cup of coffee?'

'No thanks, coffee late at night keeps me awake.'

For some reason, that amused her and she laughed and he looked at her sharply. 'Why is that funny?'

For a moment she didn't answer, then, as he continued to stare, she said, 'I don't really know – something to do with you being too sophisticated to be affected by something like that I think.' She suddenly felt herself floundering and feeling stupid.

'Doesn't go with your idea of a tough guy you mean.' He took the key from her hand and opened the blue front door with a flourish and she received the distinct impression that the absurd episode had hurt him. Handing her the key, he said, 'Thank you for coming. It's been a good evening. I've an early plane to catch so I'll say good night now.'

Suddenly formal, he turned towards the car. Thanking him again, Freya wished him a good flight and the next moment, he was in the car and away. She stood for a few seconds watching the tail light disappear, feeling disappointed that an otherwise pleasant evening had ended in a rather stupid way. He was, she thought, undoubtedly a rather prickly young man, unduly sensitive about unimportant things. She was annoyed that such a small disagreement with a stranger bothered her so much.

There was no light from Jill's flat which meant that either she was not home yet, or was already in bed. Her room suddenly felt too warm and stuffy and she opened the bedroom window, leaning out and hearing the rumble of traffic. She never liked living in London and at this moment, wished herself back in the country.

She lay in bed, going over the evening in her mind. At first, he hadn't seemed like a stranger; he was easy to talk to and had paid her the compliment of showing interest in her work. She admitted to herself that she found him attractive and was aware that attraction had been mutual, yet their parting had been nearly formal. It was, she supposed, merely a one off for Hazard, merely filling in an odd evening pleasantly. She remembered that there had been no mention of a further meeting on his return from Ireland and was annoyed to find that that was a matter for regret as far as she was concerned.

Four

On Thursday evening, the phone rang. Freya was just
about to go to bed after a busy day and picked it up with
some irritation.

'Do you like picnics?'

For a second she did not recognize the voice and
when she did, was slightly annoyed at her own
pleasure.

'Some,' she answered cautiously.

'I thought we might find a nice spot in the country.'

'That shouldn't be difficult. When?'

'Saturday. I'll call for you about ten o'clock.'

She was conscious of sharp disappointment.

'I shall be in Sussex with my father.'

The silence seemed to last a long time before he said
slowly, 'I don't want to upset that, but would it be
possible to see you there?'

'How about coming to lunch on Sunday?'

'That sounds a remarkably good idea.'

She gave him the address and directions how to get
there, aware all the time of her own pleasure that he had
contacted her. She asked him how the Irish interview
had gone and he said it had been rather sticky. 'A clever
and conceited young man who obviously regards
himself as a gift to literature.'

'You didn't like him?'

'Quite definitely not.'

'Did that come through in the interview?'

A pause before he said a trifle stiffly, 'No, of course not. I hope I am more professional than that.'

'I'm sorry, I didn't mean—'

He said in a different voice, 'No – don't say that. I'm sorry. I shouldn't have jumped on you like that.'

'OK. But do try to be less prickly. Anyway, I shall look forward to Sunday.' They fixed a time and then Freya rang off.

She wondered if her father would be disappointed that she had asked a visitor for her first weekend at home. On the other hand, she thought it might be good for him to see a fresh face. Smiling, she reminded herself that he always liked to keep abreast of all her men friends. In any case, they would have Saturday together.

At the office, a client rang to say that he thought he had discovered a rare plant and would she be interested in photographing it. In spite of the fact that the location was in the Essex marshes, she decided that it should be chased. The client was knowledgable and was unlikely to have made a mistake. It would mean going to Sussex on Saturday morning instead of Friday as she had intended.

Robin was cutting roses when she arrived, handing them to her as she left the car. 'I thought you would arrange them,' he said with his lovely smile, adding, 'It's good to see you.'

She thought he looked tired and rather pale but knew enough not to tell him so. Slipping an arm through his, they entered the house together. Over glasses of sherry, they exchanged the week's news and he was amused by her description of Jill and her American. She had always been a favourite of Robin's and he was always interested in news of her. 'If he is as nice as you think, it would be good if something came of it. She always strikes me as a little lonely.'

Finishing her drink, Freya said, 'I must go and talk to Martha and tell her—' She stopped, then said, 'Dad, I thought you wouldn't mind if a man I met at her party comes to lunch tomorrow.'

For a second his eyes clouded, then he said, 'No, of course not. You must always ask anyone you want – it's your home.'

At lunch, he said, 'Tell me about this man you've met at Jill's party. Where has he sprung from?'

'Well, first of all, he's certainly more a friend of the American, Charles Bramber, but he asked me out to dinner and that is the full extent of our acquaintance so far but he did ring up and say he would like to see me this weekend and when I told him that I would be here, he asked if it would be possible for him to come down.'

Robin smiled at her across the table. 'A fast worker, evidently. I shall be delighted to meet him. What are his interests? Shall I like him do you think?'

'He's a freelance journalist who seems to do a lot of literary interviews amongst other things. Yes – I don't see why you shouldn't get on all right.'

'I take it you've warned Martha that there will be one extra for lunch?'

'No, but I'm just about to, so I'll hear all about the visits you've had from all your girl-friends,' she said teasingly.

He shook his head and sighed. 'So kind, but I do wish they wouldn't, bless their hearts. So difficult to refuse all their invitations for tea and offers of help.'

Freya was glad to see that there was a twinkle in those clear blue eyes and she said, 'You know you love all the fuss they make over you.'

'Oh, I'm sure they mean well, but it gets a little overpowering, and that sounds very ungrateful, doesn't it?'

'Sounds like self-defence to me,' Freya said as she turned to the door.

On Sunday morning, Freya heard Hazard's car in the drive about 12.30. Robin was still over at the church but she went out to meet him and found him standing gazing up at the house. 'This is really extra special,' he said with enthusiasm as he joined her at the front door. 'I thought you said it was the rectory.'

'It was the rectory years ago but a more modern one seemed needed and when it was built, my grandfather bought this. He died soon after, but we have lived here ever since.' She led him through the hall to the garden. 'Come and have a drink. Dad will be here soon, he's still over at the church.'

Once again, she felt entirely relaxed with this man whom she had only known a short time.

'I'm looking forward to meeting your father. From what you say, he must be a wonderful man.'

'Yes, – I think so anyway. If he could only get rid of the worry about his memory, he would be so much happier. By the way, don't mention the Falklands, it only starts him being more worried.'

'Right – I'll remember.'

A few minutes later, Robin Marsdon came from the house to join them. They were sitting facing the house and saw him stop short and the colour drain from his face as he staggered briefly, then recovered. Freya was out of her chair but by the time she reached him, he seemed all right though he was still pale. 'What is it, Dad? Are you ill?'

He patted the arm she had slipped through his. 'No, no. I felt – odd for a moment. I'm all right now. Just

giddy. Don't worry. Come on, introduce me to your
friend.'

They walked arm in arm to the chairs and Freya made
him sit down before introductions were made. Hazard
rose, going to Robin's chair to shake hands. Watching
her father, Freya saw that his eyes still held a look of
confusion as he looked up at the younger man.

Hazard said, 'I'm sorry about that Sir. Is there
anything I can do for you?'

'Thank you – no. It was only momentary. I am all right
now. I suppose I can't expect to have an injury like mine
and not sustain some disadvantage sometimes.' He
touched his head lightly as he let go of Hazard's hand
and leaned back in the chair as if he were exhausted.
Freya put a glass into his hand and Hazard went to sit
down again. After a moment, Robin drank slowly, his
eyes still on Hazard. It was obvious that he was making
a tremendous effort to pull himself together as he asked
him about his work, taking a genuine interest in his
answers. Freya was still worried about him, and to give
him a chance to relax quietly, she suggested showing
Hazard the garden.

Walking beside her, Hazard asked, 'Does he often
have attacks like that?'

'No, I don't think so. Not when I am here anyway,
and I'm sure Martha would have told me if he had.'

'You're worried about him, aren't you?'

She took time to answer. 'He's had a pretty tough
time recently. He was so long in recovering from his
wound and then, soon after he was able to take up his
life again, my mother was ill and that affected him
greatly.'

For a few moments they were silent as they walked.
Suddenly she said, 'He's a difficult man to help. He
hates to be dependent on anyone.'

'It's obvious that he takes his job very seriously. Perhaps he feels that should fill all his needs.'

Freya laughed shortly. 'You've learned a bit about him already. His whole life is bound up in his religion.'

'And that makes him difficult to live with?'

He heard her sigh. 'Yes, to some extent. For me, his ideas are too narrow – too strict – too hard to live up to.'

'Does *he* live up to his own ideas?' Hazard's voice held a note of disbelief and Freya smiled as they turned and walked back to the house.

'Oh yes, indeed he does, nobody could fault him on that.'

'And you have been brought up with all those extremely difficult rules.'

'Yes, but I must have been a sore trial to him. I remember telling him I felt near God when I heard a lark singing on the Downs.' She paused to look at him. 'But perhaps *you* won't know what I'm talking about either?'

'I think I do. It's something to do with freedom and beauty.' He hesitated then added quietly, 'And God.' She nodded, suddenly feeling that this unlikely conversation had stopped them being strangers.

Freya was reluctant to leave early on Monday morning but Robin insisted that he was quite recovered.

'Do you know what caused the giddiness?'

He hesitated before answering slowly, 'No, not really. It happened so suddenly. Something seemed to hit my memory – then fade. That was when I felt giddy.' He smiled at her. 'Don't worry darling. You can see for yourself that I am all right now.'

But Freya was not sure. He seemed preoccupied and just before she left, he asked her a question which surprised her, one which seemed to give him some anxiety. 'Do you happen to know if Hazard went to the

Falklands?'

She was aware that he awaited her reply with some tenseness.

'I don't, but I should think it most unlikely. As far as I know he was never a war correspondent. Why, did you think that he might have been?'

The blue eyes still seemed a trifle confused, but he looked away, shrugging. 'I just wondered, that's all.'

That evening, Freya and Jill met for coffee in Jill's flat, each to report on the doings of the weekend.

'You first,' Freya prompted and Jill told her that she and Charles had driven into Kent to show him Ightham Mote.

'Since it was bought by an American some years ago, I thought he might be interested to see it,' she explained. 'In any case, it's a gorgeous house and I wanted to see it myself.'

'And then?'

Jill gave her a sharp glance and laughed. 'Hey – what are you getting at? I don't work at that speed. We had a leisurely dinner on the way back then sat here talking until nearly midnight. How did your weekend go?'

'I don't quite know.' Freya frowned as she spoke slowly. 'Dad was over at the church when he arrived and when he came out to the garden to join us he—' She paused, seeing again her father sway as he came through the door to the garden. 'He suddenly became giddy – as if – I don't know, but thinking about it from what he told me afterwards, it was almost as if it happened as soon as he saw Hazard sitting there. As if he had something to do with it.'

Jill shot her a sharp glance. 'Surely you must have imagined that? They had never met, had they?'

Freya shook her head. 'No, I'm sure they couldn't have done.'

'Then, why should you make that connection?'

'I didn't, not at the time. It was something Dad said just before I left this morning. He suddenly asked me if I knew if Hazard had ever been to the Falklands.'

Jill said carefully, 'That seems to me quite an ordinary thing to say under the circumstances.'

'Under the circumstances?' Freya looked puzzled.

'Yes, you know that he is always looking for something which will stir his memory – always hoping that what the doctors said about something triggering it off will take place.'

Freya looked relieved. 'Then you don't think that it could have been anything to do with seeing Hazard?'

Jill said a trifle impatiently, 'How could it be when they have never met?'

'No, I am certain that they can't have done. Even if Dad did not remember, Hazard would have done, and he obviously didn't.'

'Then, put the idea out of your mind. That head wound of his is quite enough to cause an occasional giddy fit. I don't think there is anything new there to worry about.'

Freya stood up ready to leave as Jill continued, 'It's natural that you worry about him since Louise died, but you can't change that, and you know that Martha looks after him very well indeed and she would let you know at once if he were ill.' She put her arm on Freya's shoulder as they stood together. 'No my dear, stop worrying and enjoy your new friendship. You can't undo what happened to Robin in the war. By all accounts, he was lucky to come through it as well as he has.'

Freya looked at her gratefully. 'You are a great comfort Jill. You are always so sane.'

Five

Getting to know Hazard was an entirely new experience for Freya. He was very different from any man she had met. She knew that he found her attractive, yet he made no attempt to kiss her. She was beginning to realize that he was a difficult man to know. A sensitive man who could not show his feelings easily; a man who felt strongly about anything in which he believed. In many ways, an idealist. She thought that it was this tendency which so often made him intolerant. He had strong opinions about things which mattered to him and it was impossible to shift his reasoning once he had made up his mind. The range of subjects on which they talked and argued over was wide but there was always a point she couldn't get beyond, when he would suddenly clam up and abruptly change the subject as if he didn't want to be asked any further questions. Freya asked him once what made him do this and at first, he wouldn't answer, then he said harshly, 'Something which happened in the past. I don't want to think about it.'

By the beginning of October, they were meeting regularly, often ending up in Freya's flat where she would cook a meal, afterwards sitting and talking until late before he finally left. Freya knew without any doubt that she was falling in love and made no effort to stop it happening, though she was not sure what this very self-contained man really felt about her, though the expression in those very green eyes led her to think that he felt the same way as herself. It was almost as if he was holding himself back deliberately, not allowing any further commitment. Then, one evening when he had seemed on edge, after a silence, he said suddenly, 'It's no use. I can't go on like this.'

Surprised, she asked what he meant.

Without looking at her, he said, 'You must know that I am in love with you.'

She said gently, 'How *should* I know?'

'I should have thought that it was obvious.'

Freya had just brought in the coffee tray and put it on the table before she answered quietly, 'Not obvious to me.'

He was standing by the window and now turned to face her and the expression on his face almost frightened her as he said angrily, 'I didn't want to get involved. I swore I wouldn't.'

She stood silently. He had gone beyond her. What he said made no sense.

He raised both hands in a helpless gesture. 'I was so determined not to fall in love with you. Like a fool, I thought we could go on meeting and it would remain just friendship.'

He came to her, putting his hands on her shoulders and the anger was no longer there as he continued more quietly, 'But, I can't. I love you too much. Surely that can't be so wrong?'

Freya looked into that troubled face and smiled at him. 'Why should it be wrong? I love you too. We could be happy.'

Suddenly he was pulling her close, kissing her hard and long; then, as if suddenly coming to his senses, he freed her, saying ruefully, 'I never meant that to happen.'

'Why shouldn't you kiss me? You say that you love me.' She felt confused at his strange behaviour.

'I do love you. That's the trouble. I thought I'd got everything under control but—' He put out a finger to stroke her cheek. 'But you are so lovely. Everything I want.'

The words were so very much what she needed to hear, but not in this way, not under these present confused circumstances when she didn't understand what was happening. In an effort to bring things back to normal, she went to pour the coffee into two cups, handing one to Hazard. He took it without comment.

Freya said, 'I don't understand. What has happened to make you so worried? What is wrong?'

He put the cup on the table and his voice was less strained as he looked at her. 'I'm sorry. This shouldn't have been like this. I didn't mean it to be. It was something that happened years ago.' He stopped, frowning. 'Something which changed everything for me. Perhaps all this time I've been wrong in letting it matter so much.'

'Won't you tell me about it?'

For a moment, he seemed undecided, then moved sharply saying, 'No. I can't. It's too – complicated. It's the last thing I want to do.'

Freya said gently, 'Isn't sharing part of loving?'

That went into silence until he said with some bitterness, 'Yes, perhaps, for anything normal, but not for this.'

Freya was annoyed to find herself becoming impatient. 'But I can't help you if you won't tell me.'

'You *can't* help me anyway. Nobody can.' The bitterness was still there in his voice and she was conscious of pity for him. He was so obviously distressed, so obviously unable to deal with the problem which had haunted him for so long. She wondered how it could still loom so large, how it could affect them both. She asked him, and he answered slowly, 'It's bound to. It affects everything I think or do. It is always there in my mind.' He ran his fingers through his hair distractedly. 'I want to marry you but—' he stopped and his eyes held a hopeless expression as he looked at her.

'But what? I told you that I loved you. Isn't that enough?'

He said with great seriousness, 'Is it fair to marry you with this between us?'

'If I am willing to marry you – yes – it is fair. I trust you.'

For the first time, he smiled. 'If you trust me that much, you must really love me.' He came to her, putting his arms closely round her. 'Darling, thank you for that. Do you really mean that?'

Against his chest she said firmly, 'Oh yes, I really mean it.'

He lifted her chin, kissing her gently, 'Then, will you please marry me?'

'Yes.' The word was spoken clearly knowing that he needed her reply to contain no doubt. She heard him sigh as he let her go and to ease the moment, Freya became businesslike. 'We'll have to tell Dad,' she told him.

'Yes, of course.' Then, as if it had just occurred to him, 'What do you think he will feel about it?'

It was an aspect that Freya had been pushing to the back of her mind but she said a trifle doubtfully, 'I don't really know. He always wants me to be happy.'

'How will he like it when I take you away from him?'

'Normally, he is used to me only being there at weekends, but now that he is without mother, he is bound to be more lonely.'

Hazard said more cheerfully, 'Then we must do all we can about that. Do you think he liked me?' He paused, frowning. 'You know, I wondered.'

She said at once, 'Why yes, of course. Why should he not like you?'

But she had herself, wondered the same thing. It had been such a strange day, and she had thought there had been reservations in her father's manner. She had noticed him watching Hazard when he had thought himself unobserved. Quickly, she dismissed it from her mind and for the next hour, they talked of possible future plans for themselves.

Six

They drove down to Upton St Clare in Hazard's car the next weekend on the first really cold day of autumn. A blustery wind wrenched the leaves from the trees and rain plastered the windscreen. It was a depressing day on which to bring their news and Freya suddenly realized that she was not looking forward to telling her father about their engagement. She felt an element of guilt that it should have happened so soon after her mother's death.

By the time they ran from the car to the porch, Robin had the front door open and Freya thought that he looked better than the last time she had seen him.

'What a ghastly day you've brought with you,' he said, slipping his arm through Freya's as he led them through the hall. 'I've got the fire going, come in and get warm and have a drink.'

All three stood round the blazing logs with glasses in their hands exchanging news and it was not until the first silence that Freya said quietly, 'Dad, Hazard and I are engaged.'

'Oh – no.'

She had been uncertain what her father's reaction would be, but she had not expected anything quite so definite. His manner too, was different from anything she had imagined. He stood staring at Hazard and she

saw the colour drain from his face and it seemed an age
before he moved; then, putting a hand to his head she
heard him draw a deep breath. The next moment, he
seemed to recover, putting out a hand to her and
managed to smile.

'My dear, I'm sorry. It was a bit of a shock. I wasn't
expecting anything like that.' He looked from one to the
other, saying vaguely, 'Then I must congratulate you
both.' Adding, 'It's so sudden you see.'

It was obvious that he was making a terrific effort to
pull himself together and appear normal and she felt
embarrassed for all of them. What she had hoped would
be a happy moment was filled with confusion.

Hazard asked quietly, 'Are you all right? Won't you
sit down?'

Robin turned to look at him and after a moment,
shook his head in a bewildered way, then as if he had
just heard what Hazard had said, smiled at them both.
'Yes – a good idea. Let's *all* sit down.'

Hazard said, 'I am sorry it has been such a shock to
you, but we wanted you to know as soon as possible. I
know it is a bit sudden, but – well – it just happened that
way.'

Taking a sip of his drink Robin said, 'Are you both
certain? Really sure?'

'I know that I am. I love Freya very much.' Hazard's
voice was firm as he looked across at her and his
expression left no doubt of his feelings.

Robin turned to his daughter. 'And you, are you as
sure as Hazard seems to be? Really sure, I mean?'

'Yes Dad. I am very sure.'

'Have you made any plans?'

'We want to be married soon.' That was Freya and her
father looked suddenly anxious, saying quickly, 'Oh no.
Not too soon – wait a while. It is so important.'

Watching him nervously, Freya saw confusion in those blue eyes which were always so expressive. She said, 'But Dad, we are both absolutely certain. There is no need to wait.'

Her words seemed to agitate him and he said sharply, 'But you *must* wait. Please don't fix anything yet. Please listen to me.'

He appeared so upset that she decided to go along with him for the moment. She herself was worried at the rather odd scene which was taking place. At that moment, Martha opened the door to tell them that lunch was ready, and the fact that she had to be told about the engagement eased the tension in the room.

At lunch they talked of local interests and people and deliberately Freya kept the subject going, her aim to give her father time to relax, but he was still tense as they left the table and she noticed that his eyes constantly turned to Hazard as if they were closely studying the younger man and she could see that Hazard was very aware of his close scrutiny. Altogether, it had been an uncomfortable meal and she was relieved when it was over and they returned to the drawing-room. She noticed too, that her father's hand was unsteady as he took a coffee cup from her and suddenly she remembered the giddy attack he had suffered the first time she had brought Hazard home. His head wound had caused headaches, but these had been lessening during the last two years and there had been no giddy attacks.

Rain still lashed against the window and Robin was telling Hazard that a large tree in the orchard had blown down. Freya sat quietly listening, still anxious that he had been so upset, searching in her mind for a reason, trying to reassure herself that it was merely the abruptness of their news. Perhaps she should have been more careful. Yet, his reaction had been entirely out of character. His insistence that they should wait had an urgency beyond anything normal under the circum- stances. She wondered why he felt so strongly and felt definitely that it had some connection with Hazard, though how, she had no notion. She was certain that he liked him, so it could not be that. Perhaps he thought that Hazard could not afford to marry yet, but that did not account for the note of urgency in his voice when he had begged them to wait. For no reason that she knew, Freya suddenly felt frightened, though she did not know why. Everything today had turned out differently from what she had imagined, but surely, that did not constitute a reason for fear?

The voices of the two men ceased, and Freya became conscious of the fact and pulled herself back to the present as her father stood up and looked at his watch. 'I promised Mrs Denton that I'd go over to the church to see her flower arrangements. Do either of you feel like braving the weather and coming with me? She does them so well and it means so much to her.'

It was very dark in the church and Robin switched on lights as they entered. The flowers freshly arranged that day delicately scented the air and the bright colours of the blooms glowed against the grey stone. Freya had known this lovely old church all her life and was always very aware of the sense of peace it held. She also knew how much it meant to her father and she watched him now as he walked down the main aisle to the altar to stand quietly with his hands folded in front of him, looking, she thought, in that moment, fulfilled, the strong handsome face peaceful. She had seen him look like that many times in this church and had envied the unquestioning faith which brought that expression to his face.

They all examined the lovely flower arrangements which Mrs Denton had created, then as they prepared to leave, Robin said, 'I think I'll stay for a while.'

'Dad, it's cold in here. Don't stay too long.'

'No, I won't. I'll be home in half an hour.'

Hazard held an umbrella over Freya as they hurried back to the house and neither of them spoke until they were once more standing in front of the fire. Freya threw on another log and they stood watching it blaze up.

'What do you think?' Hazard's voice held a note of anxiety and when Freya didn't answer at once, added, 'What did he mean when he said that we must wait?'

'I don't know. Perhaps it is just too sudden. Perhaps he needs more time to get used to the idea.'

He looked at her searchingly. 'You don't really believe that, do you?' He paused, frowning. 'It was something more than that which made him so—' He hesitated before ending thoughtfully, 'Made him so definite, so agitated.'

'I know, but I can't think of anything to make him feel like this. I am sure that he likes you, so it's not that.'

There seemed nothing else they could say and he pulled her down on to the settee, holding her close, stroking her hair as if she needed comforting. The only light in the darkened room was the glow of the logs and it was the way Robin found them when he opened the door abruptly, snapping on the light as he strode into the room, walking across to where they were sitting, stopping in front of Hazard.

'There is something which I must ask you.' He spoke harshly, almost on a note of panic. 'Did you go out to the Falklands during the war?'

The crackling of the logs sounded very loud in the long silence which followed. Hazard stood up slowly

and Freya watched both men as they faced each other.
Her heart suddenly thudded as she saw the colour drain
from Hazard's face. When he finally spoke, his voice
was very quiet.

'Yes, I was there. I was a freelance reporter.'

Freya heard her father let out a long breath before
turning away to move to the fire, one hand clutching the
edge of the mantelpiece as if he needed support. She
saw him put a hand to his head in a familiar gesture. He
looked so white that she was afraid that he might faint
and she went quickly to him, saying, 'Dad, what's the
matter? What is wrong? Come and sit down.'

She led him to the nearest chair and after a moment,
he looked up at her vaguely saying, 'I don't know. Not
yet. It is not all clear, but it is coming back – oh God—'
His voice held desperation and his eyes looked blank as
he became silent, just staring into the fire and seeming
unaware of her as she stood beside him feeling helpless,
and suddenly very afraid as she looked down at her
father, realizing what he had just said. The doctors had
been right in thinking that something might trigger off
his memory. It was something she had hoped for, but
not for it to happen like this. For it was obvious that he
was assuming that it had something to do with Hazard.
She turned slowly to look at him. He was sitting
forward, elbows on his knees, his hands covering his
face, and once again, fear flooded through her. This was
something she did not understand, something which
both men recognized though it made no sense to her.
Robin's face still held that blank expression, he still
didn't seem to recognize where he was. She looked
across to where Hazard still sat silently, his hands
covering his eyes.

Suddenly Robin shook his head, as if he were waking
from a nightmare then, staring down at his hands, he

said quietly, 'It's becoming clearer. I think I know now most of what happened.'

Freya was watching Hazard as he took his hands from his face. He was staring at Robin with desperation in his eyes as he waited for what he would say next, but it was a long time before Robin spoke again and what he said then as he met the younger man's eyes shattered him. 'I am sorry Hazard, but you cannot marry my daughter.'

Seven

Although the words were spoken so quietly, they seemed to fill the room as Freya continued to watch Hazard, having no idea how he would react to this situation. This whole scene did not seem real. It was almost as if none of this concerned her but was happening to someone else, that what her father had said could have no connection with her own life. Speaking only to Hazard, Robin made a statement. 'You had a row earlier that day. In the bar.' He was speaking slowly as if he were trying to make it clear to himself as well as to Hazard.

To Freya, it made no sense and she saw Hazard frown, as if he too, did not understand, but he remained silent, as if he were waiting for something further.

Abruptly, Robin stood, going to stand in front of Hazard. 'Are you going to tell me that I am wrong, that I have made a mistake and it didn't happen like that?' His voice was strong, his eyes accusing.

After a moment's hesitation, Hazard answered. 'No.' Just one condemning word. Freya saw the expression of relief which crossed her father's face and suddenly understood what he must be going through, recalling bit by bit the appalling trauma of what he had witnessed and heard during a terrifying raid which had robbed him of his memory. He certainly must be afraid to trust the accuracy of what he was recollecting now. Why did a row in a bar between two men loom so large in his mind that it had caused him such distress? What possible connection could this have to her marriage to Hazard?

Still looking at her father, she said, 'How can that matter now? After all this time, how can something like that be important now?'

Robin transferred his gaze to his daughter and she saw his eyes suddenly cloud over with uncertainty. She heard him sigh as he put a hand to his head, as if he were suddenly bewildered. 'I heard them,' he insisted.

'But Dad, it can't matter now.' She heard the note of anxiety in her own voice, the near panic, and wondered at her conviction that she must stop him before he said any more.

It was Hazard who broke the silence and there was desperation in his voice. 'What happened? Do you remember what happened?'

Robin moved his hands in a weary gesture as he said slowly, 'I don't know. That's not clear like the rest, but it will come. I am certain now that it will come and—' His voice suddenly trailed off, then hardened. 'And then I shall know what to do.' There was tremendous satisfaction in the words and in that moment, Freya realized that for her father, final recognition would mean the end of the torment he had been through for so long. Looking at Hazard she saw with surprise that he too, looked more relaxed, almost as if he had been offered a reprieve.

Robin was standing holding on to the back of a chair but now, he began moving towards the door, turning as he reached it. 'I am going over to the church for a while. Don't wait for me.'

'Are you sure you're all right?'

He smiled at her then, 'Yes, darling, I am all right. Don't worry.'

He closed the door quietly behind him and neither of them moved until they heard his footsteps on the drive, then Hazard sat forward abruptly.

'Hazard?'

He didn't answer and there was pleading in her voice as she said, 'If you know, please tell me.'

He answered evasively. 'He is not clear about any of it. Surely you can see that?' She heard the note of anxiety in his voice and without meeting his eyes, she said gently, 'No. But he will. Now that he has begun to remember, and when he does – what will it mean to you?'

She hardly knew why she asked the question, she was only sure that whatever the outcome of this puzzle, it was something which would affect both herself and Hazard and their life together.

'I can't lose you now. Won't you trust me?'

She was taken by surprise by the urgency of his words.

'Oh Hazard, of course I trust you. I couldn't marry you if I didn't.' As she said the words, she heard again her father's words, "You cannot marry my daughter".

Hazard said with some bitterness, 'You heard what he said.'

She said slowly, 'Yes, I heard and I know there must be an important reason for him to say it.'

'And already you are beginning to doubt, allowing it to influence your mind.'

He sounded angry and she said quickly, 'That's absurd. You are forgetting, I don't even know what any of this is about. How can it influence me?'

He came across to her, putting his hands on her shoulders, looking down into her eyes. 'Will you still marry me – whatever he says, whatever he remembers?'

She dropped her gaze from his as he tightened his grip

on her shoulders and he spoke again before she could answer. 'I don't think so. You love your father. You would want us to marry with his blessing. You have known and loved him all your life. You have only known me a short time.' His voice sounded entirely detached.

'But Hazard, I love you.'

'I know. Or I think I do.' He almost pushed her away from him as he continued bitterly, 'What happiness do you think we should find, marrying like that?'

'But if we loved enough—' she began and he stopped her.

'No, that's not the point. I love and want you more than I've ever loved or wanted anything, but I know now that it has to be with trust and understanding – not like this.'

'Then, tell me.'

He looked at her helplessly. 'I can't. Because it affects other people. One in particular.'

His words fell into silence until the door suddenly flew open and Robin stood there, his face suffused with anger. His finger pointed, his voice shook as he said very clearly, 'You shot him. You stood there and murdered him as he lay on the ground. I saw it all, just before I blacked out!' He strode into the room to stand in front of Hazard. 'Can you deny it?'

Hazard met those angry eyes squarely as he said quietly, 'No, I can't.' There was a long pause before he added, 'But it was not like you thought.'

Eight

Hazard's words fell into a stormy silence with both men glaring at each other. For Freya, it was a moment of extreme stress, of a sensation of being trapped, her thoughts scattered as she reviewed this odd day which was not like any other she had experienced. Nothing seemed to make sense, least of all the accusation her father had just hurled at Hazard. Her mind shied away from Hazard's own bewildering words. The angry silence in the room seemed to last for ever, with neither man showing any signs of ending it. When she could bear it no longer, she said with quiet control, 'This whole thing sounds mad. Will one of you please explain?'

For a further few seconds, both pairs of eyes remained locked, then abruptly, Robin broke away, looking at her as if he were only just aware of her presence.

'Dad?'

He gave a deep sigh. 'You heard what I said to him – you heard his reply. Is that the man you want to marry? A man who on his own admission is a murderer?'

Freya said idiotically, 'There must be some mistake.'

Her father lifted a hand in a hopeless gesture. 'How can there be any mistake when he himself admits it?'

Freya turned to look at Hazard and was shocked to see an agony of indecision on that strong sensitive face.

He remained silent and it was her father who continued speaking. 'I am so sorry darling, but you must believe me. I was there. I saw it happen.'

'But Dad, I love him. It can't be true. I know that he wouldn't – *couldn't* do that.' She spoke wildly, her eyes still on Hazard's tortured face.

'I saw him,' Robin repeated, and although he spoke quietly, it was impossible to doubt both his sincerity and his sureness. After a short pause, he continued, 'How can you feel so certain of him, of your love? What can you really know of this man whom you have only met so recently? I can understand the physical attraction, he is a good-looking young man, but what can you know of his character in such a short time? Yet, you are prepared to offer him your whole life.' He shook his head. 'I can't let you do that.' His eyes were infinitely sad as he looked at her before turning to Hazard. 'I am sorry, but I think that it would be best if you left.'

Hazard had been standing so still that when he finally moved, it was as if he had suddenly come to life. For an instant, Freya had the absurd hope that he might come across the room to her, telling her that it had all been a misunderstanding due to her father's faulty memory. Instead, when he crossed the room to her it was to say with his hands on her shoulders, 'Darling, it wouldn't be any good. I wanted it so much because I love you. I hoped it would be all right but this has smashed all that. We can't marry while this nightmare threatens us – I won't let you do that. There could be no happiness for us.'

She looked up at him to see those green eyes full of sadness and, clinging to him, she asked fearfully, 'Is there nothing you can do?' Even as she asked, she knew its futility since he had admitted to Robin's accusation.

Holding her close he said to her alone, 'I don't know.

Perhaps there is, but there is something I have to do which might help. Trust me darling. I love you.' He bent quickly to kiss her then was on his way out of the room, closing the door behind him.

She heard him go up the stairs, his footsteps in the room above and in a few minutes, come down again. The front door slammed, his car started up and she heard the crunch of gravel as he drove away down the drive, and in all that time, neither she nor her father moved. She heard his deep sigh as the sound of the car died away, then he walked to the fire and threw on another log and the movement broke the long spell of silence.

'Why did you have to do it? Why couldn't you leave it alone?' She heard the note of vicious anger in her own voice. Robin gazed at her in genuine amazement and after a pause, said quietly, 'What else could I do? My memory was clear and that gave me no choice. You must surely see that.'

She said then what she had wanted to say from the beginning. 'How can you be certain that you can trust your memory? How can you be sure that what you have remembered is accurate?'

He was gazing down into the blazing logs and it was a moment before he replied. 'I thought about that,' he said carefully. 'Even the first time I saw Hazard, he seemed familiar but I couldn't think how that could be. It gave me a terrific shock when I came into the garden that day when you brought him home for the first time.' He stopped, putting a hand to his head and Freya recollected very clearly that day and its effect on him.

'I began remembering then, but only in bits, none of it very clear, but from that day, I felt that it would come back. It did, in a series of pictures in my mind and the final one was as vivid as when I actually saw it happen, just after I fell to the ground. My last conscious thought was that I should stop what was happening. I heard the shot, then I blacked out. The rest, you know.'

Looking at him, she saw that he had aged during these last hours. He looked strained and unutterably weary and for the first time that day, she understood the tremendous strain he had been under since the facts had become clear to him. Knowing him so well, she was certain that he would feel some responsibility for what had happened. There was no doubt in her mind that, had he been able, he would have made every effort to prevent what had taken place. The fact that he had been helpless had been the main cause of his worry all this time. Now, with the return of his memory, what would he feel impelled to do?

He sat now, with his head resting on the back of the chair, his eyes closed, an expression of defeat on his face. Freya felt a moment of pity before she asked, 'What do you intend to do now?'

Without moving, he said in a low voice, 'I don't know.'

Surprised, Freya said, 'I was certain that you would—'

Sitting forward abruptly, he said sharply, 'Oh, I know where my duty lies. After all, it shouldn't be difficult to decide what is right when you have witnessed a murder.' He paused, shaking his head. 'Unfortunately, it is not as simple as that in this case.'

'I would have thought that *you* would not have found it too difficult. You always see everything in black and white with never any grey areas.' For the first time, her own bitterness showed through and Robin gave her a sharp glance. 'You are very angry, aren't you?'

'Of course I am angry. How can you trust your memory now, after all you went through then?'

He said quietly, 'Why would Hazard agree unless he knew that I was right?'

That silenced her temporarily and he continued slowly, 'No man would agree on such a matter unless it were true. I am very distressed that it has happened this way for you when you are so much in love. The only thing I am grateful for is that I knew before you married him. That would have been a tragedy.'

'What will you do?' she asked again.

There was a long pause before he spoke and then his words were very simple. 'I have to have guidance. I have to pray.'

In spite of her own violent feelings, her heart went out to him as she looked into those troubled blue eyes. What he had decided on was so absolutely right for him, inevitably for a man who all his life had complete faith and no doubts whatever about his religion. Freya looked at him helplessly. 'I still can't believe that it happened that way. Dad, I know him. He is gentle and sensitive. He couldn't do such a thing.'

His eyes were full of pity as he said gently, 'My dear, it is no good you clinging to false hopes when Hazard himself does not deny anything I said.'

Nine

Freya returned to London on Sunday evening. She had been home about half an hour when Jill knocked on her door.

'How did it go? Was Robin pleased?'

Freya held the door for her to come in and Jill turned to look at her.

'Evidently not, from the look of you.'

'No. You could certainly say that. Come in and I'll tell you.'

Jill, always a good listener, didn't interrupt as Freya talked, but she watched her carefully, seeing the strained expression, heard the sadness in her voice. At last, Freya was silent, sitting with her hands tightly clasped in her lap.

'I am truly sorry that it has turned out like this, but I still don't understand exactly what happened. It all sounds so odd. Are you certain that Robin's memory really is reliable?'

Freya gave an unamused laugh. 'I tackled him on that and he pointed out that Hazard would hardly be likely to agree that he killed someone if he hadn't.'

'No. Of course not. He must be right about that.'

'It certainly leaves little room for doubt,' Freya said bitterly. 'Yet I have it firmly in my mind that there is a mistake somewhere along the line – and don't tell me

51

that is only wishful thinking.'

'No, I won't do that, but you must admit there seems to be nothing to back up that theory.'

'I know, but I feel so certain that Hazard couldn't shoot a man the way Dad describes it – or any other way for that matter.' She moved her hands helplessly. 'Oh Jill, he's such a gentle man – very sensitive. I *know* he couldn't do that.'

After a silence, Jill said gently, 'I know you feel sure of all that but you have to admit that you haven't known Hazard very long.'

'Long enough to know that I still want to marry him.'

'Perhaps that decision was made too soon – too – physically.'

Freya shrugged. 'Yes, perhaps for some people that might be true, but you know me, I always make up my mind quickly and – I very seldom change it.'

'But this decision is very different from any other. This was a decision to make a contract for life with a man you don't really know.'

'Oh Jill, you make it sound awful, as if I'm a fool, but – I still think I am right.'

Jill took a sip of the drink on the table beside her. 'Are you saying that even with what you know now, you still would be happy to marry him?'

After a second's hesitation and with a small smile, Freya said, 'Yes, I really believe I would but – well – it doesn't apply because Hazard made it quite clear that he won't marry me now with this between us and Dad said how fortunate it was that his memory had returned in time to stop such a tragedy happening.' Freya's voice was hard.

There was a long silence before Jill said quietly, 'I think you have to be fair to Robin. All this must have been a terrible shock and strain to him. You cannot expect his reaction to be anything different from what it has been. As far as he is concerned, his beloved daughter was about to marry a murderer. He *could* only be desperately upset. Far more so when Hazard didn't deny it.'

Freya made a wry face. 'You are speaking of it as if it is a proved case.'

'As things stand, I'm afraid it is.'

'I cannot accept that. Not yet.'

'When he left, what did Hazard say?'

Freya smiled grimly. 'That he wouldn't marry me and that there was something he had to do.'

'He didn't tell you what that was?'

Freya shook her head. 'No, he didn't say any more, except that he loved me.'

Jill glanced at her with compassion, saying gently, 'Even a killer can fall in love – Freya – don't let him fool you. It will hurt all the more if you finally have to accept that it *is* all true.'

Jill studied the woman sitting opposite her. She looked ill and as if she hadn't slept. She wasn't, Jill knew, the sort of girl to fall in love lightly. However swiftly it had happened, for Freya it would be deep and lasting, for it was true what she had said about herself never changing her mind, but now she was facing an entirely unknown situation, one which she herself could do nothing to change.

'When will you see him again?'

Freya shrugged. 'I've no idea. We were to have met to choose an engagement ring.' She paused. 'But I imagine that that will now not take place.'

'Oh Freya – I am so very sorry. I wish that there was something I could do for you.'

'No, there's nothing. But it's nice to know that you are here. That helps a lot.' She gave Jill a grateful smile then asked her about her weekend.

Jill smiled. 'Charles is becoming carried away with the beauty of our stately houses and can't see too many. Incidentally, he thinks a lot of Hazard Denning. He also said that he was particularly clever at his job.'

'Which probably means that he doesn't ask as many awkward questions as some of the others he's met. Hazard did say that Charles was not easy to interview.' She was making an immense effort to make normal conversation. She was genuinely delighted as Jill talked about her new friendship with the American and couldn't help wondering how serious it would turn out to be. These were two people who had both been hurt by unhappy marriages; both would be sensibly cautious. She said during a pause, 'How badly are you smitten?'

Jill was slow to reply. 'I am afraid, rather badly, but I've no intention of rushing into anything, nor has Charles. He is only just recovering from his last mistake.'

'What happened?'

'They met when they were very young, married almost at once and within a year regretted it, finding they had nothing in common except physical attraction. Finally, as you know, she left him.'

'And you? I've never asked you, but don't talk about it unless you want to.'

'I don't mind now. Now that I've met Charles.' She shook her head, as if she found it difficult to believe in such a change of heart.

'I'm so glad for you. I hope everything goes well.'

'That's very generous considering how everything seems to be going wrong for you.'

'How much does Charles know – Hazard – I mean, how close is their friendship?'

'Not terribly close I think. They met when Hazard reviewed his first book when it was to be published over here. They liked each other and have kept in touch ever since.'

'So – Charles wouldn't know an awful lot about him?'

Hesitating, Jill said, 'May I tell him what you have told me?'

'Yes, though I don't suppose there is anything he can explain. Everything seems only too plain.'

They chatted for a while longer and it was not until Jill had left that Freya realized that, after all, Jill had said nothing about her own broken marriage.

Ten

She wakened to a feeling of emptiness she had never known before. She had expected that Hazard would phone but there had been no word from him which, curiously, did nothing to shake her faith in him although there were so many questions she needed to ask him. She had the conviction that if only they could be together, if only she could hear his voice in explanation, something could be sorted out. Her mood swung from hope to despair. How *could* there be room for any explanation for what had happened? There could be no excuses, no exoneration for having shot a man with whom he had had a row in a bar. The whole thing sounded sordid and unreal. Something she could not imagine in connection with the man she had promised to marry. Again she heard her father's voice saying quietly, 'It is no good you clinging to false hopes when Hazard himself agrees that it did happen.' Add to that, the short time they had known each other, there must surely be room for doubts. Because she had fallen in love with this man didn't mean that she couldn't be mistaken in his character. There was not a scrap of evidence to back up her conviction that it had been a different scene altogether.

The following day, she had a photographic assignment in Kent and didn't arrive home until later than usual and was not surprised to find that Charles's car was parked outside the house and later in the evening, Jill rang to ask if she would join them for coffee. Each time she met this slow speaking American, Freya liked him better, was more impressed by his quiet and unassuming manner. Tonight, he came straight to the point.

'I am so sorry for what has happened for you and Hazard.'

The words could not have been more ordinary but his voice held a deep sincerity and, not waiting for her reply, he continued quietly, 'While Hazard and I are not exactly close friends, I have always admired him and the way he works and—' He broke off with a shrug, his brown eyes studying her thoughtfully. 'Well, I find it very hard to believe from what I know of his character that he could ever behave as he seems to have done.'

'Did he ever talk to you about the Falklands?'

Frowning, he hesitated before saying slowly, 'No. As a matter of fact, he never seemed to want to discuss it at all. I knew that he had had a pretty rough time out there and put his reluctance down to that, so I never pressed him.'

'Would you know if he ever had a gun?'

Charles looked at Freya in surprise. 'Not as far as I know, and I am quite sure that in his job he would certainly not be carrying one.'

'Then, how could he have shot anyone?' There was sharp hope in Freya's voice and Charles gave her a sympathetic glance as he began to speak, then stopped abruptly. What he had been going to say was that it would not have been difficult for anyone to get hold of a gun, but he changed it to, 'In any case, I have never found him a quick-tempered man.'

Freya took the glass which Jill was handing her. 'Yet, there seems no doubt about the actual shooting.'

'Did he know the man he had a row with?'

Freya shook her head. 'I don't know. In fact, I know really nothing of what really happened there.'

'I wish I could help but because he didn't want to talk about the war, I know very little either.' Freya saw his sudden frown before he said, 'Only one thing I remember him saying, that he lost a friend in one of the air raids and that the chap's father lived in Sussex.'

'Did he say where?' Freya's voice was sharp and Charles said doubtfully, 'Yes, but I'm afraid I don't remember, except that I think it began with an R.' He thought for a moment, then added, 'It was a village, and not, I think, very far from Lewes. I'm sorry, I don't expect that's much help.'

There was a note of excitement in Freya's voice as she said, 'Yes, I think it may be. Would the name of the village be Ringmer?'

Again Charles frowned in an effort to remember. 'That could have been it. Ringmer – yes – I think it was. I do remember Hazard saying that the chap's family had lived there for years. I know he intended visiting his friend's father afterwards, but I don't know if he ever did so.'

'Did Hazard ever mention his friend's name?'

'No, I don't think so, but I know that his father was a retired Colonel, Hazard said.'

They heard Freya let her breath go on a long sigh. 'Colonel Warren. He is an old friend of my father's. He lives in Ringmer and he had a son called Victor who was killed in the Falklands.' She looked from Jill to Charles with an air of triumph. 'It has to be the same family and perhaps he could tell me something which might help.'

Jill said, 'You mean you would go to see the Colonel?'

'Why, yes. I know him you see, through Dad.'

'Did you know the son?'

'Not really well. We used to meet in the school holidays – that sort of thing.'

She was silent for a few seconds before saying, 'Victor's death was a terrible blow to the Colonel. He was an only son and he was very proud of him.'

Jill said, 'What do you think Colonel Warren could tell you?'

'He might know what really happened. I don't know, but I have to try. I suppose I am clutching at straws, but there is nothing else I can do. I only know that if Hazard said that he shot a man, then I have to find out why and how because I am certain that he would never shoot a man in cold blood.'

Eleven

The following Friday Freya drove down to Sussex taking a route which would include Ringmer, having previously phoned the Colonel asking if she might visit him. She felt a trifle guilty when she heard the obvious pleasure in his voice at the prospect. She drove through the village, turning off beside the village green to reach the pleasant stone-built house at the end of a short drive. It was already getting dusk and she sat for a few moments looking towards the lighted window, suddenly wondering why she had thought that this man could tell her anything she needed to know. With a sigh, she opened the car door, sliding out on to the gravel drive, walking slowly to the front door, beginning to wish that she had not decided to come on such a mad impulse.

He came to meet her in the hall, putting an arm round her shoulders in the warm hall in an affectionate welcome, saying there was a log fire in the sitting-room as it was getting chilly. He steered her towards it, talking all the time. He was a neatly made man, not tall but with a military bearing of which he was entirely unconscious. Settling Freya in a comfortable chair, he wanted to know if Robin was well.

'I've not seen him since the funeral and I know how grieved he is at the loss of Louise. There is so little one can offer in the way of comfort.'

'I'm sure he would be very glad to see you if you could go to see him sometime. I know he is lonely without mother. I go down nearly every weekend.'

They talked for some time of her parents and it didn't seem to occur to the Colonel that she had come for any special reason but finally, Freya said, 'I believe Victor had a friend called Hazard Denning.'

'Yes – yes he did. A close friend. It's an unlikely name that sticks in the memory, at one time, they were at school together.'

'So Victor must have known him well.'

'Oh yes, they always kept in touch, but of course, I've only seen him once since – since Victor was killed.'

He looked at Freya with a puzzled frown as if he were trying to find the connection. 'I didn't realize you had met Hazard.'

Freya said quietly, 'Hazard and I have just become engaged.'

That really caught his attention and he asked how they had met.

Now she was coming to the difficult part for she knew that he shied away from mentioning the raid in which Victor died and Robin had been wounded.

'The odd thing is that this has been the means of Dad partly recovering his memory.'

Becoming aware that she was worried, he said kindly, 'But isn't that a good thing? Isn't that what he wanted? It has been such a tragedy for him. Surely it must come as a relief to both of you?'

'A relief in one way, but it is only a partial recovery and he is very distressed because it is in some way connected with Hazard.' And she began to explain the details as far as she knew them.

He listened quietly and with increasing puzzlement

and when she stopped speaking, said with disbelief, 'You say your father accused Hazard of shooting a man simply because they had a row the night before?'

Freya stopped, aware that the Colonel watched her closely. 'Finally, Dad remembered and that's when he accused him of being a murderer.'

Colonel Warren stood up, crossed the room and came back with two glasses in his hand. Handing one to Freya, he said, 'Gin and tonic. That's what you like isn't it?'

Thanking him she took the glass, looking up as he said with some surprise, 'Rather a strong accusation, wasn't it?'

'Yes, but Hazard didn't deny it.'

The Colonel held his glass up to the light before taking a drink. 'Then you don't think Robin's memory can be inaccurate?'

Freya shook her head and he said, 'This is pretty rotten for you. Should have been a happy time for you both – now this.' There was a short silence before he said, 'But this is crazy. It simply couldn't have happened. I *know* this man – level headed, not at all the sort to lose his head and lash out with a gun.' He stopped abruptly. 'Where would he get a gun anyway? Have you thought of that?'

Freya said wearily, 'I think I've thought of everything, but I always have to come back to the same point – Hazard admits that he did shoot a man.'

After a pause, the Colonel said, 'Why did you come to me? How did you think I could help?'

Freya thrust out both hands, palms up. 'I don't know. I was clutching at straws. I hoped that perhaps you might know something that—' She broke off hopelessly. 'Oh, I don't know, it's silly, but I just felt I couldn't accept it. In spite of everything, it seems all wrong.'

'I entirely agree that it seems all wrong, but it's one thing to feel that and another thing to prove it. It sounds as if Hazard is his own worst enemy, making no effort to defend himself.'

'Yes, I can't understand that. He only agrees that he did shoot a man, but he won't say any more because he insists that it would affect and hurt other people.'

They sat silently for a minute, then Colonel Warren said thoughtfully, 'This shooting took place during the raid in which Victor was killed and Robin wounded. That is correct, isn't it?'

'Yes, because Dad says he *saw* the shooting just before he blacked out, and that was why he could do nothing to stop it.'

'He also heard the row between the two men the night before?'

'Yes, he is quite clear about that now.'

Glancing at her watch, Freya stood up. 'Dad will begin thinking that I've had an accident. I didn't tell him that I was coming here, and I think perhaps it will be better if he doesn't know.'

Putting his hand on her shoulder, the Colonel said kindly, 'I'm sorry my dear, I'm afraid I've not been any help, but one thing occurs to me, so much of this hangs on Robin's memory. Do you think if I came over, he might mention any of this?'

'I should think it quite likely because he is so worried about it.'

'If he does, perhaps I can ask a few questions which might help. If I have any luck, I'll let you know.'

In the car, Freya admitted disappointedly that she had been foolish to hope that this visit might provide any help. At the same time, it had been a relief to talk to someone who had known Hazard for a long time and so obviously held a good opinion of his character.

Twelve

The house was highlighted in her headlights as she turned into the drive. The trees were almost bare now, the drive itself a deep bronze with the scattered leaves lying on it, bright now in the car lights before she switched them off. The curtains had not been pulled and she could see the flickering shadows from the fire as her father sat near it, his eyes closed, his hands in his lap, and even from this distance the sadness of his expression was clearly marked, and as she watched, his hands came up to cover his face in a gesture of distress and she caught her breath at the pity of it, in that moment knowing that she was watching something private she was not meant to see. Opening the car door, she got out quickly and went into the house. By the time she had reached the hall, he had heard her and when she opened the sitting-room door, he was half across the room to greet her, his face lighting with pleasure at her arrival.

He said half jokingly, 'You are a little late, I was beginning to imagine all the accidents which might have happened to you.'

But it hadn't been that which had brought that expression of distress to his face.

'Are you all right?'

He looked surprised, shrugging his shoulders and

answering obliquely, but with a smile, 'Yes, my dear – as all right as I can be without her.'

There was no sensible answer to that and she didn't attempt to make one, only slipped her arm through his as they made their way to the fire together.

Returning to his chair, he asked for her news as she stood warming her hands, aware of his effort to appear normal but she felt the tension beneath the surface and after a pause, she asked gently, 'What about your memory? Has anything more come back to you?'

It seemed a long time before he replied and she watched his expression change as once more he looked distressed. Finally he said, 'I remembered his name.'

'You mean, the man who was shot?'

He nodded. 'Yes. His name was Thomas Wayland.' He paused and Freya waited for him to continue. 'A big powerful chap. I'd only spoken to him once.'

She saw him frown and asked quickly, 'You didn't like him?'

He raised a hand in protest. 'Well – I hardly knew the man but he was rather too full of himself, a bit too opinionated I thought when I saw him talking to some of the other men.'

'What was he doing there?'

'The same as Hazard – a journalist.'

After a short silence, Freya asked, 'Are you sure that he was shot?'

'Quite sure. I wasn't very close, but I saw what happened.'

Her heart felt like a lump of lead when she heard the sureness of his tone. How was it possible that there could be any mistake? Yet she persisted.

'You mean that you saw him fall when you heard the shot?'

For the first time her father looked confused and put a

hand to his head.

'That's when it happened – I mean, the bomb – when I fell and—'

His voice trailed off for a few seconds, Freya let the silence remain, then she asked gently, 'Did it happen after – after the bomb dropped – after you were wounded?'

He stared at her, the blue eyes clouded and vague and she felt mean forcing him to remember back to that awful moment. He shook his head in a helpless way and she said urgently, 'Dad – please try to think. Please try to be certain.' She was not sure in her own mind why it was important, but she was sure that she had to know.

Robin put both hands up to his face in an effort of concentration, then said slowly, as if he were living the scene again. 'After. It must have been. I couldn't move. I couldn't do anything to stop it. I heard the shot; I saw Hazard looking down at him and the gun was still in his hand.'

Freya had been sitting forward in her chair, every muscle tense, and now she let her breath go on a long sigh as she looked across at the defeated figure in the chair opposite and was suddenly overcome with remorse. She had no right to make him suffer like this. 'Dad, I'm sorry. I shouldn't have made you go back to that scene.'

Slowly he took his hands from his face and it was a few seconds before his eyes came back into focus and his next words frightened her.

'I have to decide what I must do. Now that I have remembered.'

'What you must do?'

'Yes. Now that I know who was shot.'

'But Dad, you can't *do* anything. What is there to be done after all this time?'

He sat up straighter, his voice agitated, 'Can't you see? Can't you understand? If I do nothing, then I am condoning murder.'

Freya stared at him. 'And – if you do something?' she asked almost in a whisper.

The blue eyes stared straight into her own eyes.

'If I do, then I am accusing Hazard of taking a man's life.'

His words hit her like a physical blow and she wondered why when Hazard had already admitted that he shot a man. The difference was that with those words, Robin had put everything into perspective: into the cold-blooded perspective of the law. In that second, Freya understood the appalling position her father felt himself to be in. A horrible decision for any man to face, but surely so much worse for a man of the Church. No wonder that look of torture came to his eyes. He was making the cruellest decision of his life. Surely a decision to daunt the strongest of men.

Thirteen

It had been a difficult weekend, neither of them being able to help the other. Before she left, Freya extracted a promise from her father not to do anything at present. He felt that very much as a weakness, but to appease Freya, he agreed.

She left on Monday morning driving straight to the office and did not get home until seven o'clock after a busy day. After fixing a light supper, she rang Jill. 'Are you going to be alone?'

'Yes. Come on up.'

Freya knew that Jill could not help her but she needed someone to talk to in order to clarify what appeared to be an impossible situation. Jill, always a good listener, remained silent until Freya stopped speaking. Even then, the silence remained until Jill finally said, 'How do you know that the man was dead?'

Freya was so astonished that for a moment she couldn't speak, then she said lamely, 'I never thought of that.'

'Nor apparently did Robin,' Jill said drily. 'That, of course, changes everything.'

'Yes, everything except that Hazard did shoot the man.'

'Rather less serious though.'

'Hazard *believed* that he had killed him. He never

questioned it when Dad accused him.'

Jill suggested mildly, 'Well – I don't suppose he hung about. Afterwards, I mean.'

'He would have waited.' It was not until she had spoken the words that Freya realized how inane they sounded. She sat up straighter to explain. 'What I mean is, Hazard would not just go away to leave a man to die.'

Jill remained silent and Freya gave her a doubtful look. 'All right – that sounds silly – I'm not making sense, but what I mean is—'

Jill interrupted sharply, 'What you mean is that you can't imagine the man you know either killing *or* wounding a man.'

Freya nodded silently, annoyed to find that her eyes had filled with tears. Suddenly she said almost angrily, 'You think I've been mistaken in him, don't you? You think that because I've not known him long that I am incapable of judging his character because I fell in love with him.'

'It's possible, but no, Charles is a good judge of character and he – he is prepared to give him the benefit of the doubt.'

'Oh – big deal.' Freya's voice held deep contempt and Jill said quickly, 'Have a heart. don't forget the facts – they add up to something.'

Freya sank back into her chair, the fight going out of her. 'No Jill – I'm not forgetting. I know only too well how damning they are.'

'Yet, you still believe in him.' Freya nodded and Jill continued. 'Have you heard from him? Do you know what he is doing?'

Freya said wearily, 'No to both. I have no idea what he is doing or where he is. Nothing since he left.'

'Oh Freya, I am so sorry that this should have happened to you. Charles told me to tell you he would do anything to help.'

'Please thank him but I don't think there is anybody who *can* help.' She shrugged, 'Perhaps least of all me.' And that, she thought as she stood up to leave, is the hardest thing of all. She had hoped that there would be a letter when she returned home, but there was nothing. Later, lying sleepless in bed, her mind in a turmoil, she thought of that phrase 'out of character'. What could that mean when applied to Hazard? She understood what it meant when applied to her father because she had known him all her life, or to Martha or anyone else she had known a long time, but she had only known Hazard a few months. Did she really know his strengths and weaknesses? How he would react to various situations? Because she was in love with him, was she crediting him with the character she wanted him to have? Was she deliberately blinding herself to what he really was?

In the darkness, she turned once more in the bed suddenly remembering Hazard's words on the night when he had asked her if she would still be willing to marry him with this between them, and she recollected her own momentary hesitation and his fingers tightening on her shoulders as he said sadly, 'I don't think so. You love your father and you would want to marry with his blessing. You have known *him* all your life. You have only known *me* a short while'. The inference that she could trust her father more than she trusted him was there without the words being spoken and in this lonely darkness, she wondered if perhaps Hazard had spoken a truth she had not realized. How could she reconcile these two loves which were so entirely different but both so real and so strong?

With his strict ideas of religion this new knowledge must be an intolerable burden for Robin to bear, knowing that it had been the means of wrecking Freya's happiness.

But, if the man were not dead? She clung to the thought, but even if it were true, it did not absolve Hazard from having shot him. Nothing could absolve him from that.

When eventually she slept her dreams were filled with horror. Hazard standing looking down at his victim, the gun still in his hand. In the dream, his face was filled with horror. The violent beating of her heart wakened her. The dream had been as vivid, as if she had stood beside him and as she lay in the dark, she seemed to experience the same horror that had shown in his face. It was a long time before she could compose herself and accept that it had only been a dream. Looking at the clock, she saw that it was only four o'clock. Knowing that she would not sleep again, she swung her legs out of bed and putting on a dressing-gown and slippers, went to the kitchen to make some coffee. It was, she thought, time for her to sort out her feelings and values. Whatever the strength of her love for Hazard, she could not fault her father for what he felt compelled to do. In reply to her plea that it had happened a long time ago, he would argue – and rightly – that time had nothing to do with it. If something was wrong, it was wrong for ever. Time could not change that. With his strong beliefs, he could never condone it, or lessen the guilt in his mind.

Automatically, Freya had filled and boiled the kettle and made the coffee. Now she sat at the table making no effort to fill her cup. Every muscle in her body felt taut. There was no evading the damning facts and she had to decide what her own part was to be. Judged on the facts alone, there should be no difficulty, no question. Why then was she still so convinced that there was another answer? Surely that was only madness.

Her mind felt incapable of thinking straight and suddenly she felt it might help to clarify her thoughts if she wrote down some of the details. Fetching a pen and some paper she set to work to note down anything she felt she herself could do. For several minutes she sat in front of an empty page, not knowing where to start. Her father had said that the man's name was Thomas Wayland. Not such a very common name. Supposing she tried to trace the name. Supposing that she could prove that he was still alive. Surely that would be something useful. She wrote Thomas Wayland on the empty page. Underneath, she wrote: *'If I am lucky enough to trace him, I must visit this man'*.

She sat back feeling a trifle calmer now that she was attempting something practical. What would the man's attitude be? If he had seen who shot him he could only be antagonistic and therefore a liability. This was stupid. She threw down the pen. This was useless, the only sensible thing about it was that at least she could try to trace Thomas Wayland. She looked at the full cup of coffee and stood up. By now that too would be useless and she picked up the cup and threw the coffee down the sink.

Fourteen

Freya and her partner carried out their own photographic processing and this side of her work was of special interest to Freya. She was developing shots she had taken the previous day when her secretary knocked at the door of the darkroom. 'A gentleman to see you,' she warned.

'Who is it?'

'He wouldn't give his name.'

Irritated, Freya said, 'Well, if he wants to see me, he'll have to wait. I won't be out of here for another ten minutes.'

She continued working with her usual care. It had been a difficult assignment of rare plants growing in inaccessible places and she had not felt sure of the results. With processing completed, she examined the shots critically and finally decided that they were good. Washing her hands, she suddenly remembered that someone was waiting to see her. Coming out of the darkroom, she went straight to her office.

He was sitting in the only armchair reading a magazine. She stopped in the doorway and he stood up, watching her come across the room to him.

'Oh, Hazard.'

He didn't move until she reached him, then without a word, his arms came round her, holding her closely.

Finally he said, 'I wasn't sure you would want to see me. You might have changed your mind now you have had time to think.'

'*I* haven't changed,' she said flatly, 'but I thought that you might.' She added sadly, 'I didn't even know where you were.'

Holding her away from him and looking into her eyes, he said quietly, 'You're angry with me, aren't you?'

She shifted under his hands on her shoulders and he released her and she moved away.

'Angry? No, I don't think so. Anxious – hurt – yes.'

'I'm sorry. I couldn't think what to do – what was best. All this has been such a shock. After all this time, that it should happen in this way.' His hands lifted in a helpless gesture. 'That of all people that it should be your father.'

'Oh Hazard, whatever made you do it? How could you? Whatever the row was about, it wasn't worth that.'

The green eyes stared at her with an expression she did not understand and she said impulsively, 'You're not quick tempered – I've never seen you lose your temper over anything.'

He turned away from her miserably. 'It was not temper. It was – something quite different. You must believe that.'

What he was saying didn't seem to make any sense and she said quietly, 'But you killed a man.'

He answered, 'Yes, I killed a man. I've never denied it. That is why I am not going to let you marry me. You can't understand, and it wouldn't be fair to either of us – or your father.'

'Why can't you tell me?'

'There are too many complications. After all this time it could only cause more pain and start a lot of trouble without benefiting anyone.'

His words went into a long silence and Freya watched

him walk over to the window to stare unseeingly at the traffic below. Into the silence, Freya spoke quietly. 'Thomas Wayland. Dad remembered the name.'

Hazard swung round from the window, staring blankly at her, and for a second, she thought he could not have heard and she repeated, 'Thomas Wayland, the man you shot.'

As she watched expressions chase across that lean face, she felt bewildered. Frank disbelief, doubt, finally followed by a curious expression of excitement.

'Your father said that?'

'Yes.'

For a few seconds he stood very still, then started pacing round the room, almost as if he had forgotten that she was there. It was almost five minutes before he ceased his pacing to stand in front of her, smiling for the first time. Putting a hand either side of her face, he looked down into her eyes. 'Will you trust me? After all this, *can* you trust me?'

Whatever she had expected him to say, it was not that. With no hesitation and with no doubt, she said, 'Of course I trust you.'

He bent to kiss her saying, 'Thank you darling for that. This may help.' Still holding her face, he continued slowly, 'I'll have to leave you now. I have to be in Scotland tomorrow and—' He paused. 'And after that, I know what I must try to do. I'll need time, but keep on trusting me and I will get in touch as soon as I can.' He kissed her again then turned to pick up a briefcase he had left by his chair. He turned as he reached the door. 'Darling, I love you. Whatever happens, don't ever forget that.'

She stood where he had left her, feeling bewildered by what had just happened. For a second she wondered why she had said without any doubt that she trusted him. He hadn't given her much to go on. Nothing was really altered except that she had told him that her father had remembered the man's name.

Suddenly she saw herself as a besotted teenager believing everything her loved one told her. It was the sort of attitude of which she would have been scathing, and now she admonished herself for the strength of her belief in Hazard. She sat down thoughtfully at her desk thinking of Hazard's unexpected reactions when he heard the name of Thomas Wayland. She could understand his surprise that Robin had recollected the name but she was puzzled by the look of disbelief in Hazard's eyes which had been followed by his expression of excitement. She sat with her elbows on the desk, her hands covering her eyes, concentrating on that confusing scene. How could there be any advantage to Hazard in Robin remembering that name? How could it have triggered off that sudden decision to do something which, to use his own words, 'This may help.'

Fifteen

She sat with her elbows on the desk, her hands covering her eyes, concentrating on what had happened, her mind at this moment seeming unable to cope.

Her secretary came to the door and Freya stood up as she came into the room, aware of her sharp glance.

'Headache?' Anna asked cheerfully. 'I don't know how you stand all that work in the darkroom. Can't be good for your eyes.'

Freya smiled at her. 'Maybe not, but it's fascinating work.'

Anna stood patiently by the desk while Freya read and signed the letters and when she left the room, Freya suddenly wondered if Anna too had insurmountable difficulties in her love life. With a sigh, she forced herself to go on working. At least one thing in her life was going well, for the business which she and her partner had started two years ago was steadily increasing and could now safely be considered a success. Usually Freya found all aspects of the work interesting but today, her mind continually wandered to her own problems. She longed to get in touch with Hazard but recognized that if she did really trust him, it was her task to wait, to give him time. Time for what? She could not answer that, and she could not undo the fact that he had killed a man.

77

Sighing deeply, she stood up and fetched her coat from where it hung. Why, out of all the men she had met, did she have to choose to fall hopelessly in love with the one man who had presented her with an impossible problem? Why was she so obsessed by the conviction that there was an explanation for what had happened? How do you explain away a man's life?

Her mind ran round in circles as she drove home to the flat. She was tempted to ring Hazard, then remembered that he was flying to Scotland that evening.

Time, which usually passed so swiftly, dragged by and even a good programme on television could not hold her attention and, finally, she went to bed, though not to sleep.

The next two days were devoted to rush jobs which had to be completed before the weekend and on Friday, she had an appointment with a client in Hampstead who wanted to discuss a series of illustrations for an agricultural scheme he was working on.

Unfamiliar with the area, Freya drove slowly, studying the road numbers. At the end of the road, two men appeared to be arguing, then one turned away abruptly, entered his car, slammed the door and drove away. The scene was momentary but for one instant, Freya thought that the figure looked familiar. The car too, was the right colour, but what would Hazard be doing here when he was supposed to be in Scotland? And with whom was he arguing?

She pulled herself together quickly as she reached the house she was looking for. Angry at her own reactions, she locked the car door and ran up the steps to the house. She was allowing herself to become obsessive. There must be many men who from a distance might resemble Hazard, hundreds of cars the same make and colour as his. She was being absurd.

The interview went well and all details had been completed by the time she left. Back in the car, she switched on the engine. She needed to return the way she had come; instead, she continued slowly down the road. The car, she remembered, had been parked near a lamp-post. She stopped just beyond, sitting for a moment wondering why she was doing this. It didn't make sense. Suppose it *had* been Hazard – there was no law against him visiting someone in Hampstead. But, arguing in the street? From where she sat, she could see a list of names at one side of the front door. Obviously, flats. On a sudden impulse, she got out of the car and approached the entrance with no idea of what she expected to find.

There were three small nameplates. On the ground floor lived a Mrs Wheeler. On the second, Miss Wainright. On the top floor, Mr T Wayland. Freya stood as if she were transfixed. But Thomas Wayland was dead. She stood staring at the little card. So, it could have been Hazard. It could have been Thomas Wayland with whom he was arguing?

For a few seconds, the full impact of the incident did not hit her and when, finally it did, she felt incapable of movement or clear thought. It was not until the inner door opened and an elderly woman came through that Freya moved. The woman glared at her oddly.

'Can I help you?'

Freya looked at her helplessly. 'No. No thank you. I – I must have come to the wrong address.'

With a nod, the woman continued on her way and after a moment, Freya went slowly back to the car.

Sixteen

But Thomas Wayland was dead.

In Jill's flat that evening, she made the coffee and waited for Freya to settle. 'Well, let's hear your strange tale,' she said.

Slightly irritated, Freya told her, 'I know what you are going to say about coincidences. If I hadn't got out of the car to read the name cards, I should have been prepared to settle for that and think that I had been mistaken but—'

She paused, shrugging and Jill said, 'Yes, the name cards certainly pose a problem. We can hardly take coincidence as far as that.'

'So,' Freya went on slowly, 'the Thomas Wayland whom Hazard is supposed to have killed is still alive.'

'Which means that none of the facts fit.'

'But Hazard *said* that he killed him.'

Jill stirred her coffee thoughtfully, then shook her head. 'No, he didn't,' she stated flatly. Adding, 'At least, I don't *think* he did.'

'What are you saying?'

'What I am saying is that it was not Hazard who put a name to the man he killed. It was Robin.'

Freya received that in silence then said slowly, 'Are you saying that Dad has made a mistake and Hazard killed another man?'

For the first time, Jill hesitated. 'I don't know, but it has to be that or that Hazard was wrong in thinking that the man was dead.'

Freya said hopefully, 'And Hazard didn't realize that the man was still alive? Perhaps that could account for the way he acted when Dad said the name.' She hesitated, frowning. 'Perhaps it was the first time he had even considered that the man might have lived.'

Jill looked at her with sympathy. Nothing seemed to fit with what had happened that day.

Freya continued, 'So Hazard must have been trying to trace him – to make sure one way or the other.'

For the first time, she smiled. 'Oh Jill, just think what a relief this must be to him. After all the agony of mind he has been going through all this time. And Dad,' she added with relief in her voice, 'he will feel so much happier to know that the man is alive.'

She looked at her watch and jumped up. 'I shouldn't have come. I should have stayed by the phone. Hazard will want to get in touch with me as soon as he can. I'm sure he will ring me.'

Jill, aware of her excitement and relief, watched her go with a sad shake of her head. Whatever this new turn of events led to, it did not alter the fact that Hazard had shot a man.

The phone did not ring in Freya's flat, either that night or the next and there was no sign from Hazard at all. In the end, when she could not bear the strain any longer, Freya phoned Hazard's home number. It rang for some time but finally she heard his voice. It sounded utterly weary as he repeated his own number.

'Hazard – I thought you would phone me.'

There was a pause before he answered. 'You said that you trusted me.'

Surprised, Freya said, 'Of course I trust you – I told

you, but I thought you would tell me your news, I have been waiting to hear.'

He said sharply, 'What news?'

'Thomas Wayland is alive, isn't he?'

There was a long silence before he said, 'How did you know that?'

'Because I saw you with him.'

She hadn't meant to tell him – not like that, but she was not prepared for his violent reaction. 'You mean that you followed me? How *could* you do that?' He paused, then burst out, 'My God, you say you trust me – and then – spy on me. How *could* you?' he said again.

'I *didn't* follow you. I had no idea that you would be there.'

In a slightly milder tone he asked, 'What were *you* doing there then?'

'I had an appointment at a house further up the road. It was quite by chance that I saw you. You were having a row with a man. I—'

'What a coincidence.' His voice was scathing.

'You don't believe me?'

He didn't answer and after a minute Freya said impatiently, 'I've *told* you. It *happened* like that. You asked me to give you *my* trust, don't you think that should apply on both sides?'

Finally he said in a different tone, 'All right, I believe you, but this only complicates everything more than ever. I don't know how I could have been so stupid. I made a mistake and now I am paying for it.'

'Thomas Wayland?'

'Yes, Thomas Wayland. I should have known.'

Freya was surprised to find that she was shaking. She was out of her depth now and suddenly came to a decision. 'Hazard, I don't know what you are talking about. You are not telling me anything. We can't go on like this. If you can't, or *won't*, trust me, then it is the finish as far as I am concerned.' She heard him draw a quick breath and continued before he could interrupt. 'So far, you have called the tune, made all the rules. I can't bear this any longer. We have to do this together or not at all.'

After a long silence, he asked, 'And your father?'

'My father will do what he believes to be right, quite apart from anything else, but I don't believe that *he* knows the whole story. Nor do I,' she added with some bitterness.

'Darling, thank you for wanting to go through this with me. No, you don't know the whole story, but your judgement might be very different from mine.' He was silent for a few seconds, then said with desperation in his voice, 'I am afraid of losing you and, in any case, nothing will change your father.'

She said calmly, 'Then, we shall have to face that together.'

'I don't want to place you in the position of being against him. I know how much you love him.'

'Yes, but we don't always agree on everything.'

He said on a hopeless note, 'I don't want to lose you. I love you so much.'

'If you don't want to lose me, then listen to what I say, because I really mean it.'

She heard him sigh. 'Yes, I believe you do.'

'Then, come to dinner tomorrow and give me a chance to share this with you.'

They fixed a time and this rather extraordinary conversation finished on a most ordinary note. It was not until Freya put down the phone that she realized that she was almost in a state of collapse.

Seventeen

The following evening, they met almost as strangers. Freya had taken care to look her best and Hazard arrived carrying a large sheaf of flowers which he held out to her as soon as she opened the door. She thanked him politely and held up her face for his kiss. They must, she thought suddenly, be presenting a sort of cheap comedy situation as they stood facing each other awkwardly. Somehow, she had not anticipated anything like this. She had simply thought of this meeting as the coming together of two people who needed each other desperately; as the end of a period of miserable misunderstanding which could now be put right. It was obvious that she had been over optimistic.

Hazard followed her to the kitchen, watching while she put the flowers in water.

'Let's have a drink,' she said finally as she placed the jug on the kitchen table. There was still a stiffness between them and Hazard's eyes looked guarded as they entered the sitting-room together. Glancing at him quickly, she thought there was only one way to change this and turning to him, she put her arms round his neck, lifting her mouth to his. His arms closed round her, holding her tightly against him and at that moment, she felt it was going to be all right and that words were not needed for complete understanding. When they finally sat down with drinks in their hands, Hazard said quietly, 'Where do you want me to start?'

'I want to know it all.'

'You must realize that what I am going to tell you may change your mind entirely. I am risking losing you.'

'Whatever it is it can't change what I feel for you. I know that now—' She hesitated, searching for the right words. 'Oh darling, don't you see, I'm so sure that you must have had an overpowering reason.'

His face creased into a genuine smile as he asked, 'For killing a man? Thank you for having such a cockeyed faith in me – but you are about right at that.'

He stood up abruptly, moving easily round the room, picking up ornaments then putting them down aimlessly as he prowled. Freya watched patiently. If he needed more time to sort himself out, she was prepared to give it him. She felt calmer in these last few minutes than she had since the beginning of this nightmare time. She was aware of his warning that what he was about to tell her was something so important that it would change her whole life, yet she remained calm because of her know-ledge of herself. She had always been able to face any situation as long as she knew all the facts, and now, she waited silently for whatever Hazard had decided to tell her. Finally, he came to stand in front of her.

'I think that both you and your father know Colonel Warren and his son Victor.'

Astonishment overcame her as she realized what he had said. How could that friendship have any connection with his own story? He didn't wait for her to speak but ploughed straight on. 'Victor and I have known each other nearly all our lives. We went to the same prep school, then on to public school together. After that, we lost touch a bit because he joined the army and I didn't.'

He paused, then went to sit down again, staring into

the fire, then continued slowly, 'But when we met again in the Falklands, we picked up where we left off as if there had never been a pause in our friendship. I suppose—' He looked at Freya and smiled. 'I suppose a friendship as long and as close as that can't be broken just because you haven't met all the time.'

He looked down at the hands clasped so tightly in front of him that the knuckles were white and shook his head with an air of hopelessness. 'I don't know how I can make you understand.'

Looking at that bowed head she said gently, 'Just tell me. I will understand.'

Again, he shook his head, lifting it to look into her eyes as he said, in a very clear voice, 'No, because I killed him you see.'

The sense of shock was enormous and for a few moments swamped all other feeling, then, seeing his stricken expression, she pulled herself together. What should you say to a man who has just told you that he murdered his best friend? It was not difficult because she said spontaneously, 'Then there must have been a very compelling reason.'

It was odd that at that instant she had no thought of the war which was raging in the Falklands at that time. The words were entirely instinctive and when she saw his expression change and the tension leave him, she knew that she had been right. But there was still a lot of explaining to be done and she composed herself to listen.

'There was a daylight air raid that day. The same one in which your father was injured. I heard the planes flying in low and from where I was standing, I saw Victor run across towards the air strip but—' He hesitated. 'He never reached it.'

His voice died away and he sat staring into the fire

reliving that scene and it was a minute before he continued. 'The bomb fell into a group of men and although I was some distance away, it blew me flat and I must have been knocked out for a few minutes for the first thing I remember was the sound of screaming and thinking that I must do something about it, though what I thought I could do, God alone knows.'

He put a hand up to his head and Freya saw him shudder. 'Nobody could have done anything. It was a complete shambles. All the men were dead,' he paused. 'Except Victor. He was still alive. He was conscious – lying there covered with blood and with half his body torn away.'

Freya said gently, 'You don't have to go on. I know now what you did. Oh Hazard, that couldn't be wrong – surely that couldn't be wrong.'

It was a statement, not a question, but as if he had not heard, Hazard continued slowly.

'It was his eyes – they pleaded. He couldn't speak – but they asked. Oh God – it was quite plain what he wanted and – I took his gun and shot him.' He moved his hand in a distressed gesture. 'It was the least I could do.'

The room was very quiet, the sound of a car in the road seemed from a different world. They heard Jill walk across the floor above them. Neither of them moved. Finally Hazard said derisively, 'Confessions of a murderer.'

'Don't.'

'Are you saying that you don't condemn me?'

'Condemn? How could I condemn you for a brave act of mercy for a friend?'

He said blankly, 'I took a life. I killed him.'

'Was there any chance that he could have lived?' She had to ask and he shook his head. 'No. None. I have no

doubt about that. No man would have lived as he was
then.'

Eighteen

Hazard sank back in his chair as if he felt completely drained and, seeing that, Freya suddenly realized the appalling strain he had been under for so long. In the following silence, her own mind was busy trying to assimilate all that he had said. She vaguely remembered a tall gangling boy who often stayed with the Warrens during school holidays. Presumably, Hazard. She became aware that he was watching her and he said now, 'You have a very expressive face. Why aren't you judging me? Why aren't you shocked?'

For a few seconds, she did not answer, then she said slowly, 'Perhaps because I hope that in the same circumstances I would have had the courage to do the same as you did.'

He offered her a smile of pure relief saying, 'You can't know what it's been like ever since it happened.'

'I hope I can, but of course, nobody could understand the intensity of feeling – of needing to end his suffering.'

'No. Being there – watching him, I felt I had no choice. The fact that I was taking a man's life never came into it at all. It was – simply something that I had to do for Victor.

She said as if fully realizing it for the first time, 'So, that is what Dad saw. Only, he didn't understand what he was seeing.'

Hazard said quietly, 'That is what he witnessed.'

They lapsed into silence, each with their own thoughts. There were questions Freya needed to ask, details to be filled in, but not now, in these few minutes of acute relief which they were sharing.

Later, over supper, they discussed their own plans in more detail than they had before and it was not until later in the evening that they returned to the subject of Victor's death. There were so many questions Freya wanted to ask but was afraid of their effect on Hazard who was now so much more relaxed than she had ever seen him.

Suddenly, he asked, 'What about your father? What will this mean to him?'

She had been pushing the thought from her mind. What *would* this new knowledge make to his judgement? 'I don't know,' she told him frankly. 'All his whites are so white and his blacks so black; his ideas of right and wrong are so fixed and strong and – narrow,' she added with some condemnation in her voice then, suddenly smiled, saying, 'You see, he has an almost childlike faith, and nothing shakes that.'

'I envy him that, but it must make life very difficult for him,' Hazard said. 'He must be constantly disappointed in people.'

She shrugged. 'He is an idealist, but he always makes allowances, he always tries to understand and help.'

'But,' Hazard said slowly, 'a difficult man to live with, I would imagine.'

She smiled, thinking of that wonderful face, the happiness of her parents' marriage. 'Oh yes, though I don't think my mother found it so; you see, she thought him perfect.'

'He was a lucky man – not many women could cope with that I think – and yet, *you* love him.'

Again she smiled. 'There is so much to love in him that one forgets the difficulties, the irritations he sets up. I would like to think that this will free him from all the torture he has gone through for so long.'

He said sharply, 'But you don't believe it will change anything.'

'Knowing him, I think it is unlikely, but I hope that I am wrong.' She paused before asking, 'When he was struggling to remember – why didn't you tell him then?'

'I've never told anybody,' he said slowly, and when she didn't answer, 'Can't you understand why?'

'But surely it would have been better?' she began and be broke in roughly, 'There are several reasons why it would not have been better, not least of which I have no proof that it was not done in anger. It would only have been my word.' He paused for a second, then, his voice almost pleading, 'You can't begin to know what it was like and – it had to be an instant decision.'

'It must have been so awful for you.'

'The worst thing of all was that I could not come home to tell Colonel Warren that I had killed his son. Don't you see how terrible that would have been? How could I ever have made him see that it was the only thing I could do for Victor? Much better that he should believe that his son had been killed in action. You must see that surely darling?'

There was a long silence before Freya said slowly, 'Yes, I suppose you are right. If Dad had not been a witness, nobody would have known and there would have been no complications.'

Leaving her chair, she went to stand beside him, taking both his hands in hers. 'Oh darling – what a tremendous relief. I am so very glad that you have told me. It must have been a terrible burden to bear all this time, but it is over now. Surely between us we can make

Dad understand and—' She hesitated and finished on a questioning note, 'And the Colonel need never know. There would be no sense in distressing him now.'

He leaned back to kiss her gently. 'I'm sorry my love but it's not quite so straightforward as that. I made a bad mistake in going to see Wayland.'

'But *why* did you go? I don't understand that.'

He shrugged. 'No – in retrospect I don't think I do either, except that it was a desperate idea brought on by my fear of losing you. I was snatching at straws.' He paused, finishing bitterly, 'And this one turned out to be weaker than most.'

'Was Dad right in thinking that you had a row with him that day?'

'Yes, we did have a row. A stupid one. He'd had too many beers in the bar and was being offensive to the rather timid barmaid who was quite incapable of dealing with him.' For the first time, he smiled. 'I tried to quieten him down but it was no use and I ended up by hitting him and throwing him out of the bar.'

'Did you know him or was that the first time you had met?'

'Oh yes, I knew him. He is a reporter and we've met from time to time, but we've never had anything in common and I've not seen him since the Falklands.'

'Why did you think that he might be willing to help?'

'I explained about your father being wounded and thinking he had seen me shoot a man before he blacked out. I told him that because he had seen the row the night before, he had decided that it must be him.' He stopped abruptly. 'Oh God – what a muddle it sounds now but all I wanted him to do was provide me with some proof that he was still alive. I can't think why I was such a fool.'

'You mean that you didn't mean to tell Dad the truth?'

He hesitated, then shrugged. 'I suppose that I hoped it would turn out like that.' She heard him sigh. 'You know why I told no one, but with all this being stirred up, I suppose I hadn't much hope of it remaining that way.'

He looked at her with troubled eyes. 'What I certainly wasn't prepared for was Wayland seeing it as a chance for a spot of blackmail.'

'Blackmail? Oh no.'

'He doesn't call it that of course, but he is heavily in debt at the present time and said that this could be worked out on a mutual benefit system.'

'What is he talking about?'

'It didn't take him long to realize just how important it was to me that Colonel Warren shouldn't know what had happened. This gave him just the lever he needed.'

'You mean he threatened to tell him?'

'Just that. Unless I paid off his debts. He saw it, he said, as an easy solution to both our difficulties.' Hazard spoke in a voice of complete contempt, adding, 'And yet, he used to be quite a decent chap, though I never liked him.'

Freya asked quickly, 'What are you going to do?'

He came to her and held her close. 'I'm so sorry my love. You must be wishing you had never met me, but I love you so much. Please understand that.'

She looked up at him questioningly. 'Are you saying that you intend paying this money?'

Her voice was sharper than she had intended and he let her go, starting to roam the room in his restless way, saying evenly, 'There was no decision made. I said I needed time to get the money, and in any case, I wanted time to think.'

Freya watched him carefully. 'You *can't* pay him. You *mustn't*.'

He stopped abruptly. 'You know the alternative,' he said harshly.

'Yes, I know the alternative. I wouldn't want to add to the Colonel's grief, you must know that, but surely you must know that one payment would not be the end.'

'What do you mean?' His eyes narrowed as he stared at her.

She said very quietly, 'Of course he would try again. He wouldn't be content with one payment.'

Hazard gave a deep sigh and came to rest with one arm on the mantelpiece.

'You are right, of course. I wasn't going to tell you but he told me that he saw the shooting from a distance. Too far to see who held the gun.'

'So, he didn't know until you told him?' Frowning, she added, 'What else could he do?'

Hazard shrugged. 'Heaven knows but no doubt he could cause trouble.'

For some minutes Freya remained silent, then she said with some viciousness, 'We have to stop this man.'

The green eyes were cold and hard as he said slowly, 'Yes, I agree, but not at the expense of the old man whose son I shot.'

Nineteen

Freya and Hazard talked until late but did not come up with any original ideas of how to tackle the situation, but at least Freya extracted a promise from Hazard to play for time before agreeing to part with any money. After a long silence Freya said, 'I want Dad to know the truth. I owe him that.'

It was a long time before Hazard replied, 'He will still try to stop you marrying me.'

'Perhaps, but at least he will be nearer to understanding what really happened.'

He came to stand close to her but without touching her. 'Perhaps he will persuade you.'

She lifted her hands to hold his face between them, leaning forward to kiss him gently on the lips. 'Oh no, he won't. Nobody could do that.'

He sighed deeply as his arms came round her. 'Thank you for trusting me. I couldn't bear to lose you now.'

They drove down to Sussex on the Saturday morning, using Hazard's car. When they arrived, there was already a car in the drive which Freya recognized as Colonel Warren's. She was suddenly uneasy at the two men meeting after so long a period but when they entered the room, the Colonel came forward with his hands outstretched to greet Hazard.

'My dear boy – how very nice. Robin told me you

were both coming. Such a long time since we met. Time
seems to fly.'

Freya watched Hazard carefully but he seemed to be
entirely under control as he greeted the Colonel and she
felt a sense of relief as Robin said as he kissed her,
'Philip is staying for lunch. I didn't realize it was so long
since they had met.' He turned to Hazard saying, 'Pour
Freya a drink and help yourself.'

Conversation became general and, as if by tacit
consent, the Falklands war was not mentioned. The
Colonel was interested to hear what Hazard was doing
now and they continued to talk quite easily. It was
Robin who was not relaxed and Freya wondered what
the two men had been discussing before their arrival.
Had they talked of his recovered memory? If so, there
was nothing in the Colonel's manner to indicate it
during lunch, or later when he started to tease Robin
about his attentive ladies of the parish.

'They vie with each other,' he told Hazard, 'as to who
can supply him with the best favours. I must admit to
jealousy – I don't know what he does to engender so
much admiration.'

Normally Robin would go along with this mood, but
watching him, Freya realized that he was finding it
irritating and after a few minutes, she changed the
subject to Jill and her American friend.

'I think you would like him Dad. He's an interesting
man and certainly he writes well.'

'They must come down. Yes, I would like to meet
him.'

Soon after, the Colonel stood up to leave. Turning to
Hazard, he said warmly, 'Come and see me soon if you
can spare the time.'

'Thanks very much – yes, I'd like that.'

After he had left, the cheerfulness seemed to leave the

room. It was quite dark now and Freya went to pull the curtains. Kneeling on the hearth, she threw more logs on the fire then, standing and looking at her father, said gently, 'Dad, sit down. Hazard has something to tell you that I think you should know.'

He continued to stand for a moment as he looked down at her with troubled eyes. She saw him frown and his mouth tighten before he sat down with a sigh. Then he moved a hand in a gesture for Hazard to begin.

'Thomas Wayland is alive.'

'Thank God. Oh, thank God for that.' Robin broke in before Hazard could continue and Freya realized in that moment that Hazard had made a bad start. She saw the relief in her father's face and knew that during the next few minutes that expression would be wiped from it.

Hazard said quietly, 'But I'm afraid that is not the end.'

'What do you mean?' The blue eyes studied Hazard and the brightness went out of his face.

'I mean that you chose the wrong man. You naturally assumed that the man I had a row with was the one who was killed.'

A log fell from the fire with a crash and Freya went to replace it in the silence which followed.

At last, Robin asked, 'Then, who was it who died?'

After a momentary hesitation, Hazard said, 'Let me start at the beginning, so that you can understand better.'

Robin frowned, looking confused, but he signed for Hazard to continue.

Speaking slowly and without mentioning Victor by name, Hazard built up a picture of a boyhood friendship which continued up to manhood until the time of the Falklands war. Father and daughter watched closely and silently, but only Freya understood his reluctance as he paused, then spoke only to Robin.

'You remember the bombing raid – the one in which

you were wounded. One plane flew in low and I saw it drop its bomb near a group of men. You must have seen it?' He looked at Robin who nodded, his eyes fixed on Hazard and Freya saw the struggle between fear and memory changing his expression.

Again, Hazard was silent and Freya suffered with him as he forced himself to continue. 'There were seven men in that group and the bomb killed six of them.'

In an involuntary gesture, his hand came up to cover his eyes as if even after all this time, the sight was unbearable. Robin asked, 'And the seventh?'

Dropping his hand to his side, Hazard said quietly, 'The seventh man was alive and conscious but so severely wounded that there was no possibility that he could live.'

Watching her father Freya saw understanding begin to dawn and after a long silence, he said, 'And that was the man you shot.'

'Yes.'

The room was very quiet, the only sound a log shifting and sending out a shower of sparks flying up the chimney. Finally Robin asked, 'Did you know this man?'

'Yes, I had known him all my life.' Hazard's voice was quite steady as he added, 'It was Victor Warren.'

'May God forgive you.'

Freya saw Hazard flinch as if he had been hit. After a minute, he asked, 'You think that I should have left him to die in agony?'

'You took a life.'

'Dad, you don't understand how badly wounded Victor was.'

Robin said to Hazard, 'How could you be so sure?'

Hazard said with brutal clarity, 'Half his body was blown away. No man could live like that. There was no doubt in my mind.' He paused, then added more calmly, 'It was the only thing I could do for him.'

For the first time, Robin looked at him with a fleeting sense of pity and understanding. 'You must have been haunted by a terrible sense of guilt.'

Hazard made no reply but Freya said angrily, 'Guilt? I only hope that I would have had the courage to do what Hazard did for his friend.'

There was a long silence then she asked her father in a tight voice, 'If you had not been wounded, what would *you* have done?'

He was a long time answering, then he said quietly, 'I would have tried to make his dying easier.'

'And that is exactly what Hazard did. Can't you see that?'

Hazard smiled at her, putting out his hand to touch hers as it lay near him, but he remained silently watching the old man whose face was a mask of indecision.

Still angry, she said, 'I thought you believed in a merciful God.'

He looked at her then with infinite sadness in his eyes. 'Yes, I believe that God is merciful.' The words fell into a long silence during which Freya struggled to calm herself.

Into the quietness Hazard said in a low voice, 'I couldn't have done it if I hadn't loved him.'

Robin glanced at him sharply as if he had made something clear and it seemed to Freya that for the first time her father understood something of the suffering Hazard had been through. He said gently, 'I think that I can understand how you felt – what made you do it. I find it hard to believe that it was right. It is, you see, against everything which I have been taught to believe.' He gestured in a helpless way with a hand. 'It is very difficult, very confusing.' He stopped abruptly then, almost in a tone of relief added, 'But in any case, it is not for me to judge you.'

Twenty

Nobody contradicted that statement and, as if by agreement, a long silence followed which none of them attempted to break and it was an anticlimax when Martha opened the door carrying a tea tray. It was not until then that they realized that they had been sitting in the firelight and Hazard jumped up to put on the light and take the tray from Martha who exclaimed, 'Oh, I'm sorry if I disturbed you. Were you all asleep?'

She looked at each in turn, finally her eyes settling on Robin as he stood up and smiled.

'The sight of tea will rouse us all,' he told her evasively. 'And I see you have been making one of your chocolate cakes to fatten us up.'

'And that won't do you any harm,' she told him abrasively but with a smile. Adding, 'I'm just going down the lane to see if Hannah needs anything.' She turned to Freya, 'I told you she has just come out of hospital and is on her own in the cottage.'

'Tell her I'll be down to see her later. I've brought some fruit for her. Is she all right?'

Freya and Martha talked for a few moments before Martha left.

'She's a good old girl, my Martha,' Robin said affectionately as she closed the door and Freya moved to pour the tea, saying as she did so, 'Well, it's a good job she is here to keep you in order. I don't know what you'd get up to without her.'

The complete breakaway from their previous mood brought normality into the room and during tea, in a sort of relief, they spoke only of local news in the village and since Hazard only knew a few of the people they were mentioning, he remained, gratefully, on the fringe of the conversation. Freya saw that her father was making a great effort to come to terms with what Hazard had told him. In a way, she thought, it had gone rather better than she had expected. At least her father had not shown anger, in fact, in spite of his own strong beliefs, he had shown some semblance of understanding. Men were odd, she thought, as she studied the two in front of her, both with large slices of Martha's chocolate cake on their plates. Only a short while ago, they had both been deeply concerned in the story of a man's death. A story which, for different reasons, affected each of them closely. Both these men were terribly important to her and she loved them both, but so differently. Perhaps, she thought with an inward smile, the cake provided a sort of childish comfort in an otherwise stark situation.

For the first time, Robin looked relaxed as fastidiously he cut his cake into small squares, giving the task his full attention. Hazard was obviously thinking of something else as he carefully cut his thick slice into two thin ones. Would an analyst be able to deduce something from this different approach to a simple task? Freya considered the point half seriously and Hazard looked up as if conscious of her watching him.

'Quite delicious,' he said with a smile as if this were an ordinary afternoon. Somehow the absurd incident relieved the tension in the room and when they had finished, Hazard offered to carry the tray to the kitchen.

On his return to the room, Robin said slowly, 'I wonder what Philip's reaction would be.'

'No. No. He must not know. I've been so careful all this time and told no one. You *can't* tell him now. Please.' There was real fear in his voice and Robin looked surprised, then put out a hand to touch Hazard's arm. 'Hold hard dear boy, I didn't say I was going to tell him. I agree entirely with you that there is no point in adding to his grief with such a bizarre story. It would not serve any purpose.'

'Thank God for that,' Hazard said fervently.

Robin continued, 'Whatever my own beliefs, I know you must have suffered terribly – are still suffering. I respect that and I would never try to make it worse for you or Philip. I acknowledge that what you did was done under stress and with the best motives. I can't go along with it, but as I said, it is not for me to judge.'

His attitude was far better than Freya had feared and surely this would free him from his own sense of guilt.

'Dad, have you thought what this will mean for *you*?'

He looked at her questioningly and Freya said, 'You are free now.'

He moved slowly round the room, coming to rest in front of Louise's photograph, picking it up and holding it with both hands before replacing it on the desk. 'She always believed that I would recover my memory but she never held me guilty of anything.'

Hazard said firmly, 'But you never *were* guilty.'

'If I hadn't been hit, I could have stopped you.' His eyes narrowed as if he were reliving that terrible scene. 'Yes, it was that which worried me all this time. I couldn't move, you see – so I couldn't do anything at all.'

He stood gazing down into the bright logs, then at Freya. 'You are right darling. I *am* free, and it is a wonderful feeling after all these years of guilt.' Turning to Hazard, his wonderful smile spreading, he said simply, 'Thank you for telling me. I know that it couldn't have been easy.'

He stood quietly, his hands held out to the flames then, turning to Freya, he said, 'I'm going over to the church for a while,' and made his way to the door, closing it quietly after him.

Neither of them moved until Freya came to Hazard, reaching up to put her hands behind his neck, bringing his mouth down to hers in a long kiss, finally saying, 'Thank you for telling him. You can see how much it means to him after such a long nightmare.'

Hazard smiled. 'And now he has gone to give thanks for his release.' There was something in his voice which made her draw back from him.

'Why do you say it like that?'

Looking into her eyes, he said soberly, 'Perhaps because I envy him. It must be wonderful to have that kind of simple faith.' He kissed her gently. 'I can see now why you love him. He has—' He hesitated. 'He has great simplicity – and a sort of innocence.'

Twenty-One

Robin had preached a sermon on the different levels of mercy during which Freya had found her eyes fixed hypnotically on the slim blue-eyed figure in the pulpit. He usually preached well but she had never heard him deliver one as powerful and far reaching as this, and it was not until he had left the pulpit that she felt herself relax and, glancing at Hazard sitting beside her, she was surprised to see tears in his eyes.

As soon as they reached home, Freya went to her father and putting her arms round his neck, reached up to kiss him. 'Dad that was the best.'

Smiling down at her, he said simply, 'I think your Hazard has taught me something.'

'*My* Hazard?'

'Yes. That is what you want, isn't it?'

She nodded then turned to Hazard who took her hand, saying to Robin, 'Then, we have your blessing?' Smiling, he added, 'I promise that I will do everything I can to make her happy.'

Robin came to put an arm round each of their shoulders. 'Yes, I believe that you will, and Freya's happiness means everything to me.'

It was fairly late that evening when they left to drive to London, feeling far happier than they had on the way down. They had a lot to discuss but decided that it could wait until the next evening.

Driving back to her flat on the Monday from the office, Freya became aware that the same blue car always seemed to draw up behind her at each red light. Until the third time, she had regarded it as purely chance, after that, she paid more attention and as she neared her destination, realized the car was still with her. Deliberately, she slowed and wondered what the driver would do, but he made no effort to pass and when she increased speed, he still kept behind her. Suddenly she became worried, going hastily through her mind for any photographic assignments which could have caused any hostility. Such a thing was entirely unlikely, she knew, but she found it difficult to believe it was pure chance that the car had been following her across London. Finally, when she reached her own turning, she drove past slowly and saw the driver turn to look at the name. When she finally arrived at the flat, she was annoyed to find that she was trembling, now feeling certain that she had been followed deliberately, but for what reason, she had no idea.

Early the next morning, her secretary reported that she had a call from a Mr Wayland. Should she put him through?

Conscious of a small shock running through her, Freya hesitated, her mind racing. Now she had some idea of who had been following her the evening before. Agreeing to take the call, she waited.

'Miss Marsdon?'

'Yes.'

'You probably will not know my name but—'

'Your name is Thomas Wayland and you followed my car last night.'

Believing that attack was better than defence, she

hoped that she had stopped him in his tracks. At least she had surprised him for there was a complete silence before finally, he answered. 'Well, at least that makes things easier. I very much want to come and see you.'

He had, Freya noticed, an extremely attractive voice.

'For what purpose?' she enquired bluntly.

'One reason is that you are an extremely attractive girl.'

'And your real reason?'

'I think that we may be of help to each other.'

'I find that difficult to imagine.' Freya's tone was icy.

'But I take it that you might be interested in being of help to Hazard Denning.' It was a statement of fact, and he continued smoothly, 'I suggest that at least we could meet and have a chat.'

When she did not answer, he said reasonably, 'That surely, can do no harm to either of us. In fact, it might even interest you to hear what I have to say. How about lunch tomorrow?'

Suddenly Freya was intrigued and said sharply, 'Very well. Where?'

He mentioned a restaurant near her office and, agreeing a time, she rang off, sitting for several minutes, trying to assess the conversation which had just taken place. Her first instinct was to ring up Hazard. Her hand on the phone, she hesitated then decided against it. She would keep her meeting with Thomas Wayland without telling anyone. She was curious to hear what he had to say and meeting in such a public place could do no harm.

The rest of the day, she found it difficult to concentrate and left early for home, ringing Jill as soon as she arrived, feeling the need to discuss the odd phone call with someone who would listen and advise.

Jill was intrigued.

'What do you think he wants from me?' Freya asked anxiously.

'The only thing I can think of,' Jill replied thoughtfully, 'is to try to frighten you on the extent of Hazard's wrongdoing.'

'Why should he want to do that?'

'He is probably aware that Hazard is hesitant about agreeing to his blackmail efforts. He may feel that a push from you might do it.'

'I suppose he must have been watching me for a few days, since he knew where the office was then followed me home.'

Jill said, 'Be careful tomorrow. Don't let him see that you are scared.'

'I'm not scared for myself, but I know how much this means to Hazard – that Colonel Warren shouldn't be told. Nobody could expect him to understand.'

'No, I understand that, but Hazard won't want *you* to be hurt by any of this.'

For the first time Freya said, 'I didn't tell Hazard about the phone call. I want to deal with this myself, without worrying him.'

Jill looked at her affectionately. 'You are very much in love, aren't you?'

'Yes, I am. We both are. I am proud of what he did, no matter what anybody thinks. He did what he felt to be right for his friend and, for me, that is enough.'

She paused, then said slowly, 'You know, I was surprised by Dad's reaction. In spite of all his own strict beliefs and rules, he seemed able to understand how Hazard felt and why he was able to do it.'

'And that made all the difference to the way he felt about you marrying?'

Freya smiled at the recollection of what her father had said. 'Yes, he said that Hazard, acting under stress, had done what he believed to be right for his friend, and that it was not for him to judge him.' She paused, then added slowly, 'He said that he thought Hazard had taught *him* something.'

'Meaning that he had caused him to think again himself.'

Freya nodded, saying, 'He preached a really wonderful sermon on the different aspects of mercy, and I am sure that is why he did it. I know that it affected Hazard very much.'

After a short silence, Jill said gently, 'You are very much in the middle, aren't you?'

Freya looked at her questioningly.

'I mean, you are very much the deciding factor for Hazard, it is essential that you understand Robin. You have to be—' She stopped, then continued slowly, 'I think that you have to be unsullied – untouched by what Hazard did. These two men whom you love are so entirely different – demand so much from you. You are in such a difficult position.'

'Are you saying that I allow my father to influence me too much?'

'No, not that exactly. I know you've not slept with Hazard, mostly because you know it would shock Robin.'

Freya gave a short laugh. 'Well, it's certainly not because I don't want to,' she said frankly.

'Robin wouldn't have to know,' Jill pointed out.

'No, but I'd hate to fall below his standards. I think it's because he is such a good man himself, though *he* doesn't know that. Perhaps that is why I want so much to please him, bless his heart.'

Twenty-Two

Freya slept badly that night, her mind filled with thoughts of the meeting the following day. What would the man with the attractive voice be like? Perhaps subtly persuasive. The day she had seen him argue with Hazard they had been too far away to be sure of anything except that he had looked slightly shorter than Hazard. She was determined to hold her own in a conversation and not to allow herself to be browbeaten by this man.

She decided not to be early for this appointment and the next morning, emerged from the office to walk slowly to the restaurant. She was aware that the tailored grey coat she was wearing was suitable to the occasion. She was conscious of her quickened heartbeat as she entered the restaurant to stand for a moment inside, wondering what she would do if her host had not already arrived. A man rose from a table near the window, coming towards her with hand outstretched.

'Miss Marsdon?'

She nodded, and he led her to the table and offered her a drink. Sitting down, she studied him carefully, realizing that she had had a definite picture in her mind to which the man opposite her did not conform. This man was very good looking, blond and wearing a dark grey suit with plain navy tie. Altogether neat and presentable, and again, she was attracted by his voice, saying now, 'It was good of you to come. I appreciate it.'

Prepared for a rather cruder approach, Freya hardly knew how to deal with this mildness and remained silent as the waiter brought their drinks.

'If one has something to discuss, it is always easier to make a personal contact.' Light grey eyes studied her smilingly.

With raised eyebrows, Freya asked innocently, 'Have we anything to discuss?'

'Oh yes. I would say that we have quite a lot to discuss.' He paused, the light eyes still on her. 'Things which are important to both of us.'

At that moment, a waiter presented a menu to both of them and with childish glee, Freya proceeded to choose the most expensive dishes. As they finally gave the order, her glee was slightly dampened by the uncomfortable feeling that Thomas Wayland was quite aware of what she had done as he consulted her on the choice of wine. Suddenly Freya wished that she had not come.

'I understand that although you are engaged to Hazard – and doubtless, are very much in love – you do not know each other very well.'

'Surely that cannot be of any interest to you?'

'Oh, but I think it can for on such short acquaintance you cannot have an accurate assessment of his character.'

Freya picked up her glass, taking a sip of the wine the waiter had just poured. She said coolly, 'So far I cannot see any reason for me having come here. There seems to be no point in this conversation.'

He was looking down at his glass which he was turning in his fingers. He raised his hand to stare at her. 'It was not the first time Hazard had shot Victor Warren.'

He spoke softly but Freya felt as if he had shouted the

words, hearing them with a sense of shock. She felt her mouth go dry and moistened her lips with the tip of her tongue.

His deep voice sounded sympathetic as he said, 'I am sorry. I am afraid that has shocked you.'

Annoyed that he was aware of the effect of his words, she pulled herself together with a great effort, saying chillingly, 'I take it that that is exactly what you intended.'

He shrugged. 'It is unfortunate that you are so antagonistic. My intention is to help you.'

She stared at him angrily. 'Don't be absurd. Why should you do that when all you want is to blackmail Hazard.'

For the first time, he looked disconcerted. 'Blackmail? What an accusation. Nothing like that, I do assure you. Don't forget that Hazard came to me for help in the first place and—'

'Yes, and that was the greatest mistake he could have made.'

He smiled. 'Perhaps – and, of course, one always pays for one's mistakes.'

Their main dish had arrived and he busied himself seeing that Freya had everything she needed as if this lunch was a pleasant social occasion. Glancing at her plate Freya wondered how she was going to be able to eat the delicious food feeling as she did at that moment, but, determined to make an effort, she picked up her knife and fork. Both ate silently for a few minutes, then Wayland said quietly. 'I think you forget that with what I know, I am in a position to ruin Hazard.' He moved a hand in a generous gesture. 'I haven't the slightest wish to ruin anybody, but it so happens that I need some money quickly, and if only Hazard is sensible and reasonable, we can help each other and that is the end of it.'

Freya took a further mouthful before saying anything, then spoke slowly without looking at him. 'Hazard is not asking anything for himself, only that an old man should not be told how his son died because he would not understand.'

Even to her own ears it sounded useless and inadequate and unlikely to evoke any sympathy from the man sitting opposite her, but she was totally unprepared for what he said.

'You mean that you have swallowed that story whole? You really believe that is the reason he doesn't want the story known?'

She met the derisive light grey eyes squarely. 'Oh yes. I believe it because I am certain it is true.'

He offered her an attractive smile as he reached across to touch her hand as it lay on the table.

'Hazard is a lucky man to have such a lovely girl so much in love with him,' he said as she quickly removed her hand. 'Perhaps you think I am lying when I tell you that the Falklands war was not the first time he shot his so called friend. I imagine that even if you don't know Hazard well, you must agree that he has a very short fuse?'

It was a question Freya had no intention of answering as she continued to stare at Wayland. When she remained silent, he went on smoothly. 'You see, I was there; I saw it happen. We were all three members of the school OTC and—'

She interrupted quickly, 'Are you saying that you were all three at the same school?'

He raised his eyebrows. 'Oh yes, didn't you know?'

She shook her head and he sat back in his chair with a satisfied air as the waiter came to change their plates.

'It was a stupid affair, really,' he said when they were

alone again, 'though it might have ended tragically.' He reached forward to pick up his glass and sipped his wine and Freya fought down a desire to ask a question as he watched her. Putting down his glass, he said, 'Warren was a marvellous shot and Hazard had always resented that. He was very jealous of Warren.'

Freya remained silent, realizing that it made Wayland's task more difficult and she was becoming more angry by the minute. He looked at her as if trying to gauge her mood, then said, 'It is difficult to imagine how it could have happened by mistake.' He paused. 'I mean, those sort of exercises at school are pretty carefully vetted. Besides – I was watching Hazard at the time. He shot him through the arm.'

Freya's voice was sharp with disbelief. 'You are saying, I think, that Hazard shot Victor deliberately.'

He shrugged. 'It certainly had every appearance of being deliberate. Anyway, the powers-that-be treated the whole thing very seriously.'

Freya said coldly, 'I imagine they would. *If* such a thing ever happened.'

Suddenly, he looked annoyed. 'It happened,' he told her shortly, attacking the ice-cream in front of him.

After a moment, Freya said, 'I do wonder what point you had in us meeting today.'

He didn't answer for a moment, then he said quietly, 'I can tell you exactly. It is very simple really. I made an unwise investment which went very wrong, leaving me holding the baby, without any possibility of being able to pay the debt.' He paused, shrugging. 'These things sometimes happen.' He put down his spoon carefully before continuing. 'Then, Hazard came along. Well – a bit worried to say the least, and I saw it as a godsent opportunity for us to help each other.'

He waited and when she remained silent, his tone

became more unpleasant. 'Unfortunately, and I think foolishly, Hazard refused to see things in the same light. He refused to co-operate.'

Freya said, 'And where do I come in?'

'I don't think Hazard quite realized that I was serious when I threatened to – well – spill the beans all round.'

Freya's voice was contemptuous as she said, 'I understood you to say that you were not a blackmailer.'

'Ah – there you are right, and that is where *you* come in. I have explained the position so that you can be quite clear of the position Hazard is in if I decided to make public all that I know against him.' He stopped speaking, staring into her angry eyes. 'What I have in mind is that all these difficulties can be solved if you use your considerable influence to persuade Hazard that it is in both our interests for him to – er – relieve me of my debt.'

She met this long speech in silence, then he added helpfully, 'I would be quite willing to sign a document saying it is a final payment.'

Gathering up her bag and gloves, Freya stood up, saying politely, 'Thank you for the lunch. I am afraid that you have wasted your money.' Then, turning, she walked out of the restaurant.

Twenty-Three

Back in her office, Freya sat at her desk furious with the man and his arrogance. How dare he make such accusations? She pressed her finger against her eyes, as if to blot out the words which were so vivid, in her mind, hearing again that very attractive voice saying, 'I was watching Hazard at the time. He shot Victor through the arm.'

In spite of herself, a small doubt crept into her mind, the next instant to be pushed away. Thomas Wayland must have been mistaken. Yet, how could he be? He said he had been watching Hazard. He must have been able to see what happened. He had said that 'Hazard has a short fuse'. Reluctantly, she had to admit that he did have a quick temper, but on the only two occasions that she had seen it, it had been instantly controlled. Wayland had said that Hazard was jealous because Victor was a better shot than he was. That sounded childish and totally unlike Hazard as she knew him.

She moved irritably, reminding herself how everybody kept reminding *her* how little she really knew about the man she had decided to marry. Surely she could not be so mistaken in his character. Then, why was she doubting him now? Surely she should have more faith. The phone on her desk rang and she picked it up slowly and was immediately caught up in the day's

116

business and had little time to consider her own affairs until she was driving home that evening.

Jill had put a note through her letter box. 'We are having supper at home tonight. Will you join us about half past seven? You need not let me know. Just come.'

She did not need to ask who the 'we' referred to and, for a second, hesitated, thought about the evening ahead of her and decided to go, reflecting that Charles had known Hazard much longer than she had. She would ask for his advice.

A long hot bath and a change into an attractive dress did a lot to improve her mood and when she arrived at Jill's flat, their faces told her that this was no ordinary occasion. Smiling, she looked at each of them. 'And – what are you going to tell me?' she asked innocently.

Charles said cheerfully, 'I've managed to beat her into submission and she has agreed to marry me.'

The next few minutes were filled with joy and genuine affection and the opening of champagne to drink to their future, and it was not until after dinner and they were drinking coffee that Jill looked at Freya saying, 'I've not forgotten. How did your meeting go?'

Carefully, Freya repeated almost everything which had taken place and when she had finished, turned to Charles.

'You have known him longer than I have. What do you think?'

He didn't hesitate. 'The whole thing is absurd.' He paused, frowning, 'I don't pretend to know how these things are run in English schools, but I'm damned sure that there would be strict rules for the boys who were shooting and a careless approach would not be allowed – or indeed – possible.'

He put down the coffee cup he was holding and smiled at Freya. 'Yes, I have known Hazard quite a bit longer than you and I am sure that neither of us is wrong about his character. I am quite certain that he is incapable of that sort of behaviour. He is a sensitive and caring man – often too much for his own good, and from what you told me about Victor Warren's death, he can carry friendship to its limits.' He shook his head. 'No, there must be some other explanation for that shot in the arm.'

Freya smiled gratefully. 'Thank you for that. I feel better now. I didn't really doubt him, but it was a shock, and of course, I can't prove that it is wrong, can I?'

'Why do you say that?' Jill asked quickly. 'Don't you suppose that however it happened, the Colonel would know the facts?'

Freya turned to her eagerly. 'Why, yes, of course he must know – that is if it really happened.'

As they watched, they saw her hesitate, then she said, 'But I don't want to cause any trouble in that direction – cause him any worry.'

Jill said, 'You visit him sometimes, don't you? Surely it would be easy to mention their schooldays and natural that you should want to talk about Hazard and what he was like earlier. I can't see that that could do any harm.'

They enlarged on the subject for a few minutes, then Freya, not wanting to put a damper on their celebrations, asked what their immediate plans were, and the rest of the evening was spent in pleasant argument between Jill and Charles as to how soon he could persuade her to marry him and join him in America. As Freya watched their animated discussion, she thought how much she would miss Jill and her often astringent advice, and then she reflected that she too, would be leaving here if she married Hazard. She drew herself up sharply. Why had she thought in terms of 'if' and not 'when'? Suddenly she felt depressed, as if she could not see the way forward; as if, after all, Thomas Wayland could be the means of stopping it happening; as if he really did have the power to ruin Hazard.

She sat listening to the happy planning of these friends who made up a part of her life. Everything was changing, and for Jill and Charles, the future looked pretty good. Both were experienced; both were intelligent people who were going into this marriage with their eyes open. If they cared enough they would be successful and she wished them all the joy they could have. When she thought of her own future, it appeared clouded in comparison, but she was determined to fight for that future and decided that her first move would be to visit Colonel Warren the next weekend and to entice him to tell her more about the schooldays which Victor and Hazard had shared. If he showed disinclination to talk of those days, she would not persist, but she hoped that would not be the case and was determined to remain hopeful.

Twenty-Four

Sunlight across her face wakened her on Saturday morning and for a few minutes, she lay relaxed in the gentle warmth, letting her thoughts gather slowly as her senses quickened. As usual, her first thought was of Hazard, the second, disappointment that she would not see him this weekend, though in one way, that would make it easier as it would leave her free for her planned visit to Colonel Warren. At breakfast, when she suggested it, Robin was delighted. 'I'm sure that will please him,' he told her. 'I think he is often lonely and he will love talking to you.'

It was a lovely early spring day and she decided to walk through the lanes to the village. The Colonel was gardening, looking up irritably when he heard her open the clanging gate, obviously annoyed to be disturbed, but at sight of her, he broke into a welcoming smile, coming forward, taking off his gloves, holding out both hands to her.

'You looked annoyed,' she accused him, laughing.

'Well, I didn't know it would be you, did I? I thought it was old Martin who never speaks a word of sense and doesn't listen to anyone else.'

'He certainly doesn't sound a very rewarding visitor,' Freya agreed, adding that she had called to see if he would like to come to lunch tomorrow.

'That sounds like a very good idea,' he said as he started towards the house. 'Come on in and we'll have some coffee – unless you would like something stronger?'

'Coffee will be splendid thanks. I shall enjoy some after walking over.'

'What have you done with your young man?' he wanted to know as they went into the kitchen.

'He is working over the weekend so he couldn't come down with me.' She fetched mugs from the old-fashioned dresser in the enormous kitchen, and set them on the table while he filled the kettle. 'Mrs Felton doesn't come on Saturdays?'

'No. Nor Sundays of course. Rather nice in a way to have the place to myself – do as I like then,' he said with a grin as he spooned coffee into the mugs.

'Does she keep a firm hand on you?' Freya enquired, laughing, and he nodded as he fetched milk from the fridge. 'Oh yes,' he said gloomily. 'Must always have a pudding – much rather have cheese. I don't go much on sweet things.'

'Couldn't you tell her?' Freya suggested mildly.

'Oh, I've done that. Doesn't do any good. *She* likes puddings, so we go on having them.' Suddenly, he laughed. 'But she's a good old thing. Been here for donkey's years. Thinks she owns the place, but does her best. Much too fat though – all those puddings.'

He looked round the kitchen, saying hopefully, 'I expect there are some biscuits somewhere. I must say I feel a bit peckish after all that weeding.'

Spotting a decorative tin on the dresser, Freya fetched it and put it on the table. 'Probably in here,' she said taking off the lid and peering inside. 'Digestive. Is that all right?'

'Splendid, I like those. Help yourself. Do you want to

take all this into the drawing-room?' he asked
doubtfully.

'No thanks. This will do very well,' Freya said,
perching herself on the corner of the table.

'Mind if I light my pipe?'

'Not at all, except that you shouldn't be smoking.'

He shrugged. 'Too late to give up now. Besides, I am
very disciplined, I only allow myself two a day.' He
busied himself filling and lighting the pipe, looking at
her through the smoke when he had it going.

'I'm glad you are marrying Hazard. Couldn't do
better. He will make you a good husband.' He pulled
out a chair and sat down and Freya slid off the table and
sat down opposite him.

'Everybody is telling me that I haven't known him
long enough. What do *you* think?'

After a moment, he said thoughtfully, '*He* will be
absolutely sure, I am certain of that. He feels things very
deeply – like his friendship with Victor. He doesn't
change.'

She asked, 'What was he like as a schoolboy? You
knew him then didn't you?'

'Yes, he was often here in the holidays. We got to
know him very well. He fitted into the household very
easily and Victor liked to have him here. They were very
close in spite of being so different.'

'How were they different?'

'Victor was easy going and even tempered and he
could express himself much better than Hazard ever
could and that made him easier to understand. Hazard
is quick tempered and a champion of causes and that
sometimes makes for difficulties, though he is a very
gentle man.'

'Did they quarrel?'

'No, never, and they always backed each other up.'

'Were they ever jealous of each other, I mean, if one excelled at something, like shooting, for instance?'

The Colonel shook his head. 'Both in the OTC of course, but Victor was by far the best shot.'

'And Hazard didn't mind? I mean, didn't he want to beat him?'

He looked at her almost pityingly. 'Oh no, nothing like that. It wasn't that sort of relationship. Hazard wasn't a bad shot – only just not good enough to beat Victor, who was rather exceptional.' He laughed. 'Hazard could beat him at other things – it worked out all right I think. Certainly there was no jealousy.'

He sat puffing at his pipe, a lazy cloud of smoke surrounding him. Suddenly he frowned. 'There *was* one boy though who caused some trouble. That was during camp, when they were clay pigeon shooting.'

Freya felt her nerves tighten. 'What happened?'

He said, still frowning, 'I don't know all the details, but apparently the boy came up behind Hazard as he was about to shoot, and pushed his arm so that he shot Victor in the arm.' Leaning forward, he picked up his coffee cup to find it empty. 'We'll have some more,' he offered, getting up to refill the kettle. He said with some satisfaction, 'Victor told me afterwards that Hazard went completely berserk because he knew that it was deliberate. He went for the chap and had to be pulled off him.' Measuring more coffee into the cups he said regretfully, 'Rather a pity they interfered, I thought.'

Freya asked slowly, 'Was Hazard certain that it was deliberate?'

'Oh yes, quite – several other boys saw it too. There was quite a fuss at the school. They don't like that sort of thing to happen.'

'Would you happen to know the name of the boy?' She waited anxiously for his reply.

At first the Colonel shook his head, then said vaguely, 'I know that it was a chap who was generally disliked.' He stood with the kettle still in his hand, frowning. 'Land,' he said. 'Something to do with land – his name was.'

'Wayland? Thomas Wayland. Was that it?'

He stared at her, muttering the name. 'That could be it – I'm not sure. It's a long time ago, but, what a rotten thing to do. Now *that* was jealousy, if you like.'

Twenty-Five

Walking back, Freya thought of what the Colonel had told her and of all the lies which Thomas Wayland insisted were facts. Facts which he had twisted to his own advantage. Since Victor was dead, he must have felt very sure of himself since there would be little chance of his story being disproved.

She stopped marching along the road to move to lean on a gate into a field where two horses grazed peacefully and the sight of their contentment had the effect of calming her, and she began thinking more clearly. She didn't understand why Hazard had expected Wayland to help. Certainly he must have been desperately worried to risk it. Why was seeing Wayland so important to him? He must have hoped that if he could prove that Wayland was still alive, Robin would be satisfied and after all this time, not worry any more. If that could be achieved, there would be no need for Hazard to tell his own story. Freya sighed as she turned away from the gate and continued walking. Poor Hazard, he had stepped into a hornets' nest. She hoped that he would refuse to pay Wayland any money. But if he didn't get the money, Wayland would carry out his threat. Unless— She stopped short as an idea occurred to her and a boy cycling towards her looked at her oddly.

Thomas Wayland had been a reporter for years. He was obviously not a man of principles. Surely during all that time he must have slipped up somewhere. Suddenly, she felt better. Maybe it would be a long shot, but there must be ways of finding out more about Wayland's past and she was determined to try. Something recent – something farther back in his career? Whom did she know who would have been likely to have come into contact with him? She herself came into contact with the press through her work, and her partner, Graham Mannering had a wide circle of friends. With the thought of perhaps being able to take some action, her spirits lifted. It was a slender chance, but she was determined to try to discover something which would discredit Thomas Wayland to use as a lever against him.

By the time she reached home, she was obsessed with the idea, persuading herself that it would not prove an impossible task. Robin was writing at his desk and looked up with a smile as she entered the study, a smile full of pleasure at her arrival. She looked at him appraisingly and for the first time realized that he was allowing himself to relax. Ever since the Falklands war she had only seen him looking strained and unhappy. Always carrying with him the feeling of guilt he could not shake off, but in the last weeks here had been glimpses of what he had had been like before the bombing. He could, she knew, never condone the taking of a life, but at least, he now understood Hazard's reason and accepted that he had no right to judge the younger man. He would, no doubt, pray for Hazard's soul, but he would no longer condemn him. And that, for Freya, was tremendously important.

She stood for a moment, just inside the room. 'Oh Dad.' The two words were entirely spontaneous and he said sharply, 'What's the matter?'

Reaching the desk, she smiled, taking his hand. 'Nothing at all, but you look so much better and I am so glad.'

He seemed genuinely surprised. 'It meant so much to you?' It was one of his charms that he always put a low value on himself.

She bent swiftly to kiss his cheek as she said, 'Well, of course it means a lot to me. How could it not when I love you?'

He looked up at her as he sat at the desk and his eyes filled with tears. 'I've never heard you say that before. Thank you my dear.'

Pulling himself together, he stood up, glancing down for a second at the pages on the desk. 'I've just been writing a sermon about love. There's nothing like it you know, and so often there is not enough of it.' With a smile, he added, 'I've been such a lucky man.'

They walked to the door arm in arm and he changed the subject abruptly, saying, 'Now tell me about your visit. I've no doubt he was gardening when you arrived. He spends hours in the garden. Grows wonderful flowers and puts me to shame I'm afraid.'

Altogether, Freya reflected as she drove back to London on Sunday evening, it had been a good weekend. Satisfactory from all points of view. The phone was ringing as she entered the flat and, picking up the receiver, she heard Hazard's voice.

'You're late. I rang you earlier.'

He sounded cross and she asked, 'What's wrong?'

There was a short silence, then she heard him laugh. 'Sorry darling, I get jittery if you are not there when I think you are.'

'You mean you think that I might be lying in a pool of blood somewhere after an accident?'

'You must think I'm nuts – but yes – something like

that.'

'A nice kind of nuts though. It's lovely to know that you care about the pools of blood.'

He laughed again, saying, 'I don't understand myself. I've never gone on like this before. Are you all right?'

'Yes darling, I'm quite all right, and Dad seems much better – far more relaxed about everything. How did your job go?'

'I'm still there. It's taken longer than I thought. She's so keen that I shouldn't miss any details of her lurid life that she tends to go on and on. I should be able to leave tomorrow. If so, I'll ring you. I want to take you to see a cottage on my uncle's estate which has just come empty. How do you feel about cottages?'

'Depends where they are and who is going to live in them.'

'Well, there would be me and a girl I know.'

'Sounds intriguing – yes – let's go and see it.'

They talked lightly for a few more minutes then, after a silence, she heard him sigh before saying very seriously, 'I love you so much, I can't wait much longer.'

She said gently, 'It won't be much longer, I promise you, but I want us to start—' She stopped, then finished slowly, 'I want us to start free of the past.'

A short silence before he said quietly, 'You mean Wayland. Not pay him anything.'

'Yes, I mean Wayland and not to pay him anything.'

'You know my feeling about the Colonel not knowing. I don't want that on my conscience too.'

'I know darling, and I understand that too, but at least, wait.'

'What's the point in waiting? He has made it plain enough.'

She was tempted to tell him of her visit to the Colonel and what she was trying to do but knew instinctively that he would be against her stirring up anything else. Instead, she said reasonably, 'If you don't do at once what he asks, he may be afraid to insist. Please Hazard, don't do it at once. I hate the idea of you paying him anything – I hate the thought of him winning in this way. *Please* wait and let him make the next move.'

'And if his next move is to tell the Colonel?'

She said quickly, 'It won't be. He wants the money too badly and if he *does* tell him, he knows he will get nothing. No, he won't do that.'

They argued for a few more minutes, then, with reluctance, he agreed to her request.

Twenty-Six

On Monday morning at the office, Freya knocked on Graham Mannering's door. He was leaning over his desk closely examining a file. He looked up at her entry saying, 'These are some of the best you've done on the alpines. The light was just right for this particular blue.'

Freya glanced at the shots he was examining. 'Yes, that shade of blue is always tricky – if there is too much shadow, they look almost violet.'

He continued working, setting aside the shots he wanted to use. Freya watched him with affection, old enough to be her father, they had got on well from the beginning, their enthusiasm for photography bridging the gap of generation very successfully. He had advertised for a 'leg man' after he had broken an ankle playing tennis. When what he termed 'a slip of a girl' turned up in answer to the advertisement, he seemed astonished, but, seeing samples of her work, had no hesitation in employing her. That had been the start of Freya's photographic career and she was now a partner in the firm.

Finally, he looked up. 'Anything the matter? What did you want?'

'You know quite a lot of people working in the press, don't you?'

'Quite a few – yes.' He gave her a sharp glance.

'You're engaged to one, aren't you?'

'Yes, I am but – well – I don't want to ask *him*.'

'Ask him what?'

'If he can trace a name for me.'

He studied her for a moment, taking off his glasses in order to see her better. His long face creased into a smile as he said, 'Well, if you are warning off an old boy-friend I suppose it *would* be tactless to ask the present one.'

She knew he was only teasing her but she couldn't resist saying, 'No, nothing like that. As a matter of fact, this man has been in some sort of trouble and I need to know what it is.'

It was typical of him that he asked no questions, only saying, 'Well, give me his name and I'll see if it rings a bell with anyone; I'll ask around.'

It was a long shot but she knew that this quiet man would take trouble to ask a few discreet questions, working on the assumption that unpleasant news usually travelled widely. For the moment, Freya had to be content with that.

Two days later, Graham Mannering limped into her room with a triumphant air.

'I've located your friend,' he informed her cheerfully.

'What have you found out?' she asked eagerly, and he lifted a reproachful hand. 'Have a heart – I only told you that I had located him. I haven't found out anything, except that he does not appear to be popular with other members of the press.'

'What do they say about him?'

'It's rather what they *don't* say that counts I fancy.'

'Oh, Graham – thanks. I really didn't think that you would be able to make contact so quickly.'

'There's a pub I know that a lot of these press chaps frequent. I thought someone might recognize the name.'

'And, someone did?'

'And someone did – two people, actually. Both wanted to know if we were acquainted, both were very cautious, not wanting to commit themselves.' He looked at her, one eyebrow raised. 'An encouraging sign, would you say?'

'Oh yes, very, but—'

'But what comes next. Isn't that what you were going to say?' She nodded and he went on. 'I am not aware what you want to know about this man, but I gathered that there had been some trouble about some photographs he had submitted for publication in one of the papers – shots he had no right to.'

'Any ideas what they were about?' Freya asked hopefully and he shook his head apologetically. 'No, only that they were connected with some scandal. I'm afraid that's the best I can do. I hope it's some use. I didn't like to ask too many questions.'

'No, of course not, and I am most grateful to you. You've been a great help. How about some coffee before you go back to your room?'

'Not a bad idea at all,' he said settling himself in the most comfortable chair and betraying no further interest in the task she had asked him to do. Freya smiled to herself as she rang through for the coffee, thinking that he was the most uncurious man she had ever met. The partnership was happy on both sides, but from the first, he had always assumed that owing to the difference in age their interests outside the office would necessarily be entirely different, and seldom enquired what she did in her own time. In spite of this attitude, they were friends who always worked well together.

After he left her room Freya thought about what he had told her. Not very much, yet enough to establish that Thomas Wayland suffered from a bad reputation. Something which she could perhaps, work on, though at present that was only a hazy idea, but Graham had mentioned the word 'scandal'. That might just offer the ammunition she needed. Wayland thought he had a hold over Hazard. Perhaps two could play the same game. However, if she intended doing anything, it had to be soon.

The next day, Wayland rang her at the office, giving her the opportunity she needed.

'I've been patient long enough. I'm not able to contact Hazard as he is out of the country.'

'What are you being patient about? And what has that to do with either Hazard or me?' Freya's voice sounded totally disinterested.

'That attitude won't get you anywhere,' he told her angrily. 'You know perfectly well what is at stake and how much it means to Hazard.'

'I think Hazard has made it plain that he is not paying you any money for anything at all.'

There was a pause before he said belligerently, 'Then, he must take the consequences.'

Suddenly Freya decided to bank everything on the smattering of knowledge she already had. 'Oh no, I don't think so,' she said coolly, and when he didn't answer, continued smoothly, 'You see, I am in possession of facts about you which I am certain you would not want known publicly. Facts you managed to hush up at the time but if they were known now, would finish your career.'

There was a silence before he said loudly, 'I don't know what you are talking about.'

'Oh, I think you do, but in case you've forgotten, perhaps the words photographs and scandal might revive your memory.'

In the following silence, Freya had time to realize just how foolish she had been. The full extent of her knowledge was literally in those two words. She had nothing to add to them, but she continued firmly, 'I have no wish to ruin you, though it wouldn't worry me unduly, but you can count on the fact that I shall have no hesitation in exposing what you did if you continue to blackmail Hazard.' As she waited for Wayland to speak, she saw that her hand on the phone was shaking.

'You're a vicious bitch, aren't you? I really believe you mean it.'

It was an admission that she had made her point. 'I promise that I do. All you have to do is give me your word that you will leave Hazard alone.'

He said, 'I need the money.'

'You also need your job, so you had better find another way to get it. I will give you fifteen minutes to decide. If you haven't rung by that time, you are right in thinking that I mean what I say.'

She put down the phone and sat back shakily thinking she must be mad. She glanced at the clock on her desk. Two of the fifteen minutes had gone. Suppose the phone didn't ring. What could she do then? She thought gloomily that through her impulsiveness she had created a situation she could not deal with. The hands of the clock seemed to move slowly. Ten minutes passed and she was not aware of anything but the ticking of the clock. She sat rigid in her chair, her hands clasped tightly together on the desk. Fourteen minutes. The phone rang.

'A Mr Wayland wishes to speak to you. Shall I put him through?'

'Yes please.'

She waited with every muscle taut.

'You are probably bluffing. How much do you know?'

'Enough.' She was surprised at the calmness of her voice.

'That doesn't tell me anything.'

'No, but you'd better believe it.'

'You can't prove anything.' He didn't sound convincing and she took heart from that, saying, 'You must know that isn't true.'

'But—'

'There is no but. You have a clear choice. If you want to avoid trouble, you stop blackmailing Hazard. If you don't, you know what will happen.'

After a long silence, he asked in a different voice, 'What do you want me to do?'

Taken by surprise, it was Freya's turn for silence, then she said slowly, 'I will send you a paper to be signed by both of us in which you agree to make no demands on Hazard in return for which, we remain silent on your affairs.'

He said bitterly, 'You don't trust my word,' and she answered instantly, 'Yes, that's right.'

'It's easy to hit someone who is down.'

She said quietly, 'No, not easy, but necessary.'

Twenty-Seven

Freya spent a long time in the wording of the 'document' from which she hoped so much. Finally satisfied, she typed it herself then phoned Thomas Wayland who reluctantly agreed to come to the office to sign it. While she waited, Freya got cold feet. Perhaps he would refuse; perhaps he would insist on her stating exactly what she knew of his affairs. Perhaps ... For the first time in her life, Freya poured herself a drink at eleven o'clock in the morning while she waited.

He arrived punctually and she handed him a copy of what she had written. She wanted this completed as soon as possible without it turning into a slanging match. He sat at her desk to read it, then looked up at her derisively. 'I suppose you realize that this is in no way a legal agreement?'

'Yes, of course and if you prefer, it can be made legal by a lawyer. Under the circumstances, I thought you might prefer to do it this way.'

Silently, he took a pen from his pocket and signed both copies, pushing the papers across the desk for her to sign.

'It might interest you to know that the only reason I am doing this is because something has come up which may clear my finances and I don't want anything interfering with that.' Glaring at her, he said, 'I take it you are intending keeping your side of the bargain?'

'Of course – as long as you keep yours.'

He didn't answer that but picking up one of the copies, he placed it in his wallet before standing up and moving towards the door, hesitating for a moment as if he were going to say something, then turned abruptly and went out of the room without another word.

Freya let out a long relieved sigh, not believing that it was finished so easily. Slowly she picked up the remaining paper and locked it in a drawer. The phone rang, and she picked it up.

'Darling, are you all right? I'm at the airport.'

'Hazard – oh, I'm so glad you are back. Yes, I'm all right – why not?'

'I've been worrying, in case that chap Wayland has been causing trouble. When can I see you?'

'Come to dinner at the flat tonight as early as you can make it.'

She suddenly felt weak at the knees as she put down the phone, abruptly aware of what she had done, wondering what Hazard's reaction would be, hoping he would be pleased, but by no means sure that he would be. By 6.30, she was ready for his arrival, his favourite meal in the oven, drinks ready, the table laid.

She opened the door as soon as he rang and literally flung herself into his arms, and the next moments were wordless. Finally they entered the room with their arms round each other. Freya poured drinks for them both as Hazard lay back in the armchair and she thought that he looked very tired.

'Difficult interview?'

He smiled. 'Does it show? Yes, it was – one of those women who think they write better than God. So full of herself that she couldn't stop talking.'

'But you got what you wanted?'

'Yes, eventually. But I want to hear about you. What have you been doing?' He pulled her down beside him in the big chair, sitting with his arm round her.

'Doing? Well, quite a lot I think, though you may not approve.' She frowned before settling closer against him. He turned to kiss her, saying, 'All right, let's hear the worst.'

She began with Graham Mannering and how helpful he had been, and she felt Hazard stiffen beside her.

'He knows a lot of press people,' she hastened to explain and Hazard sat up straight and asked sharply, 'But what did he tell you? What could he know?'

She had been afraid that he would ask the obvious question. Unfortunately there was not a very clear answer. Hedging, she said, 'Graham went to the pub where a lot of the pressmen go.'

'And?' Hazard was standing up now, looking down at her with troubled eyes.

'Well, apparently Wayland was in some sort of trouble recently.' She knew that such a generality would not satisfy him.

'What kind of trouble?'

'There was some scandal over some photographs.' That sounded what it was – remarkably thin.

'What kind of scandal?' he asked impatiently, obviously expecting something more definite. When she didn't answer, he said, 'Well, go on.'

She moved in the chair, feeling that this was not going to be easy. 'Come and sit down and let me tell you quietly.' He took the chair opposite hers.

She began with Thomas Wayland's phone call to the office.

'So – he threatened you. What did you do then?'

'I told him that I was in possession of facts which he could not afford to be made known.'

He gave her a sharp glance, saying, 'And, what *were* these facts?'

She didn't meet those accusing green eyes as she said, 'I told you – there was a scandal.' She continued evasively, 'The moment I mentioned it, he caved in. It obviously hit home. I made it very clear that you had no intention of paying him any money.'

Hazard pushed his fingers through his hair impatiently. 'I wish you'd left all this until I came back.'

Feeling crestfallen, Freya said, 'But it's all settled.'

He stared at her unbelievingly. 'How could it be? How could you know enough for that?'

'I didn't,' she answered frankly and he stood up, starting to pace the room.

'I don't know what you mean. You are talking in riddles.'

She explained patiently, 'Wayland is convinced that I know a great deal more than I do, so – he couldn't take the risk of me using it against him.'

Suddenly Hazard laughed. 'One blackmailer against another,' he said still laughing. 'This is crazy. I can't believe it.'

Freya went to her bag to fetch the paper she had brought home from the office. She handed it to him silently.

Smiling as he read it, he said, 'You realize this is not legally binding?'

'Oh yes, but Wayland was eager to sign because he is trying to negotiate something which will help him financially and get him out of his present mess.'

'And, you really don't know anything against him at all?'

'Well – press gossip. I intended following that up, but he phoned before I had time.' She paused, and for the first time, smiled. 'And it worked. It worked because there obviously *is* something.'

He shook his head as if he didn't believe any of it. 'The whole thing is crazy.'

'Maybe darling,' she allowed. 'But you are free. You don't have to pay the wretched man anything.'

Putting his arms round her and holding her close, he said wonderingly, 'And you did all that for me. You must love me more than I thought.' Tipping her head back, he asked curiously, 'What would you have done if he had called your bluff?'

Her arms went round his neck. She said dreamily, 'I haven't the faintest idea. Fortunately, I didn't have time to think.'

Kissing her, he said laughing, 'This I feel should go down in history as the most original case of blackmail.'

'But you *are* glad, aren't you?'

'Yes, of course I'm glad – and relieved – if it works.'

'Oh yes, it will work,' she said confidently. 'It will work because it suits him.'

Twenty-Eight

That weekend was the happiest Freya had spent for a long time; the sun shone and was beginning to have the warmth of spring, and everywhere trees and plants were bursting into new life. As she and Hazard walked on the Downs, she had the feeling that their relationship had changed and deepened. They stopped to look down at the scene below them where a small village with a church with a tall steeple appeared as if in miniature: a scene looking untroubled and peaceful. Hazard said, 'Looks ideal, doesn't it? But no doubt most of the inhabitants have as many troubles as other people anywhere else.'

'Yes, of course, but surely more easy to bear than if they were living in some depressing town.'

'For some, yes, but for others it might be too quiet and lonely. For them, to move in a crowd might make troubles easier to bear.'

Freya turned to move on, saying, 'Perhaps it is a good thing that the world is composed of so many different kinds of people.'

Hazard put his arm through hers as they walked on, asking half jokingly, 'Are we the same kind of people?'

'Yes, I think so,' she answered quite seriously and he turned to look at her.

'Are you quite certain that you want to live the rest of your life with me?'

'Quite certain.' There was no hesitation in her voice and he stopped, turning her to face him, cupping her face in his hands.

'I want you to be one hundred per cent sure. I couldn't bear it if you had any regrets later. You see—' He paused, looking deep into her eyes. 'You see, I've never felt like this before. After – after Victor, I promised myself that I would never fall in love and ask a girl to marry me. It wouldn't be fair, knowing what I had done.' He finished quietly, 'That is what I thought, but it is not what I have done.'

Meeting those green eyes steadily, Freya said gently, 'I am so glad that you didn't keep that promise.'

'But – do you really understand? I *killed* him.'

'I understand that it must have been the most difficult moment of your life. I understand that you must have loved him very much. I understand that I am marrying a brave man who I hope would do the same thing for me if I were in such dire circumstances.'

He said nothing, but the expression in his eyes as he bent to kiss her nearly made her weep.

As they walked on, he said, 'I am glad now that you know. I would have hated that to be between us, but I didn't dare hope that you could understand so well.'

'You are happier about it now, aren't you? Now that Dad knows?'

'Yes, it's a relief. Except for this fellow Wayland.'

'I don't think you need to worry about him.'

'But darling, you were only bluffing all the way.'

'But he didn't know that. I am quite a good actress. Anyway, we can't do any more, so don't start worrying.'

On Sunday, Hazard drove her to see the cottage he had mentioned. At one time, it had been two farm cottages, but farmworkers and their wives today want something more modern, and over the years, new ones had been built on the estate and for the last decade Hazard's aunt had lived there with the two cottages made into one.

On the way Hazard said anxiously, 'You may not like it. It's rather the roses-round-the-door type of cottage. You don't *have* to say yes. We could probably find something else.'

They drove through the village, then turned down a narrow lane where trees formed an archway overhead. After negotiating a sharp bend, Hazard turned into a miniature driveway and stopped.

'Here we are. Let me present Foxhammer Cottage for your inspection.' He watched Freya as she stared at it. Beams and whitewash, lattice windows and a heavy oak front door with a latch. She slid out of the car to stand, still staring.

'Definitely roses round the door,' she stated and he asked quickly, 'Don't you like it?'

She laughed up at him. 'Don't be silly – how could I *not* like it?'

She watched him fit a huge key into the old lock and swing the door open. She had expected the cottage to be empty but a few pieces of furniture remained and some rugs were scattered on the polished floors. Everything was spotlessly clean and Hazard told her that one of the farmer's wives had been looking after it.

The conversion of the two cottages had provided fair sized rooms, with kitchen and bathroom severely modern. There was a scent of wood in the sitting-room and Freya exclaimed with pleasure at the sight of the inglenook fireplace. What must have been the original stairs led by a narrow passage to two bedrooms and a bathroom. Looking out of the window in the main bedroom, Freya saw a garden just coming to life in the spring sunshine with fruit trees in a small orchard beyond. Hazard stood silently beside her, not wanting to influence her decision.

She said, 'I wish we could live here all the time.' They had already agreed that they would have to live in London during the week and the country at weekends.

He turned to her delightedly. 'Then, you like it?'

'Darling, I love it. Just think what we can do to make it lovely inside.'

She heard his relieved sigh as he came to put his arms round her saying, 'I am so pleased, and yes – we *will* make it lovely, and we will be happy here.' Holding her close, he said gently, 'I love you so much and I will do everything I can to make you happy.'

The next hour was spent in planning their home and it gave Hazard immense pleasure to watch Freya as she went from room to room, standing in the middle of each with her eyes shut, visualizing what should be done. Hazard regarded her with amusement.

'OK,' she said dreamily. 'It will have to be oak to match the old dresser.'

'What will have to be oak?' he asked looking round the room. 'You don't *have* to have what is here. You can start again from scratch.'

She looked quite shocked as she opened her eyes and went across to the dresser to stroke it gently. 'Oh no. This is so absolutely right. We must choose everything very carefully.' She turned to him with arms out-stretched. 'Oh Hazard, isn't it going to be lovely, choosing everything together and making a lovely home?' Her expression changed suddenly and she looked at him almost shyly. 'But – I've never asked you – but shall we be able to afford to buy some lovely things? I mean – it doesn't matter. I wouldn't really mind what we have as long as *you* are here. That is the only important thing.'

It was a long speech and his laugh rang out as he crossed the room to her. He said, 'I have a confession to make and—'

'Darling – it doesn't matter. Really it doesn't. We can get everything gradually as we can afford it. It will be fun.'

He hugged her tight, then shook her gently. 'Stop talking and listen.' He set her free so that he could watch her face.

'My grandfather was a very gifted and practical man and he started making cars, then aeroplane engines at just the right time. He was a rich man and when he died two years ago, he left everything to me.'

For a moment she looked stunned then she said, 'But you are a journalist – a reporter.'

He burst out laughing. 'Why shouldn't I be?'

'But you work so hard.'

'That is what makes it interesting.'

'But you could have stopped, after your grandfather died?'

'Yes, I suppose I could. I didn't want to.'

Suddenly she smiled, nodding her head. 'No. You wouldn't, would you? You are not the type to loll about doing nothing.'

Grinning at her, he said, 'No, that's right, I'm not. Well, now that is settled, let's get on with choosing all this oak we are going to buy.'

Twenty-Nine

In the car, Freya watched Hazard as he drove, the lean face concentrated on the job in hand. She came to the conclusion that he was much more relaxed. He put out a hand to take hers as it lay in her lap.

'Why are you looking at me like that?'

Laughing, she asked, 'How do you know that I *am* looking at you? You are driving and – I hope – looking where we are going.'

'Yes, I'm doing that. You are quite safe, but when I am with you, I am very conscious of you. What were you thinking then?'

She answered seriously, 'I was thinking that that dear face belongs to me; that very soon, I am going to be your wife; that I shall try very hard to make you happy, and that I love you very much.' She paused, squeezing his hand. 'Is that enough to be going on with?'

He turned briefly to look at her before replying, saying with a broad smile, 'Well, I'll have to make do, won't I?'

On their return, Robin wanted to hear about the cottage, and for the first time, Freya detected a change in his attitude to their marriage. She knew that he would never change his belief about what had happened, but, as he began to know Hazard better, he was becoming more able to understand and accept. It was he that evening who suggested that they should make a date for their wedding.

'I can see how it is between you. I don't want to stop your happiness because of my own convictions, so let's fix a date now.'

In the midst of their planning, Freya suddenly looked at her father.

'I've just realized – you can't give me away, can you?'

'Not if you want me to take the service.'

'Of course I do. It *has* to be you, and I know who I would like to give me away – Colonel Warren.'

Robin said, obviously pleased, 'Yes, that's a splendid idea and I'm sure that he would be delighted. He has known you so many years and he's never had a daughter of his own.'

'We'll go to see him next weekend,' Freya decided, 'and I hope he will agree.'

She was aware that her father watched her as they talked and wondered what was in his mind but was surprised when he said suddenly, 'What are you going to wear?' Adding, 'Nothing frilly, I hope.'

She laughed outright. 'No, you can bank on that. I'm not the frilly kind.' A sudden thought struck her. 'What happened to mother's wedding dress?'

'As far as I know, it's in that trunk in the attic.'

'Still? After all this time?'

'She certainly would not get rid of it,' he said with certainty. 'What made you ask?'

'I wondered if I could wear it.'

He remained silent so long that at last Freya said gently, 'Not if you would rather not. I wouldn't do it if you didn't like the idea.'

He looked at her then and she saw that there were tears in his eyes, but he smiled as he said, 'I can't think of anything which would give me more pleasure.'

Adding doubtfully, 'Perhaps it wouldn't fit you or, would it look too old-fashioned?'

'Perhaps it is not even there,' Freya said as she set off for the door. 'I'm going to look anyway.'

The trunk was in a far corner of the attic, a strap holding it firmly closed. She pulled it out so that she could deal with the strap. If the trunk was locked, she had no key but when the strap was free, it opened quite easily.

At first glance there seemed to be nothing but masses of white tissue paper and as she began to remove it, Freya felt a sudden sense of guilt. She imagined her mother standing beside her watching her unpack this dress which had meant so much to her all those years ago. Perhaps she would not have liked this trunk disturbed, but knowing her mother so well, she was suddenly certain that it would have pleased her that her daughter wanted to wear it at her own wedding. Kneeling in front of the trunk, Freya carefully folded each piece of tissue paper as she took it out and finally, the dress was revealed, again with tissue between each fold. Standing up, Freya lifted it out carefully making sure that the dress did not touch the dusty floor. The material was pale oyster-coloured satin, full length, slim princess style, almost dateless. A short train hung from the shoulders embroidered with seed pearls. The very simplicity of the style made it beautiful. Freya let out a breath of sheer pleasure. It had been so lovingly packed that it was scarcely creased. Now everything depended on whether it fitted.

Peering into the trunk, the dress over her arm, she saw the delicate tulle veil and the simple coronet of orange blossom which her mother had worn.

Freya's eyes filled with tears. This was a sentimental moment she would never forget. This had been a happy dress which was the beginning of a happy marriage which lasted until Louise's death. Carrying the dress, Freya went down to her room determined to find out if she could wear it. With hands which she saw with surprise were shaking, she took off the dress she was wearing and with difficulty because of the train, slipped the wedding dress over her head, conscious as she did so of a faint waft of the perfume Louise always wore.

The sleeves were long and tightly buttoned from elbow to wrist. The train was surprisingly heavy and it was some moments before she could settle the dress on her. She gave a small gasp of relief. It was a shade loose on her and a trifle too long, but otherwise, perfect. Turning all ways to look at herself, she was pleased with the result. Surely this was a good omen. If they had as good a marriage as her parents, they would be lucky indeed.

The following weekend, the weather had reverted almost to winter, heavy cloud obliterating the sun. Getting out of the car in Colonel Warren's drive, Hazard stood looking at the house, then, turning to Freya, he said sadly, 'I feel guilty every time I come here. I know I should come more often but—' He broke off, then added, 'I think of all the happy times they gave me here and that makes me all the more guilty.'

'How can you feel that when you know how pleased he is to see you?'

'Because I come under false pretences. If he knew the truth, he would not want me here.'

Freya said almost impatiently, 'You don't *know* that. Why keep thinking that way? Try to live in the present and just accept that he is pleased to see you because you were Victor's friend.'

Hazard started moving to the front door. 'Easier said than done. Don't you think that you would feel the same if it were you?'

Before she had time to answer, the Colonel had the front door open and was coming to greet them and there was no doubting the pleasure on his face.

'What a lovely surprise. Come on in out of this wretched wind. Last week it was really spring – now this.'

When they were settled with the drinks he insisted on, Freya said, 'I've come to ask you to do something very special for me.'

'My dear, if it is something I *can* do, it will give me great pleasure,' he said with a beaming smile. 'And now, tell me what it is?'

'We have fixed the date of our wedding and of course, I want Dad to marry us so, could you give me away please?'

He was so surprised that for a few seconds, he remained silent, then he said seriously, 'What a wonderful thing to ask me to do. Yes, of course I'll be delighted.'

He was so obviously pleased that Freya felt a wave of affection for this old man she had known nearly all her life.

'You having a big affair?' he asked. 'All the trimmings, bridesmaids, all that?'

Freya shook her head. 'No. We don't want a big wedding. I want the reception at home. Not too many people; people I am fond of, real friends.'

Colonel Warren looked at Hazard. 'What a sensible girl you are marrying. I've never cared for big weddings.' He hesitated, 'Well, nothing private about them, I feel.'

It was an odd thing to say, but Freya understood what he meant. It was not until just before they were leaving that he said out of the blue, 'You know, we used to think that you and Victor might make a go of it. You always got on so well.'

Feeling a trifle embarrassed, Freya said lightly, 'We

were too young to think of that. It was all parties and sport then.'

The Colonel nodded sadly. 'Yes, you were all so young. He loved parties and dancing – always very popular with the girls.' He turned to Hazard. 'You knew that, didn't you? You were together so much then – just before he went into the army.'

He continued to look at Hazard as if he were waiting for him to speak.

'Yes, he was a good dancer – we used to pinch each other's partners.' Hazard spoke lightly and Freya was aware that the old man watched him. Then, with a sigh, he shook his head. 'Seems a long time ago now. Can't put the clock back unfortunately.' Then, changing the subject, he asked cheerfully, 'Will you be wanting me in uniform then?'

'Yes, most certainly I will. I shall be so proud to walk up the aisle with you, and thank you for saying you will do it.'

Thirty

It seemed that Freya was right in her summing up of Thomas Wayland's reaction to her onslaught. It seemed that he had no wish to rock the boat while there was any chance to clear his debts by other methods, though Freya was not entirely free in her mind until several weeks of silence had gone by. The whole thing savoured of anticlimax, but that suited her very well and she felt a huge relief that it was over.

The weeks ahead were filled with happy planning which took up most of her spare time. The wedding was finally fixed for July 7th and the invitations went out. Jill had agreed to be her maid of honour and Hazard wanted Charles to be his best man. What he teasingly referred to as 'a very neat arrangement all round'.

Hazard and Freya spent time together searching for the right furniture for Foxhammer Cottage. After one foray, Freya said frankly, 'I can't get used to the idea that you can really afford to buy all these lovely things.' She laughed. 'I rather feel that we are only playing at it.'

Hazard assured her that it was giving him immense pleasure to buy her the things she wanted, adding, 'It would have given my grandfather pleasure too. He loved period furniture.'

The time flew by and the wedding dress altered and returned home ready to wear, presents began to arrive every day and there was a general air of excitement. Colonel Warren issued a dinner invitation for two nights before the wedding. It was, Freya felt, something of an occasion with Mrs Felton agreeing to stay on to cook the dinner. The Colonel had made it clear that this was to be a celebration and Hazard made a special effort to be there. Always an excellent host, Freya thought that he seemed a trifle over-anxious when they arrived, but put it down to a certain amount of doubt about Mrs Felton's cooking, being afraid that she might provide one of her stodgy meals. He seemed relieved when she came to the door to say that dinner was ready. He need not have worried for the food was delicious and well served, the champagne making the occasion into the celebration he had promised. Yet, all the time, Freya was aware that their host was far from being relaxed and she wondered if either her father or Hazard was aware of it. It was not until after coffee was served in the drawing-room that the reason became clearer.

The Colonel chose to sit in a high-backed chair and for a few moments, he looked round at his guests as if he were assessing them for a particular reason. He sat in silence, stirring his coffee, then suddenly put it down on a table near him. Looking at each in turn, he said quietly, 'I want to talk to you about Victor.'

It was about the last thing any of them expected him to say, for they all knew that it was a subject he found difficult to speak of. Freya glanced quickly at Hazard and saw that he had gone very pale. Nobody spoke and it seemed a long time before he continued slowly, as if finding the right words was difficult.

'I think you all know how much his death meant to me, and for a long time, I could not face any details; only just the official notification.' He stopped speaking, sitting staring down at the hands in his lap.

The room was very quiet; waiting. Raising his head, he looked directly at Robin as he said, 'It was your experience which finally made me want to know more. Your distress at your loss of memory – your conviction that something happened during that raid that you felt that you should have been able to stop.'

Once more, he was silent and Robin said slowly, 'Are you saying that you connected what I felt with Victor?'

The Colonel shook his head. 'No. Not then. Not until later – much later. It was then that I felt that I had to know more.'

Glancing at Hazard Freya saw that his eyes were fixed on the Colonel.

Robin asked gently, 'How did you learn more? How did you find out?'

'There are ways and means. I still have friends at the War Office who know their way around.'

'What did they tell you?'

It was Hazard who asked the question and the Colonel turned his head to look at him, but it was a moment before he answered.

'They told me that Victor's wounds were so extensive that he could not live.' There was a long silence before he added, 'I think that I was almost relieved. Victor was too full of life to have to live his whole life as a cripple. Only, you see,' he paused, 'only, he did not die from his wounds. Somebody shot him in the head.'

Freya heard the shuddering breath Hazard took, and there was a long silence before the story continued quietly. 'That puzzled me at first. I knew that he had been wounded by a bomb.' He looked across at Robin. 'That was when I connected it with what *you* had said and it began to make more sense. Though – I could have been wrong, of course.'

'Wrong about what?' Robin asked.

'Well, you see, I couldn't believe that anybody could shoot a man dying in agony out of hate or anger – so – I had to think again. To think of a more sane reason.' He stopped speaking and his voice had changed when he continued. 'So, I could only think that it had been a mercy killing.' He was silent once more, then said slowly, 'Once I was convinced of that, I always wanted to thank whoever did it.'

Hazard asked sharply, 'Are you saying that you were *glad*?'

The Colonel sat very straight in his tall chair looking directly at Hazard.

'But of course I was glad. Victor was in agony They said he would have been conscious. Wouldn't any father have been glad and grateful?' He smiled at Hazard. 'It was you, wasn't it?'

'Yes. I shot him,' Hazard said clearly, then sat forward in his chair. 'Victor *was* conscious and in terrible pain. It was the only thing I could do for him.' He dropped his head into his hands and was silent.

Freya made a movement to go to him, then checked herself. This was not the moment. This was something he had to do alone, so that he could be free. Colonel Warren stood up, going over to Hazard and putting a hand on his shoulder. 'My dear boy – thank you. You can't know what a relief this is to me.'

Looking up, Hazard said, 'I couldn't tell you. I didn't think you could possibly understand.'

'Yes, I can understand why you should feel that, but – well – I've seen a lot of active service; seen men suffering from terrible wounds. I know that Victor could not have survived so, thank God that you were there and had the courage to help him.'

He went back to his chair, saying, 'I wanted to get this clear before the wedding. You have borne the burden long enough. Now you can start again.' After what seemed like a peaceful silence, speaking slowly, he said, 'It has taken a long time to sort this out, well, for everyone's sake, it needed to be done.'

'Why did you think it was I who shot him?'

'One thing, I knew from a letter of Victor's that you were there and had met. That was one thing.' He hesitated before going on. 'The second thing was not so very difficult because I knew that you and Victor had always been very close.'

When he was silent, Freya found herself waiting for her father to say, 'But he took a life.' But he didn't and the room seemed very peaceful in the following silence, with something important completed.

On her wedding day, Freya came down the stairs with Jill behind her holding up her train, and in the hall, Colonel Warren waited for her, resplendent in his uniform. At Freya's request, they walked across to the church finally to find every pew full, every head turned to watch her. Her own eyes saw only the two men she loved so deeply as they waited for her. Her head was held high and her heart was filled with joy.

The
Love Season

One

Gabrielle Broome awoke at six o'clock in the morning to the sound of chirruping birds and remembered at once where she was. She was in her grandfather's house at Angel Creek and would be there for almost two months.

She smiled and stretched luxuriantly. It was pleasant to be woken by the birds, even though it was anti-social of them to start singing so early. She knew she would not sleep again so lay there thinking, wondering how she was going to protect her grandfather from the media attention that was already gathering apace because of his forthcoming eightieth birthday.

Not that Max needs protection! she thought. He's perfectly capable of looking after himself! It was her parents who had insisted on her being there, ringing her up at ungodly hours from the States to point out that it was her duty to try to protect her grandfather's reputation.

"You're the only one of us available, Gabby," her mother had said. "Daddy and I have our first night in a couple of weeks so we're frantic with rehearsals. We'll come over for his party, of course. You'll arrange that, won't you? I'm sure Sally will help when she can but the poor darling's run off her feet with this feminist theatre group she's mixed up in. Just keep an eye on Max for us! Don't let him get involved in anything rash!"

Gabrielle wriggled her toes under her duvet and grinned as she thought of them all. The Broomes were a theatrical family. Her grandfather, Maximilian had been a playwright and director in his hey-day, gaining a certain acclaim in the fifties and sixties when poetic drama was in vogue. Although his work was out of fashion, the texts of his plays were still sometimes on the schools' lists of examination set books and he was generally remembered with respect. But Gabrielle knew that one section of the literary establishment regarded him as an eccentric has-been so she understood her parents' concern. She just wished that they were there instead of herself to advise on the radio interviews, the TV profiles and the various public engagements that were being planned.

Why me? she wondered. I'm the only disappointment! The odd one out!

Because it was expected, she had followed her sister to drama school but soon discovered that the bright lights were not for her. Instead she had settled for teaching English and Drama which was why she was free now that the summer holidays had begun.

But how was she supposed to look after Max? Nobody had been able to do that, not even her grandmother who had died worn out from trying. Maximilian Broome was his own man and Gabrielle knew he was unlikely to listen to her.

Not that it matters! she thought. I'm here in Angel Creek and I intend to enjoy myself.

It was easily her favourite place. The River Dart has carved out many odd corners and inlets during its forty-five mile tumble from the heights of Dartmoor to the sea. Angel Creek lay a good five miles from the estuary, a quiet backwater with its own little village and a quay from which the local salmon fishermen once earned a good living. A few still fished on a part-time basis but the boats were mostly pleasure craft now or owned by wealthy incomers who had built expensive houses in the outskirts of the village or alongside the creek where their gardens stretched down to the water.

There were enthusiastic fishermen among them and her grandfather had been one in his younger days. Gabrielle supposed he was too old for that now but sensed he was restive because they were in the middle of the salmon season. She had heard the envy in his voice when he told her that his next-door neighbour was down from London to make the most of it.

She had caught sight of Craig Gillard the day before from her bedroom window. He was doing something to his dinghy which he kept moored at the landing strip at the bottom of his garden and she had watched him for a while.

She never knew quite what to make of him. There was an aloofness about Craig Gillard that made him difficult to talk to. Of course, she did not really know him, having only met him once or twice when she was visiting her grandfather.

He was attractive enough, she had to admit – a lean, muscular man with dark hair which curled around his ears and keen, observant eyes. She had been discomfited more than once by the way their gaze had lingered searchingly on her. Even thinking about him now was enough to make her fling off her duvet and leap out of bed.

It's no good! she thought. I shall have to get up. If

I'm quiet I can slip out of the house without anybody hearing.

Ten minutes later she was dressed in her jeans and sweater and running down the garden path between the rhododendron bushes to the edge of the water. Its level was high after the storms of early summer, deepening into pools under the opposite bank where oak woods spread thickly along the entire length of their quiet inlet. The chug-chug of an outboard motor broke the silence and when a dinghy came round the bend she recognized the man in it. It was Tom Narracott, one of the few local fishermen to retain family netting rights to fish in the Dart estuary.

"You're up early, Tom," she called as he swung the boat in towards her.

"So be you!" he shouted back. "I've come to tell Mr Gillard us be going after salmon this morning. The lads reckon there's a fresh run waiting to come up river with the tide and he said he'd like to come with us sometime."

"Want me to tell him, Tom?" she asked. "To save you pulling in?"

"Oh, thanks Miss Broome. That'd do me a favour. Tell him us'll be setting off from the Quay in half an hour if he's interested."

There was a gap in the hedge between her grandfather's garden and the one next door so Gabrielle scrambled through it and ran up the wide lawn towards the house Craig Gillard had built about five years earlier.

It was a beautiful, white-stuccoed house, well proportioned with a verandah running all along the front of it. It made Max's older property look shabby by comparison but she had to admit that it blended

in with its surroundings. She just wished the build-
ers had not bulldozed away the old orchard that had
been there before it. There were only three left in the
village now, even though Angel Creek had once
been renowned for its fruit growing.

Everything changes! she thought as she climbed
the steps to the porch.

Before she could ring the bell Craig appeared on
the verandah above her. "Gabrielle?" he called.
"There's nothing wrong, is there?"

"No. Tom Narracott was here to know if you want
to go fishing with him in the estuary."

"Hang on! I'll come down."

She waited until he came. "He'll be at the Quay,"
she explained, "and he's setting off in half an hour."

"Good! It'll make a change from my rod and line."

Once again she felt his eyes studying her, summing her up. She looked away, not so much from
embarrassment as from a sudden awareness of his
masculinity. He was wearing a loose shirt, unbut-
toned over brief shorts and he was tanned to a deep,
overall brown, the light brushing of hairs on his
chest and arms bleached golden by the sun.

"I knew you'd arrived," he said. "I saw you at
your window yesterday."

"Did you?" Her cheeks warmed as she had not
supposed he had seen her watching him. "I'm here
because of Max's birthday – all the celebrations – "

"Yes." He frowned. "I hope we're not going to be
invaded."

"That's partly why I'm here – to ward people off.
That's if Max will let me!"

Craig's frown deepened. "We enjoy our privacy
here," he said. "Max knows that and I'm sure you

do, too. We don't want the place overrun by television crews! Especially in the season."

She felt a prickle of annoyance. "His birthday's not until the end of August," she pointed out. "The season will nearly be over by then."

"But most of Max's interviews are before that, surely?"

"Of course. I'll try to keep people out of your way but Max will never be eighty again. We shouldn't begrudge him his bit of publicity, should we?"

She saw Craig's lips tighten. "I don't begrudge Max anything. We're good friends. Tell him I hope to bring him back a salmon for his supper tonight."

"Good luck, then! I wish I could come with you."

"You?" He stared at her. "Tom Narracott wouldn't want a woman in his boat!"

"He often took me out when I was younger! Sally and I both went with him – and with Max when he still had a boat of his own."

"But we're net fishing this morning, Gabrielle. That's not women's work. It needs strength and experience and could be dangerous. I expect Tom's like me. I never want a woman around when I'm after salmon."

"I see." A male chauvinist, she thought. I should have guessed! "You'd better be off, then," she said, "or Tom will go without you."

"Yes." He hesitated. "Perhaps another time, Gabrielle, I could take you out for a trip in my motor cruiser."

"Oh, I'll be too busy for that, Mr Gillard! I'll be keeping the television crews at bay so that they don't disturb your privacy. Good morning. And good fishing!"

She stalked away with her head held high, only losing her dignity when she had to duck through the gap in the hedge into her grandfather's garden.

Impossible man! she thought. I can't think why Max makes a friend of him! They're poles apart.

Her grandfather was still in bed when she went back into the house but his housekeeper was in the kitchen preparing breakfast. Molly Hannaford was a local woman in her late fifties, plump, red-haired and fiery, the only person Gabrielle had ever heard stand up to Max.

Gabrielle was fond of her and gave her a hug. "I've been outside. The birds woke me. It's a lovely day."

"I saw you from my bedroom," Molly said. "You were talking to Mr Gillard. He's up early."

"He's going after salmon with Tom Narracott and might bring us in one tonight. Max doesn't go fishing these days, does he?"

"He'd like to but I tell him he's too old now. They're fanatics, these men. Out all weathers. All because of a fish I'd just as soon have out of a tin!"

"Hard luck on the salmon, too," Gabrielle said, "coming all these thousands of miles to spawn, only to get caught by somebody like Craig Gillard! Max tells me he's taken a mile long stretch of fishing rights in the upper reaches of the river."

Molly gave her a shrewd glance. "You don't seem too taken with our next-door neighbour."

"Well, he was going on about Max's birthday, not wanting his privacy invaded. Who does he think he is? It's people like him who've done the invading! Angel Creek isn't a bit the same these days."

Molly sighed. "I can remember when it wasn't

much more than the old village and the big house on top of the hill. Now that's a fancy hotel and most of the old families have gone. Times change, Gabrielle, and money talks!"

"Next door's obviously loaded!" Gabrielle said. "What does he do in London that he can come down here whenever he feels like it?"

"Something in the City, I think. A stockbroker, is it? And of course, he inherited a packet when his father died."

"Lucky for some!"

"He's very good to his mother, Gabrielle. And he's often helped your grandfather with his investments."

"Then I hope Max is careful!"

"Oh, he thinks a lot of Mr Gillard – trusts his judgment. He's a very clever man, you know."

"But he's like so many of the new people! They're taking the place over and it was so lovely when Max first moved in."

Nearly twenty years ago, she thought. She could just remember the enchantment of the place when she was a little girl. Her grandmother was still alive then and used to spoil her and Sally when they visited with their parents. She supposed that Max must have seemed an invader then, a curious creature who wrote plays nobody wanted to put on any more, somebody who was looking for a retreat from the world that had rejected him, the world that suddenly wanted to remember him again.

"What would you like for breakfast?" Molly interrupted her thoughts. "I'll be cooking for your grandfather."

"Oh, just toast and coffee. I was thinking how odd

it is that everybody's so interested in Max now that he's going to be eighty."

Molly shrugged. "Well, you know the telly and the newspapers! Any anniversary and they come running! Once it's all over they'll forget him again."

"Yes. Sad, isn't it?"

"Oh, I don't know. He'll revel in all the attention and be perfectly charming to everybody. Then he'll settle back into his old ways, driving me and your family crazy!"

"So!" The voice came from the kitchen doorway. "You're talking about me behind my back!"

Both women swung round to see that Max was standing there in his slippers and dressing gown. His bushy white eyebrows were raised into his equally bushy white hair and his expression was one of comic disapproval. "What's this? Anarchy in my own house?"

"How long have you been there?" Molly demanded.

"Long enough! Come and give me a kiss, Gabby! Tell me I'm not as bad as this woman says!"

"Of course you're not!" Gabrielle ran to him and kissed him warmly. "We all love you, even though you can be such a monster sometimes!"

"Listen to that!" Max exploded. "A viper in my bosom!" But he kissed her back and held her close for a moment. "Lovely to have you here, my darling! You were always my favourite."

"Now you know that's not true! You adore Sally."

"Of course. But you're the only sensible one of the bunch, the only one wise enough to keep out of the theatre. Anyway, you're the only one here! So what shall we do today?"

"Breakfast first!" Molly said. "And there's a pile of post for you to go through."

Max groaned theatrically. "Oh, why is everybody wanting me to do things? I'm past all this!"

"No, you're not!" Gabrielle said. "You know you're enjoying it. We'll go through the post together."

They did that after breakfast, sitting in Max's snug where he kept all his books and papers and the battered old typewriter he sometimes still used to write caustic letters to the press. Most of his post that morning was confirming arrangements for interviews or suggesting themes of approach but one letter made Gabrielle pause.

"See this?" she said. "Somebody wants to put on one of your plays!"

"What?" He snatched the letter from her. "Which one?"

" 'The King's Magician' – the one that made you famous."

"Old Merlin? I haven't thought about him for years!" He was scanning the letter eagerly. "Who's this Andy Doyle? I've never heard of him. Have you?"

"Yes." Oh, I know Andy Doyle! she thought. I know him only too well! "I don't think it would be a good idea, Max," she said. "He's a free-lance – works partly for TV and partly for the stage. He wouldn't do you justice."

"Still, if he wants to revive old Merlin – " Max was looking pleased. "He says he'd like to come and see me – talk about it. No harm in that, is there?"

"You mean he wants to come here?" Gabrielle was dismayed. "Darling, don't you think you've enough on without that? We've the South Bank people coming next week to film their profile of you and on Monday you're booked to talk to the Totnes Arts Society – "

"But this is the first time anybody's wanted to do a play of mine for over twenty years! I can't turn him down without even meeting him! What have you got against him, Gabby?"

She was silent. What have I got against you, Andy? she wondered. Just that you pretended to care for me and then went off with somebody else or that you didn't even notice when I thought I was in love with you?

"I used to know him when I was at drama school," she said. "He was in his final year and very ambitious. I've seen some of his productions."

"And – ?"

She shrugged. "I suppose they were OK. A bit shallow."

Like you, Andy, she thought. All on the surface. I don't suppose you'll have changed.

Max was wearing his stubborn expression. "I may as well give him a ring. I'll ask him to come tomorrow. We've nothing on then, have we?"

"You haven't. I was going into Totnes to arrange with the hotel about your party."

"You can do that this afternoon. Take Molly! She'd like a run into Totnes."

"And what will you do?"

"Oh – potter about."

He's up to something! Gabrielle thought. He doesn't want me here when he talks to Andy. And he'll be putty in his hands, just as I was because Andy doesn't give up when he wants something.

He'll probably try to involve me, too, and expect me to be on his side.

"Well, take care!" she said. "Don't let him talk you into anything until we've discussed it, especially if he expects you to put up any money!"

Max's smile was one of cherubic innocence. "You're so like your grandmother! Just trust me, Gabby! I've had plenty of experience with theatre folk and I know what I'm doing."

But you don't know Andy Doyle! she thought. Whatever he does is for his own ends. He's only interested in you because for the moment you're in the news. He'll use you, just as he uses everybody and then he'll drop you with no compunction at all, the way he dropped me.

Two

When Gabrielle and Molly came back from Totnes later that afternoon, they found Max and Craig Gillard chatting in the snug. Craig had changed into slacks and an immaculate white shirt and his greeting was polite. But the look he gave Gabrielle was as disturbing as before, making her heart jerk disconcertingly.

Max beamed at them both. "He's brought us a ten pound salmon," he said, "so I've told him he must stay and help us eat it. You've a way with salmon, haven't you Molly?"

"You've a way with you, more like!" the housekeeper said. "I don't suppose I can cook it any better than Mr Gillard!"

"I'll come out and help you," Gabrielle said quickly. "I'd like to see how you do it."

She escaped with relief to the kitchen where she stood contemplating the sleek beauty of the silver fish lying on the kitchen table. "Does Mr Gillard really cook for himself?" she asked Molly. "Surely he has some help in that big house?"

"A girl comes in to clean a couple of days a week but apart from that he manages. He eats out a lot at the Angel Arms. Seems to prefer that since he lost his wife."

"He's been married?" Gabrielle was astonished, having somehow thought Craig Gillard too self sufficient for that.

"I thought you knew. He built that house for her but she didn't live in it more than six months, poor girl."

"Why? What happened?"

"She was drowned. He had a small sailing boat then and they were out in it together when a storm blew up. Well, you know how treacherous it can be out there. The tide was on the ebb and they were dragged down river – upended on a sand bank. She was swept away before he even saw the going of her."

Gabrielle shuddered. "That's terrible!" And it explains a lot, she thought. No wonder he doesn't approve of having a woman in a boat if there might be danger.

"It was weeks before the sea brought her body back in," Molly said. "And he, poor man, was going nearly mad with the grief and uncertainty of it. Your grandfather was kind to him, then. We all were and he's never forgotten."

Gabrielle said nothing. I must be kind to him, too, then, she thought. But he makes it so difficult! It's hard to be natural when he looks at me the way he does. She could not interpret his look which was neither approval nor disapproval but more like somebody reading a map of unknown territory he wished to explore.

The thought gave her a shiver down her spine. She stared at the clear, cold eyes of the fish he had helped to catch and wondered how long it had struggled in Tom Narracott's net.

"Poor thing!" she said involuntarily.

"Perhaps you'd rather not see me clean it," Molly said. "Why don't you go in and talk to the men instead?"

"No. I'll help with the vegetables."

"Then go out to the garden first and see if there are any courgettes ready in the frame. And bring some parsley for garnish."

Once outside, Gabrielle did not immediately collect what Molly had asked for. Instead she stood gazing towards the bend of the inlet around which lay the harbour and then the wide stretch of the River Dart. The water looked deceptively peaceful under the evening sunshine and she thought of the fish that had been caught that morning before it could swim upstream to complete its life cycle, and of Craig Gillard's young wife who had been swept away to an early death. Her grandfather had often said that the Dart could be a cruel river but she had never fully appreciated that until now.

She was subdued when she went back in and Molly was quick to notice her change of mood. "Leave all that!" she said. "Go upstairs and put on something pretty. I can manage here. Go on!" she repeated when Gabrielle would have protested. "Take a shower! Spruce yourself up!"

Who for? Gabrielle wondered as she went upstairs to her room. Craig Gillard? She realized she would have to think of him differently now but did not suppose he was a man who would welcome pity. Love, perhaps? She shied away from the word, troubled that she had even thought of it.

By the time she went downstairs again Molly's preparations were well underway. She regarded Gabrielle with approval. "That's better!" she said. "Blue always suits you – brings out the colour of your eyes. So go on in and be polite to the guest! Your grandfather will be expecting you."

Gabrielle was not at all sure that he was because she had a feeling that she was interrupting something when she joined the two men in the snug. They stopped talking abruptly and Max's eagerness to pour her a glass of sherry and his all too guileless expression made her suspicious.

"So what have you been up to while I was out?" she asked him. "Did you ring Andy Doyle?"

"Who?" Her grandfather's vagueness did not deceive her. "Oh, you mean the young man who wants to put on 'Merlin'. Well, yes, I did. He's coming tomorrow to discuss it."

"I see." Gabrielle could not hide her disapproval and she sensed that Craig Gillard was watching them both with amusement.

"Who or what is 'Merlin'?" he asked.

" 'The King's Magician'," she said. "The play that made Max famous."

"Oh, of course! The one about King Arthur. I heard a radio version of it once when I was still at school but I've never seen it performed."

"Nor have I," Gabrielle admitted.

"All the more reason to revive it now!" Max said. "I can't think what you've got against the idea, Gabby. Your young man sounded most enthusiastic."

"He's not my young man!" Gabrielle shot back. "And I wouldn't be against the idea if somebody else was doing it."

"Nobody else has offered!"

This was so patently true Gabrielle was silent and there was an awkward pause until Craig Gillard diplomatically changed the subject by enquiring how the plans for the eightieth birthday celebrations were progressing.

Then Molly called them out to supper and they were soon complimenting her on the salmon which she had poached and served with a lemon sauce and vegetables from the garden. With stuffed avocados to start with and raspberries and clotted cream to follow it was a perfect meal. Max had raided the cellar for his favourite Chablis and they all retired to the lounge afterwards feeling mellow and replete.

Perhaps it was the wine or the last rays of the sun lighting up the colours of the old Persian carpet that lulled Gabrielle into relaxing for once in Craig Gillard's company. Or perhaps it was because they were all there together and she no longer felt herself the sole focus of his eyes.

She lay back in one of the velvet armchairs and listened to him chatting to Max about his fishing trip that morning and how the pools in his own stretch of river upstream were much deeper that summer because of the earlier rains. It was some time before she realized that he was turning the conversation towards the theatre, her family and finally to herself.

"So you're teaching in Exeter, Gabrielle?" he said, having drawn that information from Molly. "What age group?"

She sat up stiffly, defensive again. "Oh, fourteens to sixteens mostly – secondary school – "

"Interesting. Especially the drama. How do you approach that with teenagers?"

"We do a lot of improvization and then we put

things together – make our own plays. The usual thing."

"Not usual at all!" Molly said. "I was invited to their last show and it was very good."

"Really?" Craig said. Gabrielle felt his intent gaze on her like an almost physical thing. "And do you write plays on your own account?"

"No!" Her reply was too quick and she saw him register the fact.

"I wondered if you might have inherited some of your grandfather's talent."

"Well, I haven't! Sorry to disappoint you!"

"Oh, you don't disappoint me, Gabrielle. Not at all!"

She saw Max glance first at her and then at Craig in amused speculation. "There's a lot more Broome in Gabrielle than she'll admit to," he said. "She could surprise us yet."

"Then I look forward to that!" Craig said.

It was late before he rose to go. Max gave a theatrical yawn. "You'll see him out, won't you, Gabby?" he said. "I'm only fit for pottering off to bed."

He beamed innocently at her but Gabrielle saw the glint in his eye as he regarded her and Craig. Oh, no, Max! she thought. You're not going to manoeuvre me into a relationship with Craig Gillard! You're not going to change my mind about Andy Doyle, either!

Outside in the porch Craig lingered. "He's really looking forward to all this, isn't he?" he said.

"Yes. I just hope he won't overdo things and tire himself out."

"You mustn't do that, either." He paused. "So –

what is it you've got against this production of his play?"

"Nothing, except that I don't think Andy Doyle's suitable. I used to know him."

"I gathered that. Perhaps you knew him rather too well."

Her face burned. "That's my business!"

"Of course. His name seems familiar so I'd like you to remember I'll always be on hand if you need any help."

"Oh, Molly and I have everything organized for Max's birthday, thanks."

"I wasn't thinking of that." He brushed her bare arm with his fingertips. "Goodnight, Gabrielle. I'm glad to have you staying next door."

He stepped from under the porch light and disappeared into the darkness. Gabrielle's arm burned from his touch and she rubbed at it fiercely, resenting the effect he could have on her. It was as if his presence kindled an answering spark that set all her senses tingling.

Max was on the phone when she went in and he called to her. "It's your mother, Gabby!" He passed over the receiver. "I've been telling her about 'Merlin' and she's delighted."

"Wonderful news, darling!" Angela enthused in her ear. "Max sounds so pleased. A production after all this time! Might there be a part in it for Sally? I don't like the sound of this women's group she's with."

She chattered on and Gabrielle listened with increasing dismay for it seemed everybody wanted Max's play to go on except her.

When Andy Doyle arrived the next afternoon she

greeted him coolly. He had driven down from London in a battered BMW and seemed as confident as ever.

"Lovely to see you, darling!" he cried as she avoided his kiss. "So unexpected, too!"

"I'm here for the birthday celebrations," she explained. "I'm on guard."

"Really?" For a moment he looked perplexed. Then he laughed. "Not from me, I hope!"

He had put on weight, she noticed. His hair was just a little too long and his cords and roll-necked sweater more shabby than casual. She thought she detected a new hardness in him, unless that had always been there and she had failed to notice it before.

"So where's the great man hiding?" he asked.

She led him to the snug where he was over fulsome in his pleasure at meeting Max and his admiration for his work. She listened to him flattering her grandfather and wondered why she had ever imagined herself in love with him.

Eventually he turned to his plans for producing Max's play. "I've some people interested already," he said. "A company I've worked with before. Of course, there's the tricky question of finance – "

"Don't look at me, young man!" Max said. "I'm practically a pauper these days."

"Ah! Well, we should be able to get a grant if we make it a regional production. I've already approached the college theatre at Exeter and they're very enthusiastic. After all, this is your eightieth year, Mr Broome. Quite a landmark!"

So what's in it for you, Andy? Gabrielle wondered and smiled wryly to herself when he went on, "You're sure to get plenty of media coverage. We could tour the area if we get a hit – might even end up in the West End! So what do you say?"

He had been pacing about the snug as he expounded his plans but now he halted in front of Max's chair, gripped its arms and stared into the old man's face. "What do you say, sir? Of course, I'll need to go through the script with you for any necessary alterations – "

"Alterations?" Max's complacent smile vanished.

"Well, it's nearly thirty years old now, isn't it? Times have changed. Poetic drama's a bit old hat these days. Personally, I admire the play. But it could do with a bit of pruning, don't you think?"

"Pruning?" Max was looking alarmed now. "I wouldn't want it cut about – "

"Oh, nothing much. Just here and there. And we'll need to find a topical angle. But with a political play like 'The King's Magician' that shouldn't be too difficult – "

"Political?" Max's eyebrows shot up.

"Of course! The powerful influence of spiritual forces! Think of the Middle East! Look, I've jotted down a few ideas – "

He drew up a chair beside Max and produced a sheaf of papers from his brief case. Max threw a glance of frantic appeal in Gabrielle's direction but she only smiled gently and said, "I'd better leave you to it. I can see you've plenty to discuss."

Outside the door of the snug she almost laughed aloud. Max won't buy that! she thought. He won't want his script mangled by somebody like Andy Doyle!

She was chuckling to herself when she went into

the kitchen. "What are you looking so pleased about?" Molly asked.

Gabrielle told her and added, "So I needn't have worried, after all."

Molly shook her head. "Don't be too sure about that! Your grandfather's as vain as the next man. If somebody wants to produce his play, he'll go along with it even if he has to fight to keep control every step of the way!"

When the two men eventually emerged from the snug Max was looking exhausted. Andy Doyle was close behind him and Gabrielle's heart sank when she saw the triumph in his face.

"Could you manage some tea, Molly," Max asked, "before this young man goes back to London? But nothing for me. I'm going up to my room for a while."

He began moving towards the staircase and Gabrielle ran after him and caught hold of his arm. "What's happened?" she demanded when they were out of earshot. "You haven't said he can do it?"

"My dear, I had no choice. This could be my last chance."

"But he'll ruin it! You know he will."

"Nonsense! I won't let him." He patted her arm. "Don't look so worried! Go and have tea with him, will you? I need to be on my own to think things out."

He began to climb the stairs and she called after him, "This is just going to upset you, you know it is!" Max did not answer so she turned away, biting her lip. What can I do now? she wondered. How can I stop it all going wrong?

Molly had brought tea into the lounge where

Gabrielle reluctantly joined Andy. "So you persuaded him," she said.

"It wasn't too hard. You didn't give me much support, though, did you?"

"I didn't intend to!"

"I thought – for old time's sake – "

"That was why! If you ruin this for him, Andy, I'll never forgive you!"

"Oh, I won't do that. It means as much to me as it does to him. Things haven't been too good recently and I need something to put me in the picture again."

"So you'll use Max because he's temporarily in the news! That's just not good enough!"

"Why? The old boy's getting a real kick out of it. I thought you'd be pleased. There could be a part in it for you, if you want it."

"I don't! I've finished with the theatre – "

"So I've heard. But I can't imagine you teaching! What happened to that play you were writing?"

"Nothing happened. And I don't want it talked about."

He looked amused. "Suit yourself!" He poured himself another cup of tea. "I saw your sister the other day in a ghastly production with her feminist group. She can do better than that. Perhaps she'd be interested. It would be an added attraction if I could feature a Broome grand-daughter in a Broome play – "

"So that's why you asked me! I wonder you haven't approached my parents, too!"

"I thought about it. But I gather they're otherwise engaged on Broadway."

Gabrielle looked at him with contempt. "I'd forgotten what a schemer you are!" she said.

"And I'd forgotten you were so beautiful." His eyes travelled over her. "You've grown up, Gabrielle. You're altogether more interesting. I made a mistake when I let you go. Still, we'll be seeing more of one another soon so we'll be able to make up for lost time, won't we?"

His effrontery left her momentarily speechless. Then she asked, "So what happened to Anthea?"

"Anthea?" It was as if he had forgotten her. "Oh, that didn't work out. She wasn't important, anyway." He stood up to go. "But I must be off. I've some phoning to do tonight – people to contact before I see your grandfather again." He held out a hand. "I'd like to think we could work together on this, Gabrielle. So won't you wish me luck?"

She hesitated, thinking that it might be as well to keep in with him so that she could watch what he was up to. "Just respect Max's play," she said. "If you do that, I've nothing against your producing it."

She took his hand and he gripped it. "Good! Let's seal that in the usual way, shall we?"

Before she could stop him he had pulled her towards him, wrapped his arms around her and kissed her firmly on the lips. Then he released her as abruptly and strode towards the door, almost colliding with Craig Gillard who was just coming in.

As the two men confronted one another Gabrielle sensed the antagonism between them. Then Andy gave a wave in her direction and called, "Until the next time, darling!"

He went. She could tell from Craig's expression that he had seen Andy kissing her and she felt stiff from embarrassment.

"Sorry for interrupting," he said. "I dropped by to

see Max but Molly told me you were in here and might be glad of some moral support. It seems I was wrong."

"You weren't wrong," Gabrielle said. "But you're too late. Max wouldn't listen to me so Andy's going to produce his play and he's already talking about cutting it. He's after the publicity because of the birthday celebrations."

"I see." Craig regarded her steadily. "And what are you after, Gabrielle?"

"Nothing. I just don't want Max to be disappointed. All I can do now is keep an eye on things so the production doesn't turn into a complete fiasco."

"Which will mean seeing a lot of Andy Doyle!"

"Not because I want to! It will be for Max. That's what I'm here for, after all."

She could tell he did not believe her and was astonished that she should care about that.

"I think you're underestimating Max," he said. "He's not likely to stand by and see his play ruined."

"But Max is underestimating Andy! He doesn't know what he's like!"

"And you do?"

"Yes."

"Then be careful, Gabrielle! I wouldn't like you to be hurt all over again."

"You're assuming I've been hurt before!"

"Well, haven't you?"

She wanted to hurl a defiant denial at him but could not meet his eyes with a lie. So she hung her head and was silent.

He came over to her then and put a hand under her chin, raising her face so that she had to look at him. "Being hurt's nothing to be ashamed of,

Gabrielle," he said roughly. "We can't always avoid it but there's no sense in running into trouble. So remember what I told you! I'll be around if you ever need any help."

It was not what he said that made her feel a frisson of alarm and expectancy. It was the entirely different message that his eyes were sending her.

Three

Two mornings later, Sally rang. "What's all this about Max's play?" she asked. "I had a call from Andy Doyle last night offering me a part." She giggled. "Morgan le Fey! I ask you!"

"You're not going to do it, are you?"

"Well, I'm considering it. It would be different. And as it's for Max – "

"It's for Andy, Sal! He only wants you because you're a Broome. Anything for publicity!"

"What's he been doing lately?"

"Not much, I suspect. Max is going to regret letting him loose on his play. He wants to cut it about and make it political."

"I see." There was a pause. "Do I detect a touch of sour grapes, Gabby?"

"No! Well – I suppose, if I'm honest, I'm only against it because it's Andy."

"I never could understand what you saw in him."

"Nor can I now! But when can you come down, Sal? I could do with some help here with Max - and everything – "

"Everything?" Sally's voice sharpened. "You're not getting involved with somebody else, are you?"

Gabrielle sighed. Her sister could always read between the lines. "I'm trying not to be – "

"Then that settles it! I'd better come down. I'll have a word with Max before I decide about the part and I'll give your new man the once-over."

31

"He's not my new man!"

"Then keep him at bay until I've vetted him! We've no performances until next week so I'll see you on Saturday if that's OK with Molly. Ask her to give me a ring, will you?"

Gabrielle put the receiver down with a feeling of relief. Sally will be on my side, she thought. Between us we'll make sure Max gets a fair deal from Andy Doyle.

Sally was three years older than herself and two inches taller. She had inherited their mother's dark hair and eyes, her dramatic good looks and vivacious temperament. Gabrielle supposed this was why she had always let her take the lead when they were growing up. Her own nature was more reserved, her colouring softer and her features more delicate so she had often felt in her sister's shadow.

It was partly due to this that she had steered clear of the stage, not because she was uninterested but because she knew she would never have the nerve to appear in public night after night. What nobody in the family suspected was her attempts to write for the theatre. Only Andy Doyle knew about that and she had regretted confiding in him ever since.

Craig Gillard had touched a nerve when he'd asked if she ever wrote plays but she had no intention of telling him that she had a drawer full of abandoned scripts in her Exeter flat. She wondered now what Sally would think of him and what he would think of her.

He remained an enigma and she had spent the last two days trying to avoid him. But his evening visits to her grandfather were becoming a habit and out of courtesy she felt obliged to join them after supper.

Anyway, she was finding his conversation increasingly interesting. It was not always about fishing. He knew a lot about books and contemporary music and art and seemed to have a finger in various cultural activities in London. She began to see why he and Max enjoyed one another's company so much.

It was only when Craig turned his eyes on her and tried to draw her into the conversation that she retreated into her shell. She could see that this puzzled him and the previous evening, when she was showing him out, he had turned to her in the porch and asked, "Why are you so afraid of me, Gabrielle?"

Embarrassment made her blush. "I'm not afraid of you."

"Then what is it? You're on the defensive if I so much as look at you!"

"That's probably it. The way you look at me!"

"How d'you mean?"

She shook her head. "I can't explain.".

"I see." She heard him sigh. "Perhaps I can. I'm sorry if I've disturbed you but you remind me of somebody. That's all it is, Gabrielle. Don't let it worry you!"

She did not like to ask of whom she reminded him but wondered uncomfortably if it might be his wife.

She wished he would go. Instead he said, "The forecast's good for tomorrow so would you like to join me for a trip down river? I want to pick up a few things in Brixham so we could have lunch there and come back up with the tide."

He waited while she considered how to refuse. "I'm not sure what Max has in mind – " she began.

"Oh, that's all right. I asked him if he could spare you and he says he can."

He's arranged it already, she thought, even before he asked me! So why should he suppose I'd want to drop everything to go out with him?

"You did say you used to go on the river with Max," he reminded her.

"Well, yes – years ago with Sally – " He seemed suddenly much too close and her heart quickened.

"Well – ?"

She had a memory of speeding down river in Max's old motor boat with the wind in her face and her hair whipping over her eyes, Sally and she both buttoned up in yellow oilskins and laughing as the wash splashed over the sides. Remembering that she smiled and knew that she would go.

"I think I'd like that," she said.

"Good. Can you be at the Quay by ten?"

She gathered that they would be going in his new boat, a gleaming blue and white motor cruiser he kept moored at the Quay as it was too big to pull in at his private landing strip.

"You'll like the Bluebell," he said, as if reading her thoughts. "She's fast and much safer for the open sea. See you tomorrow, then, Gabrielle!"

Tomorrow was now today and she was already regretting her impulse to go with him. She had dreamed about the Bluebell that night, heading out to sea in it with Craig at the wheel, on and on towards a far distant horizon. Then a huge wave had reared up from nowhere and crashed over their heads, sweeping them both away. She awoke in panic, with her heart pounding and hoped it was not a warning.

"What was Mr Gillard's wife like?" she asked Molly

while they waited for Max to come down to breakfast.

"We didn't see much of her," Molly said. "They
came in for supper once or twice and she seemed
pleasant enough."

"What did she look like?"

"Oh, tallish – blonde and very slim. They made a
handsome couple." Molly gave her a quizzical glance.
"Why d'you ask?"

"Just something he said."

So she wasn't like me, Gabrielle thought, feeling a
mixture of relief and curiosity. Who can he have
meant, then?

The question niggled at the back of her mind and
was still with her later that morning when she walked
through the village past the old church with its an-
cient yew tree and down the steep lane towards the
little harbour. But she forgot about it when she came
within sight of the familiar huddle of boats and the
water glinting silver under the sun. It was a beautiful morning and the main channel of the River Dart,
past the harbour's entrance, reflected the clear blue
of the sky.

Craig was already at the Quay, talking to Tom
Narracott. He waved as she approached and she
saw the approval in his eyes as he took in her sensible jeans and sweater and the oilskin slung over her
shoulder. "You look very workmanlike," he said.

Tom Narracott winked at her. "Oh, Miss Broome's
an old hand. Been in and out of boats since she was
so high. You couldn't have a better crew, Mr Gillard."

The Bluebell was moored at the far side of the
harbour in the deeper water so Craig led the way
down the stone landing ramp to where his dinghy

was tied. He clambered in first, then held out a hand to help her. As she took it her eyes met his and something in their expression so unnerved her she stepped in off-balance and lurched against him.

"Sorry!" she mumbled as his arms went round her. For a moment they rocked together to the movement of the dinghy and she caught the faint fishy tang of his old blue jersey and felt the warm strength of his body as he held her close.

She heard his breath beginning to quicken and pulled herself free. "It's ages since I was in a boat," she said unsteadily and sat down. "I hope I haven't lost my sea legs."

"If you have, I'll help you find them again." He leaned over her to slip the dinghy's rope from its mooring, lightly brushing her breasts with his arm as he did so. Even through the thickness of her sweater the contact was enough to set her pulses racing and she shrank back in alarm, relieved when he moved to pull-start the outboard motor into life. It spluttered protestingly before running smoothly and then they were chugging across to the other side of the harbour where the Bluebell waited.

She was a handsome twenty-five footer with an open wheel-house and a little sun-deck. Once they had climbed aboard Craig showed Gabrielle over her, obviously proud of the arrangements below decks, the compact cabin with its convertible bunks and the efficient-looking galley.

She expressed admiration for his cooker and fridge and the fact that there was enough head-room to stand upright to work. "Have you been far in her yet?" she asked.

"Not yet but I intend to. All round the south coast

sometime or across to France. She sleeps two so you could come, too, if you're interested – show me how good a crew you really are!"

He grinned at her, looking suddenly boyish and her heart leapt. But I wouldn't dare! she thought. Go all the way to France with you, sharing this little cabin where the bunks are so close together?

"We could make a start today," he said and gave her a wicked look. "Why not? Come on, Gabrielle! Up to the wheelhouse for your first lesson!"

She followed him back on deck, not knowing what to expect. Once in the wheelhouse he insisted that she sat beside him while he explained the controls to her, how he used his ignition key to switch on the power and the push button to start the diesel engine. "The throttle and gear controls are combined in one lever," he explained, "so you have to be sure you're not in gear when you push the throttle forward. Apart from that, there's nothing to it!"

"Oh!" she said and he laughed at her alarmed expression.

"I'm not suggesting you take her out today, Gabrielle! What you can do is cast off the mooring ropes for me."

The Bluebell was moored fore and aft to rings on the harbour wall. He showed her how to release the bowlines and left her to it while he went back to start the engine. She felt the cruiser shudder as the engine began to throb. "Cast off forward!" he called.

She cast off and gathered in the ropes, watching as the Bluebell slowly swung out bow first. "Cast off aft!" he shouted. She hurried to obey and the engine note quickened as the cruiser began to move away from the harbour wall and out into the open water.

"Well done, Gabrielle!" he said when she rejoined him in the wheelhouse.

She was ridiculously warmed by his praise. He's different out here, she thought. He's in his element! She watched with interest as he slowly manoeuvred the cruiser towards the harbour entrance and the wide stretch of the River Dart. Tom Narracott was waving as they slid past the thickly wooded banks of the creek and she waved back until they had rounded the corner and she could no longer see him.

It felt cooler as they headed down river towards the sea for there was a brisk breeze blowing. "Want to take a turn later on?" Craig asked. "She's very easy to handle."

"I thought you didn't like having women aboard!"

"I don't when I'm fishing."

"So what's the difference?"

"Women are too impatient. They talk too much. Anyway, I don't use a boat when I'm on my own. I settle down with my rod and line and fish from my stretch of river bank."

"So how did you like using nets with Tom and his lads?"

"It was different. It's their living, of course, but I don't know that I approve."

"Why?"

"It's too indiscriminate for me. They can spot the salmon by the wash they make so once they know where they are one lad stays on shore, holding his end of the net. Then the others row the boat out and play the net into an arc. When they've got the fish netted they all help to pull them in."

Gabrielle made a face. "It does sound a bit unfair."

"Not only for the salmon! It's unfair to rod men

like me, waiting for the fish to swim upstream!"

"But that makes you no better than Tom!"

Craig laughed. "That's another reason I don't take women fishing! You're all a lot too sentimental."

All? she wondered. So how many women have you known well enough to be able to generalize? She stole a glance at him as he sat beside her, his hands lean and competent on the wheel and his dark hair ruffled by the breeze. There was a contented smile on his face and she said, "You love it out here, don't you? So how do you square this with working in London?"

"How do you square it with teaching in Exeter?"

"That's not fair! I asked you a question."

"Then answer mine first and I'll try to answer yours."

He'd like to wriggle out of it! she thought. I know very little about him, apart from the fact that he's got plenty of money and has lost his wife. He already knows plenty about me because he's been asking Molly and Max!

"That's not fair, either," she said. "But if you must know, I don't even think about it. I'm happy when I'm teaching and I'm happy when I'm here. They're two different parts of my life, that's all."

"So what about the unhappy part at drama school?"

"What makes you think it was so unhappy?"

"Andy Doyle was there, wasn't he?"

"So? That's over and done with! And you're changing the question! You haven't answered mine yet!"

"No. I don't find it so easy." She saw his face darken. "Has Max told you about my wife?"

"Molly did." She hesitated. "I'm very sorry, Craig."

"Yes. Well, you'll understand why I can't see things as clearly as you can. This place has too many memories."

"Mostly happy, surely?"

"Whatever they are, they draw me here again and again. Then, when I've had enough I go back to London and immerse myself in work. The money market has its excitements, too, you know! I suppose what I like about Angel Creek and the river is that they never change. Or they haven't until now."

"Now?"

He turned to look at her. "You're here, Gabrielle."

The remark stunned her. Speechless, she stared straight ahead as the Bluebell cut through the water. A pleasure boat full of passengers was heading towards them on its way up river to Totnes. Several people waved from the upper deck but she did not even see them.

"Want to take a turn now," Craig asked, "before we get nearer Dartmouth and it's too busy?"

They changed places awkwardly and without a word. She had to slither past him and at one moment was almost in his lap so her hands were trembling when she took the wheel. It was still warm from his grasp and she was quite unable to think of anything to say.

"I've embarrassed you," he said. "Clumsy of me. But having you next door has made a difference, Gabrielle."

"Why? I've stayed with Max before."

"Only briefly. This time you're part of the household and I've a chance to get to know you better."

She did not answer and he added, "I've been hoping you might feel the same way about me."

They had reached the mile wide stretch of the river near Dittisham and she steered automatically, trying to sort out in her mind exactly what he was getting at and bothered by the conflicting emotions he could so easily arouse in her. Suddenly she became aware of a flotilla of small craft approaching them. They were spread out in a wide V formation and she swung the wheel over hard to avoid them.

"Steady!" Craig cried as the Bluebell shuddered and heeled over sharply to starboard. He put his hands over hers on the wheel and turned the cruiser more smoothly. The little boats passed and she saw that they were manned by students from the naval college at Dartmouth who gave an ironic cheer and raised their caps to Craig for his successful manoeuvre.

"Sorry!" she said unsteadily. "I don't think I'm very good at this."

His hands were still on hers and their thighs were touching. "Another time I'll give you a proper lesson," he said. "But just for now I think I'd better take over."

"Yes." She felt inadequate and a fool. "I wouldn't make a very good crew, would I?"

"You'd make an excellent crew, Gabrielle. It might take several lessons, though, if you're interested."

His eyes held the same expression that had so alarmed her before. It was part invitation and part challenge and she felt a tremor of excitement and apprehension.

"Well?" he asked softly. "Are you interested?"

She saw that he meant more than just boating

lessons and licked her lips nervously. "Perhaps."

He raised his eyebrows. "Only perhaps?"

"I'd like to think about it."

"Of course." He took his hands from hers. "Move over then, Gabrielle!"

They changed places again and Craig picked up speed as they headed down river towards Dartmouth. The traffic was increasing now and they were soon in the thick of it – flurries of little yachts with brightly coloured sails, motor cruisers, working craft and tourist pleasure boats. Craig was kept too busy to talk and Gabrielle sat silent beside him, wondering how to respond to his invitation.

In the distance she could see the Dartmouth ferry moving slowly across the river from Kingswear and knew they were not far from the wide expanse of the estuary. Once they were out there Craig headed towards the open sea and when they rounded the headland they were soon into a heavy swell. The wind was off the sea, hurrying the waves along with it. He reduced speed to meet them and the boat rolled and pitched. Gabrielle was exhilarated by the movement and by the salt breeze whipping her face.

He grinned at her. "All right, Gabrielle?"

"Yes. It's marvellous."

"A bit different out here! But she rides well."

"She's great!"

"When we reach Brixham we'll stop for a brew-up before going ashore. OK?"

She nodded. "Are you calling in for something special?"

He gave her a sidelong glance. "I'd better not say! It's a surprise present for Max's birthday."

"Well, you can tell me! I won't mention it."

"You may not approve. If I tell you, you won't let Molly know, will you?"

"Now you're making me really curious!"

He laughed. "Tell you what! I'll show you when I've bought it. That do?" She could get no more out of him and it was not until later that day that she discovered what he had bought for her grandfather.

Once he had berthed the Bluebell and demonstrated his skill at making tea in the galley Craig took off on a mysterious errand of his own, leaving her to wander through Brixham's narrow streets, exploring the hidden by-ways and quaint shops of the old fishing quarter.

He had suggested a cafe on the Quay for lunch and she was there before him, sitting at a window table and watching for his arrival. When he appeared he was grinning triumphantly and she could see at once what Max's present was from its shape.

"Oh, Craig!" she cried when he joined her at the table. "It's not a fishing rod? He hasn't fished for years!"

"But he'd like to! See what I've got him? It's a ten foot carbon fibre rod, very light and easy to handle. He'll love it."

"He's too old for that now! Molly will be furious."

"That's why you mustn't tell her. I've promised to take him out on his birthday. It's a secret."

"So that's what you two were hatching up! I knew you were planning something the other night!"

"You won't give the game away, though, will you?"

Gabrielle shook her head but she was worried. "Will it be safe? You know what Max is like."

"I'll be with him. I've a nice, low bank on my beat of the river and I'll make sure he doesn't do anything stupid. He's really looking forward to this, Gabrielle!"

She sighed. "You men! You never grow up!"

"No?" He pulled his chair closer to hers. "We grow up in all the ways that matter! Perhaps one day I'll be able to prove that to you."

There was a moment when she felt so held by the invitation in his eyes she was unable to look away. But this is ridiculous! she thought as she tried to stem the rising tide of sexual excitement that threatened to engulf her.

In self-defence she changed the subject. "My sister's coming on Saturday."

He raised his eyebrows. "Sally?"

"You've met her?"

"No. But I've heard a lot about her from Max."

"You'll like her. Everybody does."

And she'll like you! Gabrielle thought with sudden premonition. Sally won't feel embarrassed when you look at her or tongue-tied when you ask her a question. She'll give as good as she gets and you'll admire her for it just as everybody does. So that will be it! You'll forget all about me once you've met Sally!

Not that it matters! she tried to tell herself. It doesn't matter to me if you and Sally fall for one another! But she knew now that it did matter and was dismayed to discover how much.

Four

Sally's impending arrival threw them all into a flurry. She would be with them on Saturday in time for tea, she told Molly, and would like to stay the night. Molly spent most of that morning baking and preparing a room for her while Max was too excited to settle to anything. Gabrielle went through his post for him, finding a letter from Andy Doyle which made her as agitated as the others were.

"Oh, no!" she cried. "Sally's asked Andy to come down as well! He says he'll be here tomorrow just after lunch. How could she?"

"I expect she wants to find out how far he's got with the play," Max said. "Does he say?"

Gabrielle scanned Andy's letter. "He's approached a possible cast and fixed the venue. Now he's trying for a grant. It's all going a lot too fast, Max!"

Max patted her arm. "Don't worry! Sally and I can handle him. I hope she'll take the part. She'd be perfect as Morgan le Fey. Such dark good looks! Such magic!"

Yes! Gabrielle thought. Sally has magic all right! The atmosphere of this house has completely changed and she's not even here yet!

She was, however, delighted to welcome her sister when she arrived. Sally was late because her eight year old Metro had given her trouble on the motorway. But she was bubbling over with excitement at seeing them all again. "So lovely!" she kept saying as she went from Gabrielle to Max and then to Molly, giving them each a hug and a kiss. "Such a long time, too! You're looking marvellous, Max! So distinguished! And Gabby, darling! I love your hair cut short like that. I'd forgotten it was so pretty. Molly! I do believe you've been baking." She gave an appreciative sniff. "So when's tea? I'm starving."

She had them all laughing, fussing round her. And she does it so easily, Gabrielle thought. Sally's dark eyes were gleaming, her face alight and her whole body expressive of her pleasure at being in her grandfather's house again.

When Molly went to make the tea they all followed her into the kitchen, Sally chattering on, entertaining them with a dramatic account of her motorway breakdown and the gallant maintenance man who had come to her rescue. "So handsome!" she said. "So efficient!"

And so obviously under your spell! Gabrielle thought. Sally seemed to her to be more beautiful than ever with her high cheekbones, her finely arched eyebrows and thick, swept back hair. She was wearing a patterned, longish skirt, very full and a tight fitting bronze sweater which emphasized the slenderness of her waist.

"So what about your play, Max?" she cried. "I've always adored 'The King's Magician'. Is it going ahead?"

"We must talk about it, my darling," Max said. "Over tea. You'll bring tea into the lounge, won't you, Molly?"

He led Sally out of the kitchen, leaving Gabrielle and Molly to load the tea trolley. By the time they wheeled it in, Max and Sally were deep into their discussion and had reached the subject of Andy Doyle.

"I know Gabby doesn't trust him," Gabrielle heard Max say. "But I think he should be given a chance, don't you?"

"Of course. That's why I suggested he should come down tomorrow."

"Why did you?" Gabrielle asked. "I was looking forward to a quiet weekend with just the family."

"But we have to thrash this out between us, Gabby! I want to know what he's got in mind before I decide on taking the part." She reached out for one of Molly's Devonshire splits. "Clotted cream! Gorgeous! You don't know how I miss this in London."

Molly beamed. "And it's my home-made strawberry jam. I remembered how you always liked it."

"You're spoiling me, Molly!" Sally turned to her grandfather. "Max, you must let me have a script of the play. I'll read it tonight and remind myself of the part. Oh, I'm getting quite excited about this! It's so different from what I've been doing lately."

She launched into a description of her work with her feminist group and Gabrielle listened as she and Max talked theatre. Sally will take the part, she thought, and Max will let Andy produce his play because they both want it so badly. She hoped it would not all end in tears and was glad when tea was over and she was able to escape with Molly to the kitchen.

"Mr Gillard's not coming in tonight, is he?" she asked her. "He does seem to be making rather a habit of it."

She had not seen Craig since their boat trip. He had been off fishing with Tom Narracott again the day before and she had kept out of his way when he called in to see Max that evening. She needed time to sort herself out for she was still unsure of how to respond to his invitation and was beginning to wonder if she had read too much into it.

"I think your grandfather's asked him to supper," Molly said. "He wants to meet Sally."

"Does he?" Gabrielle was aware of a sinking feeling in the pit of her stomach. "You'll need a hand out here, then. So let's leave Sally and Max to talk until he comes."

It was a lively gathering that evening. Molly had cooked a duck because it was Sally's favourite and they ate it with fresh green peas and runner beans from the garden. Craig brought in a couple of bottles as his contribution and Max was at his most entertaining, regaling them with scandalous anecdotes about writers and actors he had known. Sally, dramatic looking in a dark red, swirling dress, capped his stories with some of her own, laughing a lot and flirting outrageously with Craig. Gabrielle smiled and smiled as she watched them, sometimes catching an amused glint in Craig's eyes as he glanced in her direction. She had little to say herself but was content to listen, storing up some of the conversation for future use.

"You were even quieter than usual this evening," Craig commented when she showed him out that night.

"I usually am when Sally's around."

"So it seems. She's quite a girl, your sister."

"I told you you'd like her."

"So you did." They were in the porch and there was still enough light for her to see the amused expression in his eyes. "I often wonder what you're thinking when you sit there, just watching and listening."

"I'm interested, that's all."

"Hmm! You're a deep one, Gabrielle Broome. I'm beginning to think Max was right when he said you'd surprise us all one day."

"Did he say that?"

"Don't pretend you've forgotten!"

She had not forgotten. In fact, she had treasured the remark, tucking it away safely in case she should ever lose faith in her ability to write.

"So Andy Doyle's coming again tomorrow," Craig said.

"That was Sally's doing. She and Max want to pin him down before he gets too far on with his plans."

"Well, if you want to avoid him, you know where to come. I could always give you that promised lesson on the Bluebell."

"Oh!" She felt her cheeks warm. "I wouldn't want to walk out while Sally's here. I haven't seen her for ages."

"Of course. But – after she's gone? You said you'd think about it."

"Yes." She licked her lips nervously. "I – wasn't sure if you were serious. I mean – about teaching me."

"Oh, I was serious, Gabrielle!" he said. "It's a long time since I've been so serious about anything." He leaned towards her in the gathering dusk and just brushed her lips with his. "So think about tomorrow, won't you?"

He went, leaving her staring after him, quite unable to move. His kiss had caused a shock of alarm but stronger than that, delight and a surge of sexual arousal that heightened the colour in her cheeks.

When she went back into the house Sally met her in the hallway. "That took you a while," she said and her eyes were curious. "What were you doing, kissing your dishy next-door neighbour good-night?"

"Don't be silly, Sal!" The rebuke came out stronger than Gabrielle intended and Sally laughed.

"Well, I wouldn't blame you if you were! I could fancy him myself." She yawned. "But I'm going up. Come and talk to me, Gabby! It's ages since we had a heart to heart. If Craig Gillard's your new man, I want to hear all about him."

Gabrielle did not feel in the mood for her sister's questions. She wanted to be on her own to think about Craig and her extraordinary reaction to his kiss. But she was too fond of Sally to refuse if she wanted to talk so she followed her obediently up-stairs.

Soon they were sitting cross-legged on her sister's bed just as they had done when they were children and had escaped from the grown-ups to whisper secrets to one another. Only now, when they talked, Gabrielle felt they had lost their old, easy confidentiality and wondered why they were both avoiding anything that touched them deeply.

Then Sally suddenly said, "I've been having a hell of a time, Gabby." The laughter had gone from her eyes and her shoulders drooped.

"With your feminist group?"

"No! It's not what I imagined but I can handle that. It's something else."

"A man?"

Sally gave a mirthless chuckle. "It usually is, isn't it?"

"You're surely not in love? Not properly?"

"Desperately. He's wonderful, Gabby. We met last year when he was directing a play I was in. But he's married and there are children. So he won't leave them. Well, I wouldn't want him to."

Gabrielle touched her hand. "I'm so sorry, Sal."

"Yes. Well – it used to be you, didn't it? You were the romantic one, always falling for the wrong people! I thought I could string them all along and have fun. It damn well hurts when it's for real."

"Yes."

"So watch out for yourself! I'm glad you've seen through Andy Doyle, but he could try getting round you again, especially now he's producing Max's play."

"That had nothing to do with me! I tried to talk Max out of it and I was hoping you'd be on my side."

"I know. Sorry about that. It just seemed a heaven sent escape route. If I take the part I'll be out of London for a while – and out of reach."

"You've definitely decided, then?"

"Not yet. I'll wait until I've seen Andy tomorrow. Will you be in on the discussion?"

"I'm not sure. I may go on the river with Mr Gillard."

"Really?" Sally's eyes widened. "So was I on the mark when I asked if he was your new man?"

"No! There's nothing between us. Nothing at all!" Gabrielle hesitated. "Do you like him, Sal?"

"Very much. Like I told you, I could fancy him myself!"

"But – if there's somebody else – ?"

"Oh, that's different! I've fancied a few men in my time and they've fancied me. But this other thing – it's hell, Gabby! So steer clear of getting serious unless you're sure it's going to lead somewhere. I wouldn't want you to suffer like me."

"Yet tonight you seemed – so happy – "

Sally gave a wry laugh. "All on the surface, my love! I'm not an actress for nothing. But you surely know that! I thought you could always see through me."

Gabrielle was silent, stunned by the revelation that her sister was not always what she seemed. *Perhaps we're not so different after all,* she thought. *We just have different ways of disguising what we feel.*

She leaned forward to kiss Sally on the cheek. "I'm glad you've told me," she said. "But you look tired now and I must get to bed. So sleep well! I'll see you in the morning."

Once she was in her own room, however, she did not go to bed. Her few minutes with Craig in the garden and her talk with Sally had left her emotionally charged and she knew she would not sleep. For a while she sat thinking and then she foraged in her case and took from it the script of a play she had been working on.

She had never been satisfied with the female lead and talking to Sally had made her realize why. Her heroine was revealing too much of herself far too soon. Re-reading the script she began to see how she could improve it and, filled with excitement, she started making alterations, cutting whole chunks of dialogue, inserting more oblique scenes that carried with them a new, sensual undercurrent, subtly changing the emphasis while keeping the main story line. She worked on and on, oblivious of the time, her mind racing ahead to the way she would build up to a passionate climax.

It was not until the grandfather clock in the hall chimed two that she realized how late it was. Exhausted by then but elated she fell into bed with a sense of achievement. Her characters were still talking in her head and would not be silent but as her eyelids closed they changed into Sally and Craig and entered her dreams.

She overslept the next morning and was the last down to breakfast, discovering that Sally had already gone out.

"She told me she was going down to the Quay," Molly said. "She hoped to see Tom Narracott if he was about. He was always so fond of her. Well, of both of you."

But Sally was his favourite, Gabrielle thought. She was more fearless than I was and ready for anything. "I'll walk down and join her, then," she said. "But I'll be back in time to give you a hand with the Sunday lunch."

It was a blustery day with a windy sky and the early morning tide was on the turn, muddying the water. The usual handful of tourists was on the Quay, waiting for something to happen, but there was no sign of either Tom Narracott or Sally. Then Gabrielle's eye was caught by a movement aboard the Bluebell. A head was emerging from below decks, a windswept head of dark hair which turned to reveal Sally's laughing face. Gabrielle shrank back as her sister completed her ascent, closely followed by Craig

Gillard who was laughing, too. Then the pair of
them made their way to the wheel-house and sat
there, side by side, just as Gabrielle had sat next to
Craig only two days before. She could tell he was
explaining the control panel to Sally, pointing out
how things worked and she turned away, swept by
a surge of jealousy so strong it made her feel momentarily sick.

Fool! she told herself as she hurried from the Quay.
It doesn't mean a thing! He's so proud of that boat
he'd show it off to anybody who seems interested.
That's probably the only reason he took me out in it.
I've been reading far too much into his offer to teach
me how to handle it.

But she could not forget the things he had said to
her and the gentle touch of his lips on hers. Confused and troubled she almost ran up the lane towards the church until the sound of the organ made
her slow her pace. People were arriving for the
Sunday morning service and she slipped in with
them, grateful for the sanctuary and peace of the
place.

I shall not tell Sally I saw her, she decided. I shall
not tell Craig, either. If he takes Sally on the river this
morning he won't want to go out with me again this
afternoon so that solves my problem of having to
refuse.

She bowed her head and stayed for the service,
telling Molly when she went back to the house that
she had not been able to find Sally so had gone to
church instead.

Molly seemed surprised, especially as Sally had
not returned, either. Gabrielle knew her sister must
still be with Craig but she only said, "She'll turn up

in time for lunch. You know how she enjoys your cooking."

Sally was late, returning flushed and wind-blown, in a rush of excited chatter. "Such a wonderful morning!" she cried. "I've been on the river in Craig's new cruiser – all the way to Totnes where we had coffee. So unexpected! What a lovely man he is!"

Gabrielle felt Max's eyes on her. "So where were you, Gabby, when all this was going on?"

"I overslept," Gabrielle said calmly. "But I made up for that by going to church. Max, can I borrow your typewriter this afternoon when you and Sally are talking to Andy Doyle? I've something I want to write up for school."

Max's bushy eyebrows shot up. "Holiday work? You mustn't overdo it, my darling. I thought you'd want to be in on our discussion."

She shook her head. "You can manage without me. I'll take the typewriter up to my room, if that's all right."

"Of course."

They were all looking at her now with varied expressions of concern. She smiled brightly back at them. "Don't worry! It's not a big job so it won't take me long."

To be away from them for a while! she thought. To get on with my play in peace while they're all so busy! Best of all, to stop thinking about Craig Gillard while I immerse myself in characters who are harmless creatures of my imagination and accountable only to me!

Five

As soon as Andy Doyle arrived after lunch, Gabrielle escaped to her room with Max's typewriter and a sheaf of copy paper. Her bed-side table was just big enough to take the machine and she sat on her bed to work, first of all reading through what she had roughed out in long-hand the night before.

Her alterations were not yet what she wanted but they had improved her play so much she began to think it might be better than anything she had so far written. Full of hope she wound the first sheet of paper into Max's battered portable and started re-typing the play from the beginning.

As always when she was writing she lost all sense of time and clattered on and on, revising as she went, completely absorbed. Much later, when somebody tapped on her door, she called, "Come in!" thinking it must be Sally.

She did not even look up until Andy Doyle said, "So this is what you're doing!" He strolled uninvited into her room and picked up the pages of script she had piled on the bed beside her. "Another play, I see."

"Leave that!" She snatched the pages from him. "Who told you I was up here?"

"Your lovely sister. She said to tell you tea's ready."

"Well, you needn't have come up! You could have shouted from the bottom of the stairs."

"I did, but you didn't hear me. That typewriter

makes a hell of a racket! It's a museum piece!"

"It belongs to Max." She began putting her papers in order.

"I wanted to see you, anyway," Andy said. "You've been hiding away all afternoon. Not from me, I hope."

"You didn't need me there. I imagine you got round Sally and Max easily enough."

"Well, Sally's accepted the part and I'm doing the play."

"There's no more to be said then, is there?"

"Oh, come on, Gabrielle! I hoped you'd be in on this, make it a real Broome family affair – "

"I told you before. I'm not interested."

"But I am – very. Especially in you. I might even be interested in this play you're writing – "

"No, thanks." She pushed her papers into the drawer of her bedside table and snapped it shut. "Shall we go down? They'll wonder where we are."

She made a move towards the door but he barred her path. "Sally knows we're up here," he said softly. "Of course, she may be wondering what we're doing – "

"Get out of my way, Andy!"

His eyes narrowed and something in their expression made her uneasy. But then he moved to let her pass. "Another time, then," he said as he followed her downstairs. "I can wait."

The others were all in the lounge and Gabrielle saw to her embarrassment that Craig was there, too. His eyes went from her to Andy before he looked pointedly away.

"Whatever have you been doing, Gabby?" Sally cried. "We've been waiting ages."

"She was writing a play," Andy said. "It took all my charm to persuade her to come down. Didn't it, Gabrielle?"

He laid a possessive hand on her shoulder. Irritated, she shrugged it off.

"A play?" Sally queried. "What sort of play?"

"I told you," Gabrielle lied. "Something for school."

"Oh, that!" Sally lost interest at once. "Well, do come and have tea! I must set off for London soon."

"Me, too," Andy said. "But I'm looking forward to coming back!" and he winked suggestively at Gabrielle.

Over tea he started talking about his plans for the play now that he and Max had reached agreement. He would begin rehearsals as soon as he was sure of a grant which he hoped to get partly from the Arts Council and partly from a London consortium of businessmen who liked to put money into theatrical ventures.

"It makes them feel arty," he said, "and they enjoy taking a risk. They give free seats to all their friends and hardly miss the money if they back a flop. With a name like yours, Mr Broome, they'll be glad to get involved."

Max looked gratified but Craig shot a keen glance in Andy's direction. "Have you approached them yet?" he asked.

"Not directly. I've a friend who knows one of the group so I'm putting his name forward as producer. But it's really all my show."

"I see." Craig said no more but Gabrielle could tell from his expression that he was displeased about something. Much later, when tea was over and Sally and Andy had gone, he took Gabrielle's arm and led her into the garden.

"I came looking for you this afternoon," he said, "in case you wanted to escape with me on the Bluebell."

"Oh! I didn't think you'd want to go out again after your trip with Sally."

"That was unexpected. You were invited."

She flushed. "I'm sorry, I had some work to do."

"So I hear. You escaped in your own fashion by writing a play!"

"For school," she said hastily.

"Of course!" She realized he had seen through her subterfuge. "You don't have to hide things from me, you know, Gabrielle. I've had some experience with writers so I know how secretive you can be."

"I'm not a writer! Or not yet!"

"You're Max's granddaughter! That must count for something."

She bit her lip. "You won't tell him, will you? I've not written anything good enough yet – "

They had walked down to the bank of the creek where they stood watching the play of light on the water and the midges dancing under the trees.

"I won't tell him," Craig said, "But Andy Doyle might. He knows, doesn't he?"

Gabrielle sighed. "I told him once, years ago and he saw what I was doing today."

There was a pause. Then, without looking at her, Craig said, "If you wanted me to, I could block this request he's making for a grant."

"What?" She was bewildered. "With the Arts Council?"

"No! With the business consortium. I'm pretty

sure it's the one I helped set up a few years ago."

"You put money into the theatre?" She recalled that she had gathered from Craig's conversations with Max that he was involved in various cultural activities in London. "But that's marvellous! I'd no idea."

He shrugged. "I like to put my money into things that interest me. The point is, Gabrielle, if you don't want Doyle to produce Max's play and he's approached us for cash, I could make sure he doesn't get any."

"I see." Gabrielle frowned as she considered that.

"I don't usually have much to do with the allocation of funds. But I told you his name seemed familiar so he could have tapped us before." Craig regarded her steadily. "So what d'you think? It's up to you."

Gabrielle shook her head. "I don't know, Craig. Max would be terribly disappointed. So would Sally and it wouldn't stop Andy. He'd try to get the money from somewhere else."

"You'd rather he went ahead, then?"

"No! I wish he wasn't doing it! But as it is – " She looked at Craig appealingly, wanting him to understand. "Don't you see? It means so much to them!"

"I see it means a lot to Andy Doyle!" Craig turned abruptly towards his own garden. "I shouldn't have spoken. So forget what I said, Gabrielle! I'll take the short cut back. Say goodnight to Molly and Max for me, will you?"

"Craig – " Gabrielle ran after him as he made for the gap in the hedge. "Don't go like that! I'm thinking of Sally and Max. I'm not bothered about Andy – "

"Aren't you? He seemed very friendly with you today."

"He means nothing to me now!" She caught at Craig's arm and moved closer. "You must believe me!"

His expression was inscrutable. "Does it matter if I believe you or not?"

"Yes," she whispered. "It does matter."

There was a moment when they seemed to sway towards one another and she caught her breath, thinking he was going to kiss her again. But he only reached out a hand to stroke her cheek. "Then I'll believe you," he said roughly. "I wouldn't like a lack of trust to come between us, Gabrielle."

She put a hand to her cheek to cherish the spot he had caressed. What is happening to me? she wondered as she watched him duck through the hedge and stride up the lawn towards his own house. Surely I'm not letting myself fall in love with this man?

She was a long time getting to sleep that night and it was almost a relief the next day to be kept so busy she had little time to think about Craig. Max was booked to give his talk to the Totnes Arts Society that evening and had left it to the last minute to make notes. She ended up making them for him. He was in his most perverse mood and as she was driving him into Totnes she despaired of getting him there in time.

But when he appeared he was looking serene and confident and very much the grand old man of letters in his velvet dinner jacket and maroon bow tie. His silver hair gleamed, his cheeks glowed pink and his eyes sparkled.

"Come along then, Gabby!" he cried. "I thought

you'd have had the car at the door by now!"

Behind his back Molly rolled her eyes at Gabrielle who laughed. "You look marvellous!" she said. "All the ladies will fall in love with you."

He was a great success at the meeting, surrounded by admirers afterwards and photographed for the local press. Even the cynical journalist who interviewed him seemed awed. Gabrielle watched him revelling in all the attention and realized how much he must have hated being out of the public eye for so long.

On the way home in the car he sat silently beside her and she thought at first he was tired. Then he suddenly said, "I felt a dreadful fraud tonight, Gabby."

"A fraud?" She was astonished. "Why?"

"It's years since I've produced anything worthwhile. I gave up too soon because I couldn't change with the times."

"You still have your reputation! Nobody can take that away, Max."

"A reputation only lasts as long as you're remembered, my darling."

"So? Everybody's remembering you now!"

He gave a mirthless chuckle. "Only because I'm going to be eighty! I'm a fossil, Gabby, and they're taking me out to see how well I've been preserved!"

She made comforting noises but could think of nothing really encouraging to say and they were almost into Angel Creek before Max spoke again. "Still, I'd better give them a run for their money! When are the South Bank people coming?"

"On Wednesday to talk about the programme and Thursday and Friday to do the filming. You'll enjoy it, Max. And you're not a fraud. Or not to me and the family."

He patted her knee. "Ah! We Broomes always stick together. And we'll leave our marks, such as they are. You'll leave yours, too, Gabby, I'm sure of that. Just don't wait too late to make it, my darling!"

If she was to make her mark through her writing, Max did not leave her much time to concentrate on it. He pulled out all his old theatrical reviews, photographs and programmes the next morning, wanting her to help him choose what would be most useful to back up his television appearance. In the middle of it all, the BBC rang to say they had found the original radio version of 'The King's Magician' in their archives and needed his permission to repeat it during the week of his birthday.

"Only if they pay me again!" Max said, chuckling with delight. "Today's rates, too! You tell them that, Gabby!"

They were still busy that evening when Craig called in to tell them he had to go back to London for a while. "There are things I must see to," he said. "I'm leaving in the morning so I've come to say good-bye."

"Are you sure you're not escaping from our television invasion?" Gabrielle teased. He was looking unusually sombre and she hoped to raise a smile. When he did not respond she wondered if he might still be annoyed with her for appearing to support Andy Doyle the night before.

"We'll miss you!" Max said. "How long will you be away?"

"Not for long. A week at the most."

"Then you must give me some advice before you

go! Gabrielle's been helping me choose a few items for this TV film and I'd like to know what you think of them."

He monopolized Craig for the rest of the evening and it was not until he was about to go that Gabrielle had some time alone with him.

"I'll go back through the garden," he said. "It's a lovely evening so will you walk down with me?" His eyes were telling her he had something to say and she wondered what it might be. Once they were outside in the warm darkness of the summer night he took her arm. "I didn't want to leave, thinking I might have upset you yesterday."

She stared at him. "I thought you were angry with me."

"No." He laughed awkwardly. "I believe I was jealous."

"Jealous?" Her heart missed a beat.

"I couldn't bear the way Doyle was looking at you. And when I thought you were on his side – "

"But I told you! If I'm siding with anybody it's with Max and Sally. I don't want them to be disappointed."

"I see that now and I'm sorry." He tightened his grip on her arm, drawing her closer. "You're beginning to mean a lot to me, Gabrielle. I didn't realize how much until last night."

"Oh!" She stared straight ahead, aware of the movement of his body against hers and of the persistent hammering of her heart.

"So I shall miss you when I'm away. I've some business to attend to. I can keep in regular touch by phone and fax but for some things I have to be there."

"I see."

"Then there's another – private matter." They had reached the bottom of the garden and he turned her to face him. "But when I come back, you must tell me if you want to go on with your boating lessons – and with our friendship. I need to know, Gabrielle. You'll have plenty of time to make up your mind, unless you've made it up already."

She understood what he meant and sensed his tension as he waited for her reply "I'm – not sure," she whispered at last and heard him sigh.

"Well, don't be too long deciding." He drew her gently towards him and ran his lips over the line of her eyebrows. "Goodbye, Gabrielle. Try to think of me when I'm away."

Then he was gone and she walked back to the house in a dream. Why didn't I tell him? she wondered. Why didn't I say that of course I'd like to go boating with him? What am I holding back for if I'm really falling in love? Is it because of what Sally said about being sure?

Life became so hectic during the next few days she hardly had time to miss him. But in the evenings, after the television people had departed for the Angel Arms where they were staying and she was released from Max's demands she thought constantly of Craig and wondered what he was doing. She was glad to have her writing to turn to then, but even that could not always banish her memories, in particular of his moments of tenderness in the garden when he had thrown her into such emotional confusion.

Once the filming finished and everybody involved had returned to London, Max became restless and irritable. Molly was sharper with him than usual and Gabrielle realized for the first time how much they were all missing Craig. She wished he would come back so that she could take up his offer of boating lessons or anything else he might want to teach her.

It was the anything else that invaded her dreams and even her writing, making the heroine of her play say and do things that astonished her. She blushed sometimes when she checked the script through and wondered what Craig would think of it if he read it and if she dared show it to Sally.

Her sister had not been in touch since her visit and neither had Andy. But that Saturday afternoon they both rang.

Sally came on the phone first and Max took the call in the snug, coming out afterwards quite bewildered by her message which had something to do with the financing of the production of his play.

"She said Andy's having trouble getting his grant," he told Gabrielle, "but that we're not to worry because she's going to see Craig. What's he got to do with it, Gabby?"

Gabrielle's heart sank. Surely Craig hadn't blocked Andy's request – not after she'd told him how much the production meant to her grandfather!

"Don't worry!" she reassured Max. "Sally must know what she's doing."

But she was bothered and unable to settle to anything. When the telephone rang again about half an hour later she flew to answer it before Max could get there.

It was Andy Doyle, sounding so angry she was glad she had taken the call. "So what's going on,

Gabrielle?" he demanded. "What are you and your boy-friend playing at?"

"What do you mean? What boy-friend?"

"Your next-door neighbour. He's stopped the grant I thought I was getting from the business consortium I told you about. Seems he's part of it. So why couldn't he have told me that to my face? The Arts Council won't confirm their funding unless I get outside backing to match it. I've been left with a cast and a theatre and made to look a fool!"

"I'm sorry, Andy – " Gabrielle began.

"Sorry!" He gave a cynical laugh. "You probably put him up to it!"

"No! It was nothing to do with me! He's not my boy-friend, either."

"Really?" She could hear the sneer in his voice. "He fancies you, though. I could tell. But you'd better watch out there, Gabrielle! I've been making enquiries about your friend, Gillard from a bloke who knows him. He's got a woman in tow, nicely tucked away in a flat in Surrey and he visits her regularly. I don't suppose he's told you that!"

"Why should he?" Her heart had plummetted but she kept her voice steady. "It doesn't matter to me."

"Well, that's good because I've asked your sister to try sweet-talking him round. If he's as susceptible as he seems, Sally shouldn't have too much trouble!"

Gabrielle put the phone down, unable to listen to any more. So Craig had another woman and might even be with her at that moment – his private business! Andy might be lying but somehow she feared he wasn't for it was unlikely that a man like Craig Gillard would have remained unattached for so long after the death of his wife.

That hurt, but what hurt even more was that he hadn't listened to her about the grant and didn't seem to care if he disappointed his old friend, Max. No doubt he would deceive Sally, too, making all sorts of promises he had no intention of honouring. In return for what?

Gabrielle's face burned as she realized how near she had come to taking his interest in herself seriously. She knew better now and determined not to make the same mistake when he came back expecting an answer from her.

Six

All through that weekend Gabrielle was left wondering what was happening in London, whether Sally had seen Craig and what had taken place between them. Max prowled about, asking questions she either could not or dared not answer and all the time she was conscious of feeling betrayed.

It doesn't matter! she kept telling herself. I didn't commit myself so it doesn't matter how many women he has hidden away in Surrey! He can have as many as he likes – even Sally if she wants him. I will not let it matter!

But although she managed to suppress her feelings during the day, at night, when she slept, they slipped out of her control and let Craig into her dreams. Then she was in the garden with him, being kissed under the trees, or they were making love in his little cabin on the Bluebell. Worse still, she was back in the dream when they rode the waves together until they were swamped by the huge one that crashed over their heads and they were drowning – drowning –

She awoke sweating then, unashamedly wanting him beside her so that she could put her arms around him and be reassured of his safety. "Fool!" she groaned, realizing that, despite everything, he meant more to her than she cared to admit.

It was late on Monday before Sally phoned again. Gabrielle was in her room, working on her play when Max suddenly banged on her door. He called, "Can I come in?" and had bounced inside before she could answer.

He was grinning broadly. "Everything's going to be all right, Gabby," he said. "Sally's just rung. The money's available so the production's going ahead. She says there'll be one or two changes but Craig will tell us all about them when he arrives tomorrow."

"Craig? Coming tomorrow?" Gabrielle's heart gave a lurch. "Did she say what the changes are?"

"No. She was rather mysterious. Excited, too. I can't think what Craig's got to do with it, can you?"

Gabrielle did not answer. So what has he got to do with it? she wondered. If he blocked the grant originally, why has he changed his mind? Because of Sally?

She was trying not to imagine what might have happened between Craig and her sister when she realized that Max was looking over her shoulder at what she had just typed.

"What's this?" he asked. "It doesn't look much like school work to me!"

"Oh! It's nothing." She attempted to cover the page. "Just an idea I've been roughing out."

Max gently removed her hand. "Hm!" he said as he began to read. "Powerful stuff by the look of it."

"I haven't got it right yet, Max!"

He noticed the rest of the script on her bed and picked it up. "I'd like to read this, Gabby."

"No! It's not good enough."

But he was already glancing through the pages of type. "Mind if I take it down to the snug?"

"It's not finished. I'd rather you didn't."

Max's eyes twinkled wisely at her. "Somebody's got to read what you've written sometime, my darling. This isn't your first play, is it?"

"No. But the others were just exercises, to see if I could do it."

"And this one – ?"

"I'm not sure. I think it's a bit better."

"Then why not let me be the judge? I'm an old hand, after all. I know how difficult it is to be objective about one's own work."

She could tell he meant it kindly but she still shook her head. "When it's finished, Max. You don't mind – ?"

He sighed and handed the script back to her. "You're a chip off the old block, Gabby! I should have known. But promise me you'll let me see it when it's ready!"

"All right." She smiled up at him. "I promise."

"And that you'll let me hand it over to somebody else if I think it's worth an airing?"

This was more alarming. "Oh! I'd have to think about that!"

Max leaned over and kissed her on the forehead. "Just go ahead and get it finished!"

That's all very well! Gabrielle thought after he had gone. He doesn't leave me time to start, let alone finish! If 'The King's Magician' goes ahead he'll have us both running round in circles. Then there's Radio four wanting an interview and the Sunday papers needing up-to-date photographs for their colour supplements! Not only that, Craig's coming back!

She realized that it was this that was throwing her into confusion and had put a stop to any more work on her play that evening. Her brain buzzed with the problem of how to react to Craig when she met him again. How could she behave naturally, knowing he had another woman somewhere? Then there was Max's play! What right had he to interfere in the financial arrangements? Nobody had asked him to!

She knew she was deliberately working herself up into a state of indignation against Craig because she did not want to admit to the more primitive messages her body was sending her. Craig was coming back and she was glad! She wanted him to come, wanted her night time dreams to come true and feared she might not be strong-minded enough to hold out against him if they ever became a possibility.

She was kept busy the next day arranging photographic sessions for Max. A feeling of urgency was beginning to pervade the house for tomorrow would be the first of August and his eightieth birthday was only three weeks away.

When Craig looked in on her late that afternoon she was still working in the snug. Her heart leapt at the sight of him but she greeted him coolly. "Oh, you're back!" she said. "How was London?"

"Much as usual. I hear you survived the filming."

"Yes. Now it's photographers! Have you seen Max?"

"Only Molly. I wanted to have a word with you before I spoke to him."

"Really?" She wished she could control the beating of her heart as easily as the tone of her voice.

"I owe you an explanation, Gabrielle. You must have wondered why I didn't take your advice about not blocking Andy Doyle's grant."

"You don't owe me an explanation! It's Max who

can't understand what's been going on."

"But Sally rang you, didn't she?"

"Only to say the money was available. She didn't say how or why. I suppose she got you to change your mind."

"No. We were already making other arrangements. I wondered why Doyle had made his application through somebody else. It was because he blotted his copybook with the consortium a couple of years ago. That's why I remembered his name. There was some trouble about missing funds. When I pointed out he was involved again we decided we couldn't let the grant go through. But I didn't want to disappoint Max."

"So?"

"I got the others to agree to it on condition that Doyle stood down from any direct control of the money. He took a huff at that and pulled out."

"But now there's nobody to direct!"

Craig smiled. "Sally knows somebody who'd like to take over. She's going to bring him down to meet Max at the weekend. She says he's very good and he admires Max's plays, 'The King's Magician' in particular."

"I see." Gabrielle was troubled. "Andy must be furious."

"He is. But there's not much he can do about it now. He needn't have pulled out."

"No." Gabrielle still felt uneasy. Andy was not the sort of person to take a slight lying down. And who was this man Sally was bringing to meet Max? Surely she wasn't being rash enough to involve her lover?

"You're looking worried," Craig said. "Is there something wrong?"

She shook her head. "What are you going to tell Max?"

"Only as much as I need to. He'll probably be pleased to have somebody else directing. He and Doyle didn't really see eye to eye, did they?"

"No."

"And you won't be bothered with him again, either." When she did not answer, Craig frowned. "There is something wrong, isn't there? Has anything happened while I've been away?"

"Of course not." She avoided his eyes and began gathering up the letters she had typed. "I must finish what I'm doing here. Why don't you go and find Max? I know he's anxious to hear about the new arrangements."

Craig gave her one of his penetrating glances. "You're looking tired, Gabrielle. Max is pushing you too hard. I shall tell him I'm taking you out on the river tomorrow."

"No! You mustn't do that!"

"Why not?"

"There's too much to do here."

"Nonsense! If the weather's good, I'll come and fetch you at ten! I hope you'll have something to tell me then."

She started to protest but he was already leaving the snug. Then let it rain! she thought and glanced out of the window where dark clouds were beginning to obscure the sun. Oh, please let it rain because I daren't trust myself alone with him, knowing what I know and feeling the way I do! He'll want an answer and what can I possibly say?

She was vexed when Max invited him to supper that evening. She contrived to escape early to her room, for just sitting next to Craig at table had thrown her into such a turmoil of delight and apprehension she had hardly been able to say a word. She knew it would not be wise to go out with him the next day even though she wanted to. So why couldn't they just be friends? She tried to argue herself into believing that perhaps that was all he intended but she could tell from what she had read in his eyes and from her own shameful feelings that she was deceiving herself.

The rain came overnight but had cleared by the next morning. Promptly at ten, Craig was at the door. Before Gabrielle could get there Max had let him in and she heard him telling Craig that of course it was all right for him to steal Gabrielle away for a while and that they were not to hurry back on his account.

There was a wicked gleam in her grandfather's eyes as he watched them go. "He's in good form today," Craig commented.

They were walking across Max's lawn to the gap in the hedge and the grass had a new, damp springiness under their feet. Craig's dinghy was beached at his landing strip and they were going to use it to get from their inlet to the harbour where the Bluebell was moored.

"That's because his play's going ahead," Gabrielle said. "Was he surprised that you were involved?"

"Not really. He knows I often put money into the Arts."

"Why do you?" she asked as he dragged the dinghy to the water's edge and waded in, pulling it after him.

"Because I'm not creative and I admire people who are."

"People like Max?"

"All sorts of people, especially those who need a bit of help to get going. That's what the consortium's all about."

He held the dinghy steady and reached out a hand to help her. When she stepped in without losing her balance, he laughed. "Well done! I knew you'd soon find your sea legs."

He scrambled in himself and pushed off from the bank, then jerked the outboard motor into life.

"But what's in it for you?" she asked, still curious. "Is it like Andy said, that you get a kick out of mixing with theatre folk and taking a risk?"

He shrugged. "We're not a charity, Gabrielle. It's always a business arrangement and we don't take on anything that hasn't a chance. It's swings and roundabouts, I suppose." He smiled at her. "But where shall we go today? Up river?"

"Anywhere." She was suddenly glad she had come, glad to be chugging towards the bend of the inlet in the cool of the morning with the breeze in her hair. The wooded banks were sparkling after the rain and she knew that she was glad, most of all, to be with Craig again.

They would go to Totnes, he decided, after they had reached the Quay and had boarded the Bluebell. They would have lunch there in the Dartmouth Inn and, if Gabrielle wanted, she could take the wheel for part of the way. He would explain the controls more carefully to her this time. "You did say you would think it over," he said. "Having lessons, I mean."

She knew he meant more than boating lessons and that this was when she should make it clear she could not commit herself to a deeper relationship. But he was wearing his boyish, carefree expression and her resolve crumbled.

"All right," she said weakly. "I'll have another go if you want to risk it. But it's just for today."

"Why?" He looked disappointed. "I could do with an efficient, regular crew."

"I'm not promising that, Craig!"

"No?" The challenge was in his eyes again, making her heart turn over. "We'll have to see about that."

He let her take the wheel almost as soon as they were out of the harbour and she found a new confidence as they headed up river. He explained things to her as they went and was a good teacher, calm and unflurried. It was not until they were nearing Totnes and had to manoeuvre around Vire Island that he took over again.

"That was good, Gabrielle," he said. "Another time I'll let you bring her in but it's too busy here today."

The town's limestone bridge was already in sight but Craig was stopping before that, pulling in at the old Town Quay with its easy access to the Dartmouth Inn from the street called The Plains. This was a new approach for Gabrielle. She was used to arriving by car and she watched admiringly as he edged the Bluebell slowly in until he found a mooring.

"I'll never be able to manage that!" she said.

"Of course you will!" He grinned at her. "When we go back, you could try it at Angel Creek. But the fresh air's made me hungry so let's go and find lunch!"

The Dartmouth Inn boasted its own paved square with troughs of flowers and hanging baskets and, in the middle of it, a twelve foot high drinking fountain with an old fashioned lamp on top. They found a window table from which they could admire the setting and watch the people who came and went.

"Is this where you brought Sally for coffee?" Gabrielle asked as she studied the menu.

"No. I saved this place for you."

"Oh!" She felt her cheeks warm. "You've been here before, then?"

"Once or twice. I knew you'd like it."

"I like everything in Totnes. It's so old and it has so many unexpected byways. Shall we walk up to the castle afterwards? It's years since I've been there."

"Of course." He smiled indulgently. "But what would you like to eat? I can recommend the venison. They serve it laced with a black-currant liqueur."

"Now you're spoiling me!"

"Not nearly as much as I'd like to!" He laid a hand over one of hers. "I missed you when I was away."

She gave a laugh which sounded brittle even to herself. "And Max missed you! He was impossible in the evenings." I missed you, too! she thought but did not dare to say so and looked down at the menu in case her eyes were giving her away.

The wine waiter approached their table and the dangerous moment of intimacy passed. They were careful with one another after that, keeping their conversation general over lunch. Craig told her about some of the theatrical ventures his consortium had helped finance and she made him laugh with stories about her drama classes at school. They kept off the subject of Max's play and Gabrielle did not ask the one question to which she most wanted an answer. But although Craig's other woman was not mentioned it seemed to Gabrielle that her invisible presence was with them all the time, making it impossible for her to relax.

She could tell that Craig noticed her unease but it was not until much later, after they had walked up the steep High Street, under the East Gate arch with its famous clock and had made their way to the Castle grounds that he commented on it.

As he took her hand to help her climb the mound to the Norman keep he suddenly said, "So what is it, Gabrielle? What's wrong?"

She had stopped to catch her breath. "Nothing. Nothing's wrong."

"Don't pretend! Before I went away I thought I was getting somewhere with you at last. You'd stopped shying away like a frightened fawn and begun to treat me almost naturally. So what's happened to change all that?"

She shook her head. "Nothing's happened. You're imagining it."

"I'm moving too fast for you, is that it?"

She stared at him dumbly, not knowing what to say. They had reached the top of the mound and he drew her into the shadow of the circular stone wall. "If I'm moving too fast it's because I don't want to lose you. Not now I've found you. Don't you understand, Gabrielle? You're becoming all I want."

Then his arms went round her and he was holding her close, seeking her mouth with his and teasing her lips apart until she responded and clung to him, swept up and helpless.

Until she remembered and pulled herself free.

Flushed and shaken she whispered, "No, Craig! I'm sorry – "

"What?" Not understanding, he would have cradled her to him again but she stiffened and pushed him away.

"It's no good. Don't you see? I can't – "

"Can't?" He stared at her uncomprehendingly. "Why not?"

"You must know why not!"

She turned from him and began running down the steep slope of the mound towards the entrance gate and did not once look back to see if he was following her. Out in the street she slowed her pace and eventually he caught her up "I don't understand," he said.

"Then leave it! Please! I'd rather not discuss it."

"But we must discuss it!" He grabbed her arm and swung her round to face him. "For a moment back there you wanted me as much as I wanted you. I could tell you did!"

"Let me go! People are looking."

"Let them! I want to know what happened to change you while I've been away!"

"Nothing! It's what happened to you! I surely don't need to tell you about that!"

He let go of her arm and stared at her in bewilderment. "So you did want Doyle to have that grant!"

"No!" she almost shouted at him. "Oh, forget it, Craig! It doesn't matter. None of it matters!"

She began hurrying down the street and was at the Quay before him. When they boarded the Bluebell she pleaded a headache and sat in the little cabin for the voyage back, feeling miserable and frustrated. That moment in his arms had released a rush of desire so piercing she was left physically aching and ready to run to him if he should call.

When he did not she stayed where she was, reminding herself of Sally's warning not to become involved in an affair unless she was sure it would lead somewhere. And she was not sure of Craig, however much she wanted to be.

They were nearing the harbour of Angel Creek before he shouted down to her. "You may as well try taking her in, in case you don't get another chance. Or are you still pretending to have a headache?"

She flinched at the sarcasm in his voice but climbed up on deck all the same. "I'm not much good at parking a car," she said. "So I warn you it will be your fault if I scrape the Bluebell."

"Just do what I tell you and you'll be OK."

Cool and impersonal, he sat next to her when she took the wheel. They were coming in against the tide so he told her to stand off a few yards from the harbour wall and cut the engine so that the wind could drift the cruiser in sideways. Once she had swung the bow in he left her and went to make the bowlines fast before pulling the stern into position.

When all was secure he returned to the wheelhouse. "You see?" he said. "You'd make an excellent crew. So I shall not give up trying to persuade you."

The manoeuvre had left her elated and not a little proud of herself. "I enjoyed that," she admitted, then hesitated. "I'm – sorry about earlier. But I'd like to think we could still be friends, Craig."

"Of course." His smile was enigmatic. "I don't pretend to understand so you mustn't expect me to give up, Gabrielle. You ought to know me better than that by now!"

Seven

Craig called on Max as usual during the next couple of days but Gabrielle took care not to be alone with him. It was enough to hear him talking and laughing with her grandfather and to have to endure the scrutiny of his eyes over supper.

She was perversely vexed when he did not invite her out again even though she would have refused if he had. Two photographers were arriving for their sessions with Max on the Friday, one in the morning and one in the afternoon.

Max fussed about, undecided what to wear until Gabrielle and Molly persuaded him to dress the way he usually did, in his comfortable cords and sweater. He was taken in the snug with his books, outside in the garden and down by the water's edge, remaining surprisingly co-operative throughout.

The arrival of Sally and the new director the following day posed rather more problems as there was only one spare bedroom and they needed to stay the night. Craig came to the rescue with the offer of a bed in his house, saying he did not mind which of them took it up. Molly was grateful but Gabrielle wondered if Sally had intended sharing her bed with this mysterious man they had yet to meet.

They were expected soon after lunch but did not appear until almost four o'clock. "We made a late start," Sally explained. "Sorry about that."

She was looking radiant, the white cotton dress she wore setting off her vivid colouring. Gabrielle had only to see the expression on her face when she turned to the man beside her to know that he was, indeed, her lover.

"This is Hal," Sally said. "Hal Lawrence. He'll do wonders for your play, Max!"

She introduced them all, bubbling over with her usual enthusiasm. But Gabrielle sensed a change in her, a new seriousness beneath the surface gaiety. She wondered if this had something to do with Hal who was older than she had imagined, tall and lean with a haggard look about him and hair already streaking with grey. But when he smiled his face lit up and from the way he gripped Max's hand she could tell he was genuinely pleased to meet him.

"It will be an honour to direct your play, Mr Broome," he said. "We must talk about it."

Sally laughed. "He's talked about nothing else all the way down! So go on, you two – off to the snug! We'll catch up on all the gossip." She put her arms around Gabrielle's and Molly's waists and gave them both an affectionate squeeze.

"But you'll be wanting your tea!" Molly said. "So I'll leave you two girls to talk while I go and make it."

Left to themselves, Gabrielle and Sally wandered out on to the patio where they sat on the old wooden seat Max had installed there years before. The weather was sultry, a brooding sort of day with a hint of mist over the river and Sally leaned back with a sigh.

"Lovely to be here again," she said. "So quiet after London!"

"It hasn't been! What with television crews and photographers!"

"Poor you! And now another visitor." She gave Gabrielle a sidelong glance. "What d'you think of Hal?"

Gabrielle was careful. "I haven't seen enough of him to say. More to the point – what do you think of him?"

Sally smiled. "You've guessed, haven't you? You must think I'm mad, bringing him down here."

"Well, I've wondered. I thought the idea of taking a part in the play was to escape."

"It was. But I couldn't bear the thought of being away from him. I've tried, you know. I stopped seeing him for a whole week after I went back last time and I didn't get in touch again until we needed somebody else to direct. When he called for me this morning the first thing we did was go to bed. I'm a fool, aren't I?"

Gabrielle laid a hand on her arm. "No. I understand."

"Do you?" Sally laughed, a bleak sound. "When I'm with him nothing else matters. It's only afterwards I despair, when I can't tell how it will all end." She stood up restlessly. "But enough about me! Let's walk down to the water. I want to know what's been happening here. Is your dishy next-door neighbour in residence again?"

"Yes." Gabrielle stood up, too. "He's offered you or Hal a bed for the night if you want it."

"Really?" They began to walk down the sloping lawn to the inlet. "That's kind of him. I suppose I'd better not shock Molly by suggesting Hal shares mine!"

"Does Craig know about you two?"

Sally shook her head. "If he does, he hasn't let on." She looked at Gabrielle questioningly. "Are you still going out with him?"

Gabrielle flushed. "We've been boating once or twice."

"No more than that? I thought, from the way he spoke of you in London – "

"He's Max's friend, Sal! Anyway, I think he's already attached."

Sally raised her eyebrows. "What makes you think that?"

"Andy told me he has a woman friend in Surrey, somebody he supports in a flat and visits regularly."

"And you believed him? I'd want more proof than Andy's gossip! Although, come to think of it – " Sally paused.

"Yes?"

"Craig did say he was going down to Surrey the day after he met me – "

"I see."

Sally took her hand. "Don't look so doleful! That doesn't mean a thing! I'll see what I can find out when I go back to town. OK?"

Gabrielle tried to smile. It's true then, she was thinking. He does have a reason for going to Surrey.

"Of course," Sally said, "you could always ask him."

"I couldn't do that!"

"Why not? Would you like me to?"

"No! You mustn't, Sal!"

Sally sighed. "People kept telling me Hal was married but I didn't believe them until it was too late."

"It's not too late for me!"

"Good. You keep it like that, Gabby, until you're sure!"

They heard someone calling and turned to see Molly waving from the french windows that led into the garden.

"It looks as if tea's ready," Gabrielle said. "We'd better go in."

But is it already too late for me? she wondered as she and Sally walked up the lawn together. If Craig persists, I could easily become as besotted with him as Sally is with Hal.

Molly took tea into the snug for the two men as they did not want to break off from their discussion and it was almost suppertime before they emerged, well satisfied with one another's ideas for the play.

Max was beaming. "It's so good to have somebody who can take a fresh look at 'Merlin' without wanting to chop it about!" he said. "I can safely leave my play in this young man's hands."

"Didn't I tell you?" Sally cried. "He has the magic touch, just like Merlin himself."

She put an arm through Hal's and smiled up at him, her face momentarily transparent with love. Gabrielle saw Max give her a quick glance before he asked, "But where's Craig? Isn't he coming to supper tonight? I want to thank him for arranging all this. You too, my darling!" he said to Sally, "After all, you were the one who recommended Hal."

"Oh, I can always recommend him!" Sally said. "Would you like us to fetch Craig for you? He's offered one of us a bed for the night so we should let him know who's coming."

"Hmm!" Max said to Gabrielle when Sally and

Hal had left them. "There's more going on there than meets the eye. Is she serious this time?"

"Well, you know Sally!" Gabrielle said. "I shouldn't let it worry you!"

Max sighed. "I can't help worrying about you two. Your parents are so far away and I'd like to think you were both going to be happy. Something's gone wrong between you and Craig, hasn't it?"

"There was never much between us to go wrong!"

Max gave an impatient click of his tongue. "I may be a selfish old fool, Gabby, but I'm not blind! If there's anything I can do, you will let me know?"

"Of course. But there's nothing. You and I have more important things to think about, anyway, now that 'The King's Magician's' going ahead. Tell me what you and Hal have decided!"

The talk over supper that evening was all about the play. Gabrielle was happy to let it go on around her because it kept Craig's attention from focusing upon herself. When their eyes occasionally met there was a question in his which she pretended not to notice. She did not even move to see him out that night because Hal went home with him after accepting his offer of a bed.

But the next morning they both arrived early with the suggestion that the four of them should take a trip down river on the Bluebell before lunch. Gabrielle could hardly refuse in the face of everybody else's enthusiasm. She did try saying she should stay and help with the Sunday lunch, an excuse that was immediately waved away by Molly.

"And you can't let me down!" Craig said. "I've been telling Hal what an excellent crew you make.

So come on, Gabrielle! We'll take the dinghy to the Quay and meet the others there."

He was clearly jubilant. He grabbed Gabrielle's hand and began racing her down the lawn towards the gap in the hedge, laughing when she called out to him to stop.

"I told you I wouldn't give up," he said when he slowed at last to a walk. "I knew you wouldn't come out with me on your own but you'll be quite safe if Sally and Hal come, too."

"Will I?" When he looked at her with that ardent expression in his eyes she did not feel safe at all.

"As safe as you want to be." He drew her through the gap in the hedge to his own garden and stood for a moment looking down at her, the laughter gone from his face. "I hope you'll soon trust me enough to forget about being safe. There are times when it's better to take a chance, Gabrielle. Life doesn't throw many of those our way."

She stared at him trying to work out what he meant. Then he moved abruptly. "Come on! Let's get the dinghy launched or they'll be at the Quay before us."

All the way from their inlet to the harbour Gabrielle was silent, pondering over the conflicting advice she was being given, Sally urging caution and Craig what amounted to a gamble. But once they were joined by the other two she was swept up into the excitement and laughter of getting everybody across the water to where the Bluebell was moored and safely aboard her.

The plan was to cruise down river to Dartmouth and call in there for coffee. Gabrielle and Craig would take turns at the wheel. The weather was still heavy and close so Sally and Hal commandeered the sun-deck and sat there, wrapped in one another's arms, oblivious to everything going on around them.

They were some way on when Craig raised his eyebrows at Gabrielle. "I see your sister's not as cautious as you are," he commented.

Gabrielle was steering and stared straight ahead. "So I learn from her mistakes!"

He chuckled. "And is Hal one of them?"

"That's for Sally to say."

"He's married, though, isn't he?"

"I believe so."

"And you think he's a mistake!"

"I didn't say that! I'm not Sally. I can't answer for her."

"But," Craig persisted, "he'd be a mistake from your point of view."

She considered what she should reply to that. "Let's say I wouldn't want to come between a man and his wife," she said at last. "In fact, I'd think twice about starting a relationship with any man who was committed to somebody else."

This was so close to what she supposed Craig's own position to be that she held her breath, gripping the wheel hard to stop her hands from trembling.

"Even if you fell in love with him?" Craig asked.

"I wouldn't let myself fall in love with him!"

He laughed. "It's as easy as that, is it? You can turn love on or off like a tap whenever it happens to be convenient?"

She flushed. "Now you're twisting what I said!"

"Yes. And I'm sorry." He moved closer to her on the wheelhouse bench. "I admire your principles,

Gabrielle. But I think you're deluding yourself. I don't know why you're holding back from me but I could tell that day in Totnes, that you'd come part-way to meet me already." He put a hand on her knee. "So what went wrong?"

She pushed his hand away. "Please! Don't distract me when I'm steering!"

"You think I might be committed to somebody else? Is that what you were trying to tell me just now?"

"I don't know what to think because I don't know anything about you!"

"I see." Out of the corner of her eye she saw that he was frowning. "We all have commitments, Gabrielle and sometimes we can't talk about them. I'm not romantically attached to anybody, if that's what's worrying you." Their shoulders were touching now and she could feel his breath in her ear. "You must believe me," he murmured. "If I weren't free to love you, I wouldn't be here with you now." His arm went round her waist and he drew her closer, making her heart quicken. "You do believe me, don't you?"

"For heaven's sake, Craig!" she protested. "The river's getting busy – "

"So? You can handle it. You're not my special crew for nothing!" He ran his lips over her cheek and nuzzled at her ear. "Special in every way," he whispered, making her so agitated she hardly knew what she was doing.

"Stop it!" she said helplessly. "If you can't be-have, you'd better take over! We're almost into Dartmouth."

"In a moment – " He turned her face to his and

kissed her, letting his lips linger.

"Careful!" She pulled away in panic. "We'll run into something!"

"Not us! We can do it together! Move over a bit!"

Still holding her, he slid along the seat and reached for the control lever with his free hand. To her consternation he pushed it forward to full throttle, then gripped the wheel and began helping her steer, weaving deftly in and out of the river traffic.

"Not so fast!" she cried. "Are you crazy?"

"Of course! Crazy for you!" He laughed and held her tighter, alarming her with his unexpected recklessness as they sped down river. It was not until they were coming into Dartmouth harbour that he began at last to slow down and look for a mooring. By then Gabrielle was breathless, stimulated by his nearness and by the rush of air whipping her cheeks and the ridiculous things he had whispered in her ear.

"You don't play fair, do you, Craig?" she said when he was easing the Bluebell in. "What was all that about being safe if I came out with you?"

"As safe as you wanted to be!" he reminded her. "That still holds good, Gabrielle."

She gazed at him with parted lips, realizing from the gleam in his eyes and the racing of her pulse that safety was the last thing either of them had in mind at that moment.

His voice was husky when he said, "But we'd better go into that later!" He cut the engine and let the cruiser drift quietly to her mooring. "Can you manage here if I get Hal to help me make fast?"

She nodded and he left her at the wheel, emotionally in a turmoil, longing for his return yet still fearful. Can I believe him, she wondered, when he says he's not attached to anybody else?

When he came back he took her hands in his and pulled her to her feet. "You see?" he said. "We did it together and it was easy. It could all be just as easy, Gabrielle."

She came to him shyly but could not resist when he ran his hands over her body and claimed her mouth with his. For what seemed a long time they rocked together to the movement of the Bluebell, delighting in their discovery of one another and lost to everything as their hands and lips gently explored.

Then Sally called from the sun-deck. "Come on, you two! What are you doing up there? Aren't we going ashore for coffee?"

Dazed, they pulled apart then and stumbled down on deck, hand in hand.

Sally eyed them in mock disapproval. "So!" she said. "This is what you were up to!"

Gabrielle was incapable of speech but Craig gave a sheepish grin. "Well, what d'you expect when we had you and Hal for an example?" he said.

"What? You didn't need any encouragement from us!" Sally glanced at her watch. "But we'd better get moving or we'll be late for lunch and upset Molly."

Once they had scrambled ashore she contrived to get alongside Gabrielle and linked arms with her, letting the men walk on ahead. "So what's going on?" she asked. "I thought you were playing safe until I'd found out more about Craig."

"I was. But he told me on the way down that there's nobody else."

"You actually asked him?"

"Not directly. Something I said made him tell me

and I think I believe him."

"You only think?"

"Well, he did say something about people having commitments they can't talk about."

"Meaning there's something he doesn't want to talk about?"

"Perhaps. The trouble is, Sal, I seem to be falling in love with him. And I didn't mean to."

Sally sighed. "We never do! I think I'd better make a few enquiries to be on the safe side. So try not to get in too deep until you've heard from me. Although, from the look of you just now, I'd say you're out of your depth already!"

"Was it so obvious?" Gabrielle glanced at Craig, striding along in front of them, straight-backed and lithe in his jersey and jeans. Desire stirred in her as she remembered the warmth of his body against hers and the searching tenderness of his mouth. "It'll be difficult to avoid him," she said. "He's always in and out from next door – "

"Can't you say you're busy?"

"He gets round Max who tells him I'm not! Of course, he could be called back to London again on business – "

"Or to Surrey!"

The two sisters looked at one another. "You're right," Gabrielle said. "So I'll try not to get in too deep. But it won't be easy. What are you going to do about Hal?"

Sally shrugged. "Go on as before, I suppose. We'll be busy with rehearsals so I'll have to see him. He wants to push ahead with the play now and put it on soon after Max's birthday if we can get the theatre."

"But that's marvellous! Max will be thrilled."

"Hal hates a long rehearsal period. He has other projects in the pipeline, anyway. We'll be bringing the company down to Exeter for the final rehearsals, so you could come along too, if you like."

"Oh, I would! Thanks."

Sally gave her a sly glance. "It would give you a taste of the theatre again. Max tells me you've written a play."

"Oh!" Gabrielle was embarrassed. "It's nothing much – "

"He thinks it could be good. Want me to read it?"

"Not yet. It isn't finished. I told Max that."

"Then I'll give you a deadline! The next time I come I'll expect to see a completed script. So you keep yourself busy with that until I make sure Craig Gillard's on the level. Promise?"

Gabrielle laughed. "All right." She saw that Craig and Hal were waiting for them to catch up and that Craig was indicating a cafe. "He's found somewhere for coffee," she said and could not control the ridiculous surge of joy and expectancy that hurried her along the busy street towards him.

Eight

Promising Sally that she would try not to get too involved with Craig was all very well. Avoiding him not only proved impossible, it also went against all Gabrielle's instincts now that her passions had been stirred. Just seeing him made her feel weak at the knees and when he was not around she thought about him all the time, not even working on her play completely shutting him out.

To her relief, first the weather and then the BBC came to her rescue. At the beginning of the week the sultry heat broke up into thunderstorms, making any river trips an impossibility so she had only to see Craig when he called on her grandfather. They welcomed the downpour which they said would swell the pools and draw the salmon up-river in time for the birthday fishing trip.

When Craig suggested going by road to Totnes for a meal in the Dartmouth Inn she was able to say she was busy. The BBC were recording the radio interview with Max at their Bristol studios on the Wednesday and she was helping him compile a list of relevant dates so that he had everything at his finger tips.

"You're not putting up barriers again, are you?" Craig asked, suspicion in his eyes.

"No. This is important for Max. The interview goes out just before the repeat of 'The King's Magician' so it has to be good."

"Hmm!" She had seen Craig to the door as usual. The driving rain made lingering in the porch uncomfortable but he drew her to him and kissed her briefly. "I shall not be fobbed off this time, Gabrielle!" he warned. "You and I have moved on a stage since Sunday."

"Have we?"

"You know very well we have!" He kissed her again, more fiercely. "So don't pretend you've forgotten!"

She had not forgotten and that was the trouble. She remembered all too clearly everything that had happened between them and the things he had said to her, going over and over them in her mind when she was awake and haunted by them in her dreams when she slept.

Max was in a difficult mood on Wednesday morning. "Why are they dragging me all the way to Bristol?" he grumbled. "Why can't they record the interview here?"

"Because they've better equipment there! Cheer up, Max! It'll be fun. We can make a day of it."

Gabrielle was driving as usual and she felt her spirits lift as they left Angel Creek and headed towards Exeter and the M5. She loved the village but it was beginning to feel claustrophobic, the close relationship between herself, her grandfather and Molly, and the growing intimacy with Craig somehow hemming her in. It was good to be going somewhere different for a change, especially as the rain had stopped and a fresh breeze from the west was driving the clouds away.

"Craig will be up-river this morning," Max said enviously, "trying out his pools. I'd rather be with him than going to the BBC."

"But he's taking you fishing on your birthday!"

"Yes. So whatever you do, don't let Molly find out! We're setting off very early that morning before she gets up or she'd try to stop me."

"You will be careful, though, won't you?"

"Careful?" Max rolled his eyes. "Craig's fussing like a mother hen. I mustn't leave the bank! I mustn't wade in! How am I supposed to play a salmon if I can't wade in?"

He grumbled on but Gabrielle only half listened. Talking about Craig had brought him to mind again, making her wonder what he was doing and if Sally had been able to find out anything about him. She had been expecting a call from her sister ever since she went back to London and was beginning to hope that perhaps there was nothing discreditable to discover.

So when Sally rang that evening she went to the phone quite unprepared as she had been in the middle of telling Molly all about Max's day in Bristol.

Sally came to the point at once. "Sorry, Gabby," she said. "Craig's woman exists all right. Her name's Helena and she's a writer."

"Oh!" That was all Gabrielle could say.

"Hal found out for me. He knows one of the consortium Craig's mixed up with. It seems the affair's been going on for years, even before Craig's wife was drowned." When Gabrielle said nothing she asked sharply, "Are you still there, Gabby?"

"Yes. Yes, I'm here." In her mind she was hearing Craig say, "I've had some experience with writers so I know how secretive you can be – "

"Well," Sally said, "I should keep out of it if I were you, especially as it's been going on for so long."

"Yes. Did Hal find out her second name?"

"His contact didn't know it. Craig only refers to her as Helena."

There was a pause. Then Gabrielle asked, "How old is she?"

"No idea. She can't be all that young if it's been going on for years. What will you do – ask Craig about her?"

"I don't know." I can't ask him! Gabrielle was thinking. I don't want to listen to any more of his lies! I don't think I ever want to see him again. She was full of misery, not so much because Craig's woman was a reality as because he had so blatantly denied her existence.

"So will that be all right?" Sally was asking, jerking her back to attention.

"Sorry?"

"If Hal and I borrow your flat for the weekend when we come down to look at the theatre?"

"Oh! Well, yes, I suppose so. When did you say?"

"A week on Friday. Haven't you been listening? We'll try to get down mid afternoon because we want to look for digs for the rest of the company while we're there. They'll all have to be in Exeter soon."

"You'll need the keys of the flat, then." It was almost a month since Gabrielle had been there and she thought back to what sort of state it might be in. "I didn't leave much food," she said. "Well – a few tins and stuff in the freezer. I'd better meet you there." And tidy the place up, she thought and put a clean cover on the duvet, not altogether sure if she liked the idea of Sally and Hal taking over her bed.

"No need to fuss!" Sally said. "We'll manage. Thanks, Gabby. It'll be nicer there than in an hotel. See you Friday week, then! Try not to be too upset about Craig! He's not worth it."

Yet without him you and Hal wouldn't be working on Max's play! Gabrielle thought as she put down the receiver. She felt slightly sick because Craig had betrayed her trust. Yet at the same time she could not help hoping there might be some mistake, that he could explain this Helena if she could only find the courage to ask about her.

But when he called in that evening, triumphantly bearing a fifteen pound salmon he had caught in his favourite pool and gloating over the way the rain had improved his fishing, she could not face him. She hid away upstairs, bashing away at Max's old typewriter with tears of disappointment running down her cheeks.

The next morning he came looking for her, finding her in the vegetable garden where she had been sent by Molly to pick the last of the runner beans.

"Want some help?" he asked. For a moment he worked between the rows beside her, dropping the beans into her basket and agitating her because he was so close.

"I've nearly enough already," she said and would not look at him until he took the basket from her and put it down on the trampled earth.

"You're retreating again, aren't you?" he said and swung her round to face him. "So what is it this time?"

She hung her head. "Nothing – "

"Don't lie to me, Gabrielle!"

"Then don't you lie to me!" she flashed back. "These things you can't talk about – what are they – ?"

His face darkened. "Things? What are you getting at?"

"A place in Surrey – a woman called Helena – ?"

He was suddenly still. "Helena? Who's told you about her?"

"Never mind! She's a writer, isn't she?"

"So? I've helped several writers through the consortium."

"Paying their rents – visiting them regularly – ?"

Craig caught her wrist. "Look – I told you there was nobody else who meant anything to me – "

"She must mean something!"

"There's only you, Gabrielle! Can't you believe that?"

"No! I can't! It's been going on for years, hasn't it, even when your wife was still alive. How could you, Craig?" She jerked her hand away and picked up her basket. "I'm not going to be taken in like that, even if she was!"

"Gabrielle!" He pulled her back to him, knocking the basket from her hand and spilling the beans on to the earth. "I'd like to tell you but I can't just yet. There are other people involved. You must trust me!" His arms went round her and he held her close, kissing her forehead, her cheeks and then her lips until she relaxed against him with a sigh as desire quickened and the old magic took hold.

"I can't do without you," he murmured. "And you can't do without me, you know you can't."

His hands slid under her sweater to her bare shoulder blades and she shuddered as his fingers traced the pattern of her spine. "I want you so!" he muttered. "I've wanted you ever since that morning when you stood under my balcony, looking up at me – "

He was pressing her back against the bean canes and she felt the fallen pods scrunching under her feet. "The beans!" she cried and pulled away from him. "We're spoiling them – "

"We can pick some more! We can do it together, like on the Bluebell. We could do everything together, Gabrielle. Wouldn't you like that?"

Of course I'd like that! she thought. But how can I be sure of you after what Sally's told me?

Troubled, she stared into his face as if she could find the answer there and saw his lips tighten. "Well?" he asked.

She shook her head. "I don't know. I don't like secrets, Craig."

"But if I promise to tell you as soon as I can – ?"

She hesitated. "Perhaps."

"Then that's good enough for now!" The taut muscles of his face relaxed. "It'll mean I'll have to go away again for a few days – "

"And miss such good fishing?" She wished she could recall the gibe when she saw the hurt in his eyes.

He reached out a hand to smooth her tousled hair. "You mean more to me than a few fishing trips," he said sombrely. "I hope I'll be able to convince you of that." He picked up her basket and began collecting the fallen beans. "We'd better do something about these or Molly will come looking for us."

He left that same afternoon, telling no-one where he was going, not even Max. Gabrielle suspected he was off to Surrey to see the mysterious Helena and kept wondering what she was like and what the relationship was between her and Craig. He had seemed so sincere in his protestations of love for herself she found it difficult not to believe him. Yet he had apparently deceived his wife for years.

The disturbing thought occurred to her that perhaps her drowning had not been an accident. Suppose she had found out about Helena? Anything could have happened that day on the river if she and Craig had had a violent quarrel.

No! Gabrielle thought. I mustn't think such dreadful things! Didn't Molly say how heart-broken he was when his wife was drowned?

She dismissed the idea from her mind but could not shut out Helena so easily. She was becoming an obsession and Gabrielle could not stop thinking about her, especially what kind of writer she was and if she had been published. She slept badly that night and could settle to nothing the next day so she asked Max if he would mind if she went to Exeter to clean up her flat and collect any post that might be there.

She spent the afternoon working out her frustration in an orgy of tidying and polishing and before she left looked out some of her earlier attempts at playwriting in case she felt inspired to improve them. With Sally's deadline in mind, she had almost completed her revisions of the play her sister and Max wanted to read.

Tired and more at peace with herself she returned to find her grandfather in a state of excitement. He had had a phone call from the theatrical magazine 'Stage', he told her, wanting to know all about the forthcoming production of 'The King's Magician', who was going to direct it and how it would be subsidised.

"Such a lot of questions!" he said. "The young woman was most interested. She'd heard all about you and Sally and how Craig is being so helpful – "

"Craig?" Gabrielle glanced sharply at Max. "What had she heard about him?"

"That he's part of the consortium. Such a pleasant young woman! She congratulated me on my birthday. And she was very impressed that we have Hal Lawrence directing. Seems he's quite a catch."

Gabrielle frowned. "I hope you didn't say too much."

"I didn't need to, my darling. She knew most of it already. She's promised me a good write-up in this week's issue so we must order a copy."

Gabrielle knew how difficult it was to persuade the local newsagents to order anything different from their usual stock of papers so she did not even try. Max soon forgot about it, anyway. The weather turned very warm and he took to sitting out in the garden instead of in the snug, reading and dozing on his old wooden seat and waiting for Craig to come back. But Craig stayed away all that weekend.

Now that most of her grandfather's interviews were over, Gabrielle had more time to herself, so she worked at her writing in an effort to stop thinking about Craig and Helena. When that failed she strolled down to the Quay to chat to Tom Narracott.

"What's this I hear about Mr Broome going fishing on his birthday?" Tom asked. "'Tis a few years since he was up river."

"I know. Mr Gillard's taking him."

Tom chuckled. "He told me. Seems he's having

trouble getting your grandfather to say he'll keep to the bank. Wants to go wading in like he used to."

"He shouldn't be going at all! Molly wouldn't let him if she knew."

"Well! You're only eighty once. Don't you worry, Miss Broome. He'll be all right with Mr Gillard. A good man, he is. You can trust him to look after your grandfather."

It seems everybody can trust him except me! Gabrielle thought as she walked back to the house. She was beginning to feel ashamed of her doubts and wishing that Craig would come back so that she could tell him so.

She had still heard nothing from him so when the phone rang late on Wednesday afternoon she hurried to answer it, thinking it might be he. But it was Andy Doyle and she could tell from the triumph in his voice that he had something unpleasant to tell her.

"Seen today's papers?" he asked. "Bit of a shock for Mr Broome, I'll bet."

"What? What do you mean?"

"The story broke in the 'Stage' but the tabloids have picked it up. I warned you against your friend, Gillard, didn't I?"

"I don't know what you're talking about, Andy!"

"Well, if you haven't seen a paper yet you'd better get along to your newsagents before they sell out! It'll be all over the village by now."

"What will?"

"Oh, I won't spoil the surprise by telling you!" She could imagine his spiteful grin at the other end of the line as he rang off.

Dismayed, she put down the receiver, wondering what Max could possibly have said to the journalist from the 'Stage' to have interested the tabloids. And why was Andy Doyle so pleased with himself?

She snatched up her purse and ran out of the house and down the lane to the newsagents, getting there just as the shop was about to close.

There were only a few papers left and she began feverishly searching through them.

The girl behind the counter watched her curiously. "Looking for the bit about Mr Broome's play?" she asked. "Not very nice, having that sort of thing written about you, is it? Want me to find it?" She took the papers from Gabrielle and began thumbing through them. "There's only a paragraph in this one but a half page here. See?"

Gabrielle scanned the headlines with horror. "Broome play funded for sex," one read, and the other, "Financier in scandal over arts funds."

"I'll take these," she muttered, her face hot as she fumbled in her purse. "But it will be a mistake – "

"That's what I told everybody who's been in. I mean, we all know Mr Broome."

"Yes. Well – thanks – "

She escaped with relief from the shop, stopping on her way back to read the reports in full.

They were both written in a sickening tone of righteous indignation, questioning the way Craig's consortium allocated its grants. The insinuation was that its members were not above favouring their friends and their mistresses. A 'reliable source', quoted in one paper, had revealed that a large sum of money, disguised as a bursary, had been given to a woman writer whose lover was a well-known financier and one of the group.

The heaviest attacks were reserved for Max's play,

the reports suggesting it was only being subsidized because Max had two nubile granddaughters who were only too happy to use their charms on his behalf. One was the lover of the financier concerned and the other was sleeping with the director. "Have a happy eightieth birthday, Mr Broome!" the paper concluded. "We think you deserve it!"

"This is monstrous!" Gabrielle blurted out. She was certain who the "reliable source" had been and that her grandfather had corroborated the story in all innocence. So this was how Andy was taking his revenge!

I mustn't let Max see these! she thought and pushed the papers into the refuse bin when she reached the house. She wondered if Sally had seen them or Craig. He would be furious if he had.

Because it's so unfair! she raged inwardly. Even if we were lovers, Craig isn't the sort of person to use his influence like that!

Then she remembered, uncomfortably, that he had offered to block Andy's request for a grant if she had wanted him to and had afterwards persuaded the consortium to agree to it when Andy withdrew. So who had he been hoping to please by doing that, herself or Max? And why? Because he believed in the play or because he hoped eventually to get her into his bed just as he had his friend, Helena?

She was tormented by doubts again, especially when Craig did not come back and she heard nothing from him. It was Sally who rang that evening, asking if she had seen the press reports. She had tried to ring Craig at his flat, she told Gabrielle, but could get no answer.

"Because I think he should sue," she said. "He

can't let them get away with this! What does Max say?"

"He doesn't know. I threw the papers away. I've a feeling Molly may have heard something in the village because she's gone all quiet."

"Well, I think it's rotten! It could spoil the birthday celebrations."

"Will it hurt the play, d'you think?"

"Hal says not, that any publicity's good publicity. But I'm not so sure. When are the parents coming over? They'll be livid."

"Next week sometime. They're letting me know."

"Andy Doyle's at the bottom of this," Sally said. "You can be sure of that. What a worm he is! D'you want me to pass the word around so that he gets blacklisted?"

"No. Leave it, Sal! The less said the better. It'll be forgotten as soon as the next story breaks."

But not by me, she thought. Or not until Craig comes back and tells me that none of it is true, especially the part about the money doled out to the financier's mistress who happens to be a writer and whose name can only be Helena!

Nine

Craig returned the next day and found Gabrielle sitting by the water's edge at the end of Max's lawn where she was correcting the final draft of her play. She stuffed the script into her brief case when she saw him and jumped to her feet. "We thought you were never coming back," she said.

Her relief was mixed with apprehension when she saw that he was carrying copies of the offending tabloids and that he looked angry.

"You'll have seen these, I expect!" he said and threw them down at her feet. "I've just come from Buckinghamshire where I've been pacifying my mother. Some kind person made a point of showing them to her. I shall sue, of course."

Gabrielle was dismayed. "But you mustn't! I've kept them from Max so he doesn't know anything about it."

"How the devil did it all start? I've given the editors a blast and they say they picked it up from the 'Stage'."

"Yes." Gabrielle hesitated. "I'm afraid Max is partly to blame. Somebody from the magazine rang him to verify the facts – "

"Facts! These aren't facts! This is libel!"

"I know. Andy must have put them on to the story and Max won't have realized what they were after."

"So where were you, Gabrielle? What was Max doing answering the phone?"

She felt her own anger rising. "I was in Exeter. I can't be watching him all the time!"

Craig frowned. "Well, it's done now. I don't suppose it was your fault," he added grudgingly.

"Oh – thanks for that!"

"But you can't expect me to do nothing about it. There's the reputation of the consortium to consider."

"But what about Max? It's his birthday next week. You could ruin it if you sue. And what about Sally? And me? We care about our reputations, too!"

"Of course you do! But we all know there's no truth in any of this."

"Do we? I only know what concerns us, that you and I aren't lovers! But Sally and Hal are! His marriage has already been damaged by it. D'you want their affair splashed all over the tabloids again? As for the rest of it – "

"The rest of it?" There was an ominous glint in Craig's eyes. "You mean about me and my woman friend! I've already told you there's nothing in that."

"But you haven't, have you? You said you'd tell me when you could. That's why you went away. Well, now you're back."

"Yes." He looked uncomfortable. "I've spoken to Helena."

"And?"

"She said she'd like to see you first – that she'd rather tell you herself."

"What?" Gabrielle felt a blaze of anger sweep through her. "You mean I have to present myself to her to prove I can be trusted to keep your guilty secret, whatever it is?"

"It's not like that, Gabrielle!"

"It seems like that to me! Well, you can forget it!

If you can't tell me yourself I don't want to know! I don't want to meet your mistress, either!"

"Helena is not my mistress!"

"I don't care if she is! You can have as many mistresses as you like so long as I'm not one of them! No! Don't touch me!" He had attempted to take her arm. "You'd better go in and talk to Max. He'll be glad to see you. So don't let him down, too! If you upset him by suing the press over this, I'll never forgive you, Craig!"

She stormed away from him and ran up to the house. Upstairs in her bedroom she flung herself upon her bed and pounded at her pillow. How dare he! she raged. How dare he suggest I should meet that woman! And how can she have the gall to imagine I'd want to meet her?

It was a while before she calmed down. When she did, she realized she had left her briefcase containing the script of her play on the bank of the inlet. She peered from her window but Craig was nowhere to be seen so she supposed he must be with Max.

She slipped quietly out of the house, only to find that her briefcase was not where she had left it. So had Craig taken it? Her face felt hot at the thought of his reading her play for she knew she had revealed more of herself in it than was prudent. She would have to ask him if he had picked it up and wondered how she could bring herself to do that after the accusations she had flung at him.

In the end she went along to the snug, thinking it might be easier to confront him if Max was there, too. But her grandfather was alone.

"Oh!" she said. "I thought Craig was with you."

"Craig?" Max looked surprised. "Is he back, then?"

"He was in the garden so I assumed he was coming in."

Max regarded her thoughtfully. "Is something the matter, Gabby?"

"No. I left the script of my play down by the water, that's all. He could have picked it up."

"I see. You're very flushed, my darling. Are you sure there's nothing wrong?"

"Of course! Don't fuss so! If Craig comes in, will you ask him if he's got my briefcase?"

"You could ask him yourself, couldn't you?"

"I'd rather not."

"Ah! So there is something wrong."

"Just ask him, Max! And get it back for me! I don't want him to read my play!"

She hurried from the snug and up to her room. He's got it, then! she thought. And he's the last person in the world I wanted to read it!

It was some time before Craig called at the house. Molly let him in and Gabrielle could hear him laughing with her in the hallway and then the housekeeper saying, "She must be upstairs. Why don't you take it up to her?"

Alarmed, Gabrielle hurried out of her bedroom to the landing, only to see Craig already halfway up the stairs. He was carrying her briefcase and she backed nervously away as he climbed purposefully upwards, smiling at her.

"You dropped this," he said. "I saw you looking for it from my window so I thought it might be important."

"Not very!" She took the briefcase from him, muttered an ungracious, "Thanks," and would have shut her bedroom door against him had he not already blocked the frame with his broad shoulders.

"So this is where you do your writing," he said as he took in Max's old typewriter on her bedside table and the pile of manuscripts on her dressing chest.

"When I have time." She hugged the case to her, standing her ground so that he could not come farther into the room.

She saw the amusement in his eyes as he noted the possessive way she was clutching her briefcase. "I didn't open it, Gabrielle," he said.

"Oh?"

"I was tempted to but I decided I'd rather wait until you wanted me to read whatever was inside it."

"Which isn't likely to happen!"

"Then I respect your privacy."

She had an uneasy feeling that he was putting her in the wrong. "Are you trying to prove something?" she asked.

He raised his eyebrows. "Why should I want to do that?"

"You know very well why! You didn't read my manuscript to make me feel guilty for asking questions about your private life!"

"Somebody else's private life," he said gently.

"But you're involved in it, aren't you?"

He sighed and took a step towards her. "Come and see Helena with me!" he said. "She'll explain."

"No!"

"But why not? She's perfectly charming and she wants to meet you. You're both writers, after all."

"I'm not a writer! I keep telling you that!"

"But you will be. Just as I know you and I are meant for one another." He took the briefcase from her and tossed it on to her bed. "Why fight against it, Gabrielle?"

His arms went round her but when he would have held her close she jerked away. "Don't! I'm not such a fool as to let you get round me like that again! So will you please leave my room?"

"But Gabrielle – "

"Please go!"

"We can't go on like this – "

"Go, Craig!"

She turned her back on him and did not see him leave but heard his feet clattering down the stairs. Then she shut her bedroom door and leaned against it, closing her eyes in an effort to obliterate the memory of the disappointment in his face when she had turned him away.

Afterwards she was shaken by the depths of her misery. When there had been coldness between them before there had always been the hope that Craig had only to explain and everything would come right. Now he had challenged her to accept an explanation from somebody else and her refusal to do that had a frightening finality.

She was glad that Sally and Hal were coming to Exeter that weekend so that she could talk things over with her sister. They had arranged to meet at the flat and she was there before them on the Friday afternoon with milk and bread and fresh fruit, a cake that Molly had baked and a bunch of roses from the garden.

"You're an angel, Gabby!" Sally cried. She kissed her sister, then held her at arm's length. "But you're looking a bit wan. Not fretting over Craig Gillard, I hope?"

Gabrielle managed a smile. "I'm trying not to."

"You must tell me everything!" Sally turned to Hal who was bringing in their cases. "Be a darling and put the kettle on! I'm dying for a cup of tea."

"He won't know where anything is!" Gabrielle objected.

"He'll soon find out." Sally subsided gracefully into one of Gabrielle's wicker chairs. "He's very adaptable. So – what's been happening?"

Gabrielle told her, pouring out all her doubts about Craig and her uncertainties as to whether she had been mistaken in refusing to meet the mysterious Helena.

"But how can I?" she asked. "Would you want to meet one of Hal's mistresses?"

"I've met his wife," Sally said. "I liked her very much. That's why I'd hate to hurt her."

"Does she know you're here with him now?"

"She knows we're in Exeter but not that we're together. She thinks it's just work. Hal's managed to persuade her that those beastly stories aren't true."

"That's another thing," Gabrielle said. "Craig's threatening to sue the newspapers so it could all start up again. I just don't know what to do about him, Sal."

"I see." Sally considered. "Then we'd better get down to basics. How much does he really mean to you?"

Gabrielle looked down. "More than I like to admit."

"Then take him up on his offer! Call his bluff! Go and see this woman! You'll be able to tell if there's anything between them. Even if there is, you'd be no worse off."

"I suppose not – "

"Trust your instincts! You've always been good at summing people up. Which reminds me – have you finished that play?"

"Yes." Gabrielle reached for her briefcase. "I've brought you the script."

"Good girl! Can I show it to Hal if I like it?"

"Only if you really do. If you think it's any good, I'll let Max read it." She hesitated. "So – you think I should see this Helena?"

"Well, I would. Better to find out than be forever in the dark. There's nothing worse than suspicion, Gabby."

"No." At that moment Hal came in carrying a tray. "But here's your tea. I won't stay for it, Sal. You'll want to get along to the theatre and I've masses to do. The parents are arriving on Tuesday and they've asked me to book them in at the Angel Arms. You'll be down for the birthday, won't you?"

"Try and stop me! Can I bring Hal? He could sleep next door again."

"Ah – " Gabrielle looked doubtful.

Sally smiled. "Don't worry! We'll be diplomatic. And thanks for the flat. It's lovely."

"Thanks for your advice."

"Well, what are sisters for?" Sally tapped the playscript. "I'll be in touch about this, Gabby."

When she was driving back to Angel Creek, Gabrielle wondered how she could tell Craig if she changed her mind about meeting Helena. Suppose he's changed his, she thought, or has even given me up altogether. After all, I did tell him to go.

The idea that he might have taken his dismissal seriously bothered her, especially when he did not call in to see Max that evening. She was subdued over supper, noncommital when Molly asked about Sally and Hal, and the cause of a burst of irritation from her grandfather because she had not enquired from them how his play was progressing.

"Really, Gabby!" he exploded. "You've lost interest in everything since your stupid quarrel with Craig! It's time you two got it settled so that we can get back to normal. We've a lot to do before next week!"

"I know! Don't keep telling me!" Max's rebuke was suddenly too much and she jumped up from the table, feeling tears stinging the backs of her eyes. "Stop trying to push us together, will you? I'll be glad when your birthday's over so that I can get away from here!"

She rushed from the room into the kitchen and immediately felt ashamed. Molly came after her and put a comforting arm round her shoulders. "You mustn't let him upset you," she said. "He's fond of you, so he worries."

"Yes. I'll tell him I'm sorry. It's just – "

"You've been overdoing things. And those newspaper stories can't have helped."

Gabrielle stared at Molly. "You know about them?"

"I found the papers in the bin when I emptied the rubbish. I'm glad you kept them from your grandfather."

"It wasn't true, you know, about me and Craig – "

"I know that. But you think a lot of him, don't you? And he thinks a lot of you."

"I'm not sure of him you see, so I hold back and he can't understand."

"Well, it's always best to be sure."

"He hasn't ever brought a woman friend next door, has he?"

Molly shook her head. "Not that we've seen."

"And his marriage was happy?"

"I'd have said so. Of course, you can never really tell from outside."

"No." Gabrielle gave her a hug. "I'm sorry I blew up just now. I'll go and apologize to Max."

"Just give him a kiss. He'll understand. To tell you the truth, I'll be glad when his birthday's over as well. The preparations have been going on for long enough!"

"Let's hope next Saturday won't be an anti-climax, then!"

"Oh, your mum and dad won't let it be that! They'll liven things up when they arrive."

"Yes." Gabrielle was filled with a rush of relief at the thought. "It'll be marvellous to have all the family together again."

She went to make her peace with Max but discovered he had left the dining room and wandered out into the garden. As she walked down the lawn towards him Craig appeared through the gap in the hedge, making her hesitate. But her grandfather had already seen her and beckoned her on.

She went up to him and kissed him. "Sorry, Max," she whispered in his ear. "I didn't mean what I said."

"I know you didn't, my darling."

She saw that Craig was watching them quizzically. "We missed you at supper tonight," she said and gave him a tentative smile.

"I was just coming over. I've been fishing in the

estuary with Tom Narracott and we waited to come up with the tide."

"You're still in plenty of time for coffee," Max said. "I'll go on ahead and tell Molly you're joining us."

He left them and there was an uncomfortable silence. Then Craig said, "That was a bit obvious, wasn't it?"

"He thinks we've quarrelled."

"And haven't we?"

"I don't know. What do you think?"

He seemed to consider. "I think we've reached the stage when anything could happen."

"Depending on what?"

He made no reply but she read the answer in his eyes. "Sally thinks I should meet your friend, Helena," she said.

"Sally's a sensible girl."

"So – if I do – ?"

"If you do, I'll be delighted. So will Helena."

"But it can't be until after Max's birthday. My parents are arriving soon and there's a lot to arrange."

"Just let me know when you're free!"

She smiled again, more easily. "Until then, if we could – well, just be friends – ?"

"I'll do my best!"

She saw that he was laughing at her and coloured up. "You know what I mean, Craig!"

"I know exactly what you mean. So I'll try to hold my passions in check until you give me leave. It'll be difficult, of course!"

"Oh!" She could not help a rueful laugh. "Why do you always twist what I say when I'm trying to be serious?"

"Because you're so delicious when you're serious!" He reached out a hand and touched her cheek. "If I didn't laugh at you sometimes I'd be grovelling at your feet. And that wouldn't do much for my image, would it?"

He took her hand and began leading her back to the house, twining his fingers with hers. The contact was reassuring and she was warmed by it. "About your image," she said. "You're not really going to sue the papers, are you?"

He was a moment answering. Then he said, "Would it worry you so much if I did?"

"It would upset Max, perhaps ruin his birthday. And I'd never live it down at school."

"I see."

"Hal's in trouble with his wife already, so he and Sally wouldn't want the stories raked over again. Anyway, if it was Andy Doyle's doing, he's the one who ought to apologize."

"Difficult to prove though, Gabrielle. Still, I see your point. I won't make a move unless I have to."

With that Gabrielle had to be content. And nothing more might have been said about the matter had not the stories appeared again in the Sunday papers that were featuring Max in their colour supplements. He had ordered both to be delivered and was down early that morning, eager to read what had been written about him.

Ten

It was difficult to decide who was the most angry. Max roared his rage and rang for Craig who came over at once. His cold fury was even more alarming so Gabrielle left them in the snug, considering what was to be done.

She was more angry with herself and sought consolation from Molly in the kitchen. "I should have guessed the Sundays would pick it up," she said. "If only I'd get hold of them first I could have taken out the bits that mattered. Max was really only interested in the colour mags."

Her worry increased when Sally phoned later that morning from the Exeter flat. "Hal's afraid somebody might work out where we are," her sister said. "He had a hard enough job convincing his wife before this. Has Max seen the latest?"

"Unfortunately. He was really looking forward to reading the articles about him and the supplements have done him proud. Yet the main papers have focused on this beastly story!"

"So what will he do?"

Gabrielle sighed. "He and Craig are hammering that out between them. I've left them to it."

"Well, would it help if we made a detour and called in on you on our way back to town? Hal thought we ought to decide on a common policy."

"Good idea! What we most need is an apology, especially from Andy Doyle!"

Not that that's likely to happen! Gabrielle thought as she put the receiver down. So perhaps a dignified silence on our part would be better.

She was astonished when Max thought differently and touched that he was more concerned about the insinuations made against herself and Sally than about the suggestion that he was profiting from his friendship with Craig.

"I will not have my granddaughters smeared like this!" he raged. "I shall demand a retraction and if I don't get one I shall sue!"

Gabrielle had taken coffee into the snug for the two men. "And what about you?" she asked Craig.

"I'm with Max over this. Now that he knows I imagine your objections don't hold any more."

She poured their coffee before answering. "And what about Sally and Hal?" she asked. "What about your friend, Helena? Aren't some things best left alone?"

"But none of this is true!" Max cried, smacking his palm on to the papers on his desk. "It's all a damned lie!"

"Some of it might seem to be true," Gabrielle said gently.

"You mean about Sally and Hal? So they're lovers! What of it? That's not the reason Hal's directing my play. It's because he's such a damned good director!"

"We know that," Gabrielle said. "But does his wife? Imagine how she'd feel if it all came out in court."

"If she's got anything about her she'll stand by him!" Max fumed. "As for this rubbish about Craig! You don't believe any of that, surely?"

Gabrielle could not look at Craig when she replied. "I'm reserving judgement."

Max exploded then. "So this is what your quarrel's been about! I'd have thought better of you, Gabby. Can't you recognize an honest man when you meet one?"

She was stung to a quick retort. "I recognized a dishonest one in Andy Doyle but you wouldn't listen to me. Now look what's happened!"

"This is getting us nowhere," Craig said. "Gabrielle and I know where we stand, Max, and it's got nothing to do with any of this. I suggest we wait until Sally and Hal arrive. If they agree, I'd like to approach the papers through the consortium. That should keep personalities out of it. We could demand a retraction of the stories and an apology."

"And if we don't get it?" Max asked.

Craig shrugged his shoulders. "Then we'll have to think again." He looked at Gabrielle. "Would you be happy with that?"

"It might work," she said. "The main thing is to stop this going any farther. For that to happen we'll have to shut Andy Doyle up somehow."

"Yes – well – I might have an idea about that, too."

He would not say what it was and was no more forthcoming when Sally and Hal arrived that afternoon. They were in time for tea and as it was a warm, sunny day, Molly brought it outside on to the patio and they all sat round the old garden table under the flowered umbrella Gabrielle remembered from her childhood.

"This takes me back," Sally said. "We were here when grandma bought this umbrella. You said it was an extravagance, Max, and that you'd never use it. I wish she could see you now!"

"So do I, my darling," Max said wistfully. "I could do with her common-sense sometimes. Not that Gabrielle hasn't filled in very nicely," he added quickly. "She's very like her grandmother, you know."

"He means I try to keep him in order," Gabrielle said and they all laughed.

Whether it was because of the sunshine or Molly's cream tea the tensions of the morning vanished. They were relaxed with one another and when Craig explained his plan of action to Sally and Hal they were happy to fall in with it.

"Leave everything to me!" he said. "If you're approached by the press refer them to the consortium and make no comment."

"Very sensible," Sally said to Gabrielle when they were clearing away the tea things. "In fact, your Craig strikes me as being a pretty dependable type all round. You might do worse. Have you taken him up on his offer?"

"To see Helena? I said I'd go with him once the birthday's over. So what about you? How was your weekend?"

"Blissful! But we've been working as well. We've seen the theatre and arranged for rehearsals. We've even found a few places for the cast to stay. More important – we've both read your script."

"Oh?" Gabrielle held her breath, unable to ask what they had thought of it.

"It's marvellous, Gabby. Such unexpected passion! Is the girl in it me or you? We couldn't decide. She does the sort of things I get up to but she thinks more like you."

Gabrielle smiled her relief. "I didn't realize she was either of us."

"I'd love the part. And Hal's itching to get his hands on the play and direct it. There's a company he's worked with before that might be interested."

"Not so fast! I want Max's approval first."

"Just don't go all bashful and hide it away again! Make a few copies so that we can pass it around! If Max's play goes well and breaks even we could ask Craig's consortium for another grant."

"No!"

Sally looked astonished. "Why not?"

"We couldn't possibly! Not after the recent scandal! I don't want any favours from Craig or his consortium! If the play's up to production it must be done by somebody who doesn't know me or that I'm related to Max or even to the parents. Don't you see?"

Sally was clearly baffled. "No, I don't! Why so independent? Everybody knows somebody in the theatre!"

"Yes. That's why we get people like Andy Doyle screwing things up! But I'm glad you like my play. I'll let Max read it and see what he thinks. OK?"

Sally sighed. "Have it your own way! But I know what I'd do if I had somebody like Craig Gillard eating out of my hand!"

"You're not me, though, are you? I wouldn't want him like that, anyway."

"But you're in love with him. And he's in love with you. That's obvious. I shouldn't keep him waiting too long, though, not if he's got another interest somewhere."

"You were the one telling me to be careful!"

"Careful, yes! But there's no need to go into purdah!"

After Sally and Hal had left for London, Gabrielle took the script of her play up to her room and stowed it away safely. She would let Max read it once the excitement of his birthday was over and might even show it to her mother and father when they arrived.

She wondered what they would think of Craig and what he would think of them. They would all meet at the party on Saturday. Craig had promised to bring Max home from their fishing trip in plenty of time to get dressed for it but she was concerned that their early morning start might exhaust him.

"He really should have a rest when he gets back," she told Craig that evening when she showed him out.

"Don't worry, Gabrielle! I won't let him get too tired. We'll be going up-river in the Landrover and driving across the fields to my beat so he won't have much walking to do. There's a gravel spit under the bank near the best pool so he can fish from there."

"Is the pool very deep?"

"Deepish, especially since the storms. But it's not dangerous. I'll keep an eye on him." When she still seemed unconvinced he added, "If you're bothered, we could have a run up there tomorrow and you could see the place for yourself."

"I've a lot to do, Craig."

"Oh, come on! You can spare an hour or so in the afternoon. I'll be busy earlier on, getting in touch with the other members of the consortium. Don't forget to keep Max away from the phone in case anybody starts asking questions!"

They had gone out the back way and walked down

Max's lawn together. The sky was reddening beyond the inlet and the sun was already invisible behind the trees. He hesitated near the gap in the hedge. "Does a friend get a goodnight kiss?"

She thought of what Sally had said about not going into purdah and smiled. "If it's just a friendly one."

But even a friendly kiss, she discovered, could be disturbing when it called up memories of earlier, passionate ones. His mouth was warm and soft against hers and she closed her eyes involuntarily, swaying a little towards him. He released her abruptly. "Goodnight, Gabrielle!" he said huskily. "You'll come tomorrow?"

"Yes."

He went and she was left staring after him, startled by the urgency of the desire he could so easily arouse in her. I'm already lost then, she thought, Helena or no Helena!

He called for her soon after lunch the next day. She had thought they might be taking the Bluebell up river but he explained that the Landrover would be quicker and that he wanted her to see exactly what he planned for Max.

"In any case," he said, "the cruiser will only pass under Totnes bridge when it's low tide. We might find we couldn't get back. That wouldn't worry me, of course!"

She saw from his wicked look that he was thinking of the two bunks in his cabin. "It would worry me!" she said firmly as she climbed into his Landrover.

His beat was a long way up river, past Totnes and the little village of Staverton to where the Dart looped towards Buckfastleigh. The mile he owned was only approachable across the fields and she could understand its attraction for him when he parked the Landrover in the shade of one of the oak trees that gave the river its name. It was a magical place, very quiet and away from any sign of habitation, the water lying still and tranquil under the heat of the August afternoon.

He took her hand to lead her along the bank towards his favourite pool. "You should have brought your rods," she said and then remembered. "Sorry! I forgot."

"Forgot?"

"That you don't like female company when you're fishing."

"Ah! That might depend on the company." He pointed out the gravel spit below them. "This is where I'll take Max. Shall we sit for a while?"

He found her a grassy patch where she sat, staring down into the depths of the pool. "Are they in there?" she asked.

"Oh, they're there all right. If you're quiet you might see them."

He sat down beside her and after a while moved closer and put an arm round her. She hardly noticed for she was staring hypnotized into the peaty dark of the pool where the midges danced and there was no sound. Then there came a rippling of the surface of the water, making her catch her breath.

"See?" he murmured in her ear.

"Yes," she whispered back.

Her head was close to Craig's and she hardly dared breathe as she followed the pattern of the ripples. Then suddenly they erupted into a fountain of spray as the salmon jumped, its silver body arched and gleaming in a shaft of sunlight. Gabrielle jerked back with a gasp of delight and clutched at Craig's arm.

"How wonderful!" she cried. "But how can you bear to catch them when they're so beautiful and so free?"

"Oh, Gabrielle!" he groaned and tightened his arm around her. "How could I ever bear to let you go, when you're even more beautiful?"

His kiss this time was not a friend's but a lover's, sensual and demanding. He eased her down on her back and moved his mouth to the hollow of her throat where her shirt was open at the neck. She felt his tongue exploring the cleft between her breasts and shuddered, running her hands through his thick, dark hair. Helena did not matter any more, nothing mattered except Craig and the overwhelming urge that swept over her to give him whatever he wanted.

He raised his head and looked down at her, his eyes heavy with desire. "Sorry," he muttered. "I got carried away."

Oh, so did I! she thought. But I don't care! All I want at this moment is for you to love me and I don't care any more if Helena was your mistress.

She would have pulled him back to her again but he resisted and sat up. "I gave you my word, Gabrielle," he said, "so I'll keep to it. There'll be plenty of time for us after we've seen Helena and there are no more secrets." He held out a hand to her. "So we'd better get back before I'm carried away again! You know now where I'll bring Max and I've shown you my favourite pool."

"Another of your secrets?" she asked as he pulled her to her feet.

"There'll be no more to come between us. I swear that, Gabrielle! Everything's going to be in the open from now on."

"Everything?"

A tall order! she thought. I couldn't possibly tell you what I was feeling just now. You still believe Helena matters to me and she doesn't any more. I don't know why I ever felt she was so important.

She slipped a hand through his arm as they walked to the Landrover. On the drive back they said little for it was as if that moment of intimacy had said everything for them. When they parted at Angel Creek he gripped her hand tightly. "You're going to be busy with your parents tomorrow," he said. "So I'll keep out of your way."

"They'll want to meet you."

"And I'm looking forward to meeting them. But you know what I mean – "

"Yes." She raised her face for his kiss which was gentle and a friend's again. "Thanks for showing me your pool. Max will love it."

His eyes darkened. "It will mean more to me after today, Gabrielle. We must go there again."

"I'd like that," she whispered and fled before he read in her eyes what she really meant.

Later that night, Sally phoned and Gabrielle could tell from her voice that something was wrong. "It's all over, Gabby," she said, "and I don't know how I can bear it."

"You mean – you and Hal?"

"The Sunday papers were the last straw. His wife was so upset he said he couldn't put her through any more. I knew she'd win if it came to a choice between her and me. Because of the children, you see."

"I'm so sorry, Sal."

"I expected it to end sometime but not so soon. And not like this."

"What about the play?"

"Oh, that's all right. We're professionals, after all. But he won't be coming to Max's party."

"You'll come, though?"

"Of course. The show must go on, mustn't it?" Sally's voice broke and Gabrielle yearned to comfort her.

"Couldn't you come down straightaway?" she asked.

"No. We're too busy rehearsing." Sally blew her nose and made an obvious effort to control her voice. "So what about you?" she asked. "How is it with you and Craig?"

Gabrielle reflected before answering. "Friendly," she said at last.

"I suppose that's something. I hope you'll have better luck than I've had."

I hope so, too! Gabrielle thought and wondered how she would fare if it ever came to a choice between herself and Helena who had been Craig's friend, if not his mistress for so many years. Surely her claim would be much stronger than her own!

Eleven

Gabrielle's parents flew into Heathrow very early the next morning and were met by Sally who had found them somewhere to stay overnight. They were soon on the phone to Max to reassure him of their safe arrival and rang again later on to commiserate with him over the newspaper stories.

"Not to worry, darling!" Angela comforted. "At least they've reminded everybody that you're still very much alive! We'll be with you tomorrow. Rupert's hiring a car."

"But what time will you get here? I'm going to be on the radio tomorrow afternoon at half past four."

This was the interview Max had recorded in Bristol. The transmission of 'The King's Magician' was scheduled for the following day and he wanted Rupert and Angela there to listen to the programmes with him. He fussed about the next morning, convinced that they would forget or be late.

"I'm going to tape it all," Gabrielle said, "so it won't matter if they're not here in time."

But this would not do for Max. Everybody had to be there, even Craig, so Gabrielle was getting anxious when her mother and father had still not arrived at four o'clock.

Then there came the hooting of a car horn outside and they all rushed to the door to see Angela and Rupert Broome climbing out of a bright red Peugeot.

"Darlings!" Angela cried as she swept towards

them with arms outstretched. "The traffic! And I'd
forgotten how narrow your lanes are!"

She was all in white, from her sandals to her
flowing skirt and jacket and even her earrings. She
was tanned to a deep, golden brown which set off
her hair, blonde now instead of dark and styled in a
bubble of curls. They all gaped at the transformation
as she advanced on them and kissed them in turn.

"You're more beautiful than ever!" Max said. "But
whatever have you done to your hair?"

"It's for the play, darling. Is it too ghastly?" She
paused in front of Gabrielle. "How pretty you look,
Gabby! Doesn't she look pretty these days, Rupert?"

Her husband was close behind her. He folded
Gabrielle in his arms and gave her a kiss. "She always looks pretty," he said and smiled fondly down
at her.

Gabrielle was relieved to see that he looked much
as usual and as handsome as ever. "Hello, Dad," she
said and gave him a hug. "Lovely to see you! Such
a long time, too!"

"Too long!" Max cried. "But come in, do! It's time
for the programme. Molly, go and switch on, or we'll
miss it!"

Craig had been hanging back in the porch but
Angela noticed him. "Who's your friend, darling?"
she asked Gabrielle. "Aren't you going to introduce
us?"

"Oh!" Gabrielle said. "This is Mr Gillard from
next door. He's Max's friend. Craig – my mother and
father."

They shook hands. "I've heard a lot about you,"
Craig said.

"Really?" Angela's eyes appraised him. "I've heard

about you, too, from Sally, but I'd like to hear much more."

"Later!" Max cried. "The programme!"

He shepherded them all into the lounge. Molly had already switched on the radio and Gabrielle had previously inserted a cassette to record. Craig contrived to find a seat on the sofa next to her. "So!" he murmured in her ear. "I'm Max's friend, am I?"

"Ssh!" she whispered for the announcer was giving details of Max's interview and they all settled down to listen.

Gabrielle watched her grandfather's face as the programme progressed and she could see that he was pleased. By the end of it he was smiling and almost purring with pleasure. "Well!" he said. "I didn't do too badly, did I?"

"You were wonderful!" Angela enthused. "I'm sure your play will be wonderful, too. When's the South Bank show?"

"Not until next week. Will you still be here for it?"

Angela made a face. "Afraid not. We shouldn't really be here at all. Our understudies are standing in for us because we couldn't miss your birthday. Has Gabrielle been helpful?"

"I couldn't have managed without her!"

Gabrielle felt her mother's eyes on her and moved a little away from Craig who was sitting very close with his arm along the back of the sofa.

"Good!" Angela said. "I can see she's enjoyed being here. Haven't you, darling?"

"I always do," Gabrielle said and stood up. "But you'll be ready for tea. I'll help Molly bring it in."

She escaped to the kitchen and away from her mother's observant eyes. There would be questions, she knew and she wondered how much Sally had told her. When Molly and she brought the tea trolley into the lounge she saw that Angela had moved to the sofa and was deep in conversation with Craig.

Her father was chatting to Max and she was struck by the way he was getting to look more like him, his nose a little more aquiline and his forehead more prominent where his hair was receding. The realization that her father was growing older chilled her and her hand shook when she passed him his cup.

"Sorry!" she said. "I've slopped some in the saucer. I'll get you another."

"No. This is fine." Her father looked at her with interest. "But what's this I hear about a play you've written? Sally says it's good."

Max raised his bushy eyebrows. "Sally's read it already? Gabby wouldn't show it to me!"

Gabrielle blushed. "I've only just finished it. I was keeping it until after your birthday."

"But why? We'd all like to read it." Max seemed suddenly struck by a good idea. "If you duplicated copies we could each take a part and give a dramatized reading of it after supper tonight."

"Oh, no!" Gabrielle said. "I wouldn't want that!"

"Want what?" Angela had caught the tail end of their conversation. "What's this that Gabby doesn't want?"

Max explained while Gabrielle wished herself anywhere but at the centre of attention. She caught Craig's eye and sent him a message of frantic appeal.

He responded at once. "Actually, I was going to suggest you might all come next door for drinks this evening."

"What a lovely idea!" Angela said and turned to

Gabrielle. "I'm not really in the mood for dramatics tonight, darling, although I'm sure your play's quite splendid. Rupert can read it and tell me all about it."

To Gabrielle's relief the subject was dropped and when Craig was leaving them she followed him out into the garden. "Thanks for rescuing me," she said. "I'd have hated that."

"I could tell. But you'll have to come out of hiding sometime, Gabrielle."

"That's what Sally said. So I'll let Max read the play and my father, if he wants to."

"Yes." Craig gave her one of his penetrating glances. "You're close to him, aren't you? And much more like him than your mother."

"Sally's more like her, although that's not so obvious now that Mother's gone blonde." Gabrielle hesitated. "You and she seemed to be getting on very well."

"Did we?" Craig raised an eyebrow. "No doubt you'll soon find out why."

But it was not until Gabrielle escorted Angela and Rupert to the Angel Arms that night that her mother told her about her conversation with Craig. She was tired of the States, she said and wanted to come back home. She and Rupert were considering setting up their own company and for that they would need financial backing. Sally had told them about Craig's consortium so she had asked him if they would consider an application from them.

"You asked Craig for money?" Gabrielle was appalled. "Mother, how could you?"

"Commercial backing, darling! Not money in the strict sense. A purely business arrangement."

"It comes to the same thing!"

"Not if they get a return for their investment. Craig's been very helpful with Max's play and he's obviously very taken with you, so I thought – "

"Well, don't think! We've had enough trouble with the press already. We don't want another scandal!"

Angela looked put out. "I thought you'd be pleased if we came back home. We see so little of you and Sally."

"Of course I'd be pleased! But you must find another way! Keep Craig out of it! Please!"

She was horrified that her relationship with Craig might become even more complicated and wished he had no money so that she could love him just for what he was. It seemed to her that his wealth was the chief cause of all their difficulties, even to the way he was supporting Helena. Surely it wasn't also going to affect her pleasure in having her parents over for Max's birthday?

She was edgy for the next few days, worrying whenever Craig was around in case her mother might approach him again. Max was no help. He became more and more excited as his birthday cards started to arrive, demanding that they should be displayed where everybody could see them. Only the repeat of his radio play disappointed him because he said the actors' voices sounded old fashioned, too plummy and upperclass.

"He's getting himself worked up!" Molly grumbled to Gabrielle. "He'll make himself ill if he doesn't watch out."

It's a good job she doesn't know about the fishing trip! Gabrielle thought. Craig had drawn her into the conspiracy because he was afraid Max might oversleep on his birthday morning. She was to set her alarm for five thirty and make sure he was dressed and ready for a six o'clock start. In the event, Max was up before her and already in the porch waiting for Craig when she went looking for him.

"Happy birthday, darling!" she said and kissed him. "Have a lovely day!"

It was a clear August morning, a little crisp with a hint of autumn in the air. When Craig pulled up in the Landrover he had Max's birthday present with him and Gabrielle saw her grandfather's eyes gleam when he realised what it was.

"I've looked out my old rod and tackle," he said.

"Well, now you won't need it," Craig told him. "Give it to Gabrielle to take back in!" and he winked at her as Max passed over his bundle.

"Look after him!" she said. "Get him back home in good time!"

"Don't worry!" Craig grinned in anticipation. "We'll be first at the party."

She waved them away and watched them drive up the hill towards the main road until the Landrover disappeared around the corner. When she went back in she was troubled by an unexpected feeling of foreboding which she was unable to shake off all day.

Molly was furious when she discovered where Max had gone and Angela and Rupert were disappointed when they arrived with his presents. They all looked despondently at their parcels and piled them up on his desk in the snug so that he could open them when he returned.

They cheered up when Sally arrived from London. She was in time for a late lunch and they sat around after it, catching up on their family news. Sally made no mention of Hal except in the context of Max's play and Gabrielle was not able to get her alone to ask her about him. Occasionally, when their eyes met, she caught in her sister's a bleak expression that made her yearn to comfort her.

Craig had packed a lunch for himself and Max and intended returning no later than four o'clock. As the afternoon wore on Gabrielle kept looking at her watch, wondering where they were and what they were doing. When the phone rang at half past three, she jumped to her feet and hurried to answer it.

"Gabrielle?" It was Craig's voice, sounding breathy as if he had been hurrying. "Something's happened."

"What?" She felt a cold hand at her heart. "What is it? Not Max?"

"I'm on the car phone. He's OK but he's on the wrong side of the river – "

"What? What d'you mean?"

"He was fishing from the spit and hooked a salmon. He was having trouble so I went to the car for the net to help him. But he waded in."

"Oh, you said you wouldn't let him do that!"

"I did warn him! He stumbled somehow and went down – got dragged along. I went in after him but there was a current – "

"Oh, Craig! You promised to look after him!"

"I've got him out but he's across the river and I daren't risk bringing him back through the water, he's so cold. You'll have to come in the cruiser!"

"What? I can't!"

"You must, Gabrielle! Get Tom Narracott to help you! You know where we are."

"I can't do it, Craig!"

"You can! You've done it before!"

"Not without you!"

"You'll be OK. Just remember all I told you. And listen! You'll need an ignition key. I keep a spare under the control panel – feel around for it – !"

"What about Totnes bridge? You said the cruiser can't go under it at high tide – "

"It was high this morning – won't be high again until about nine tonight. You should be OK but you may have trouble getting all the way up to us so tow the dinghy in case – !"

"I can't do this, Craig!"

"I'm relying on you, Gabrielle." His voice softened. "Just be careful, my darling. I must go – get back to Max – "

"You'll be cold, too."

"Never mind about me! Just come!"

Gabrielle put the receiver down and ran, dazed, back to the others. "It was Craig," she burst out. "Max has been in the water. I've to take the cruiser to fetch him."

"I'll come with you," Rupert said at once.

"We'll need the dinghy."

"He shouldn't have gone!" Molly cried but Gabrielle and her father were already hurrying from the room.

Sally came running after them. "What can we do?"

"Ring his doctor – and the hotel at Totnes! Say we'll be late!"

If we ever get there! Gabrielle thought as she and Rupert ran down Max's lawn and through the gap in the hedge to where Craig's dinghy was moored.

She was glad of her father's strength to help launch it and to jerk the outboard motor into life but their progress seemed agonizingly slow as they chugged towards the harbour. Tom Narracott was nowhere to be seen and there was no time to go looking for him so she knew she would have to manage on her own. She headed straight for the Bluebell, clambered aboard and threw a rope down to Rupert so that he could secure the dinghy to the stern. When he joined her on deck she asked him if he'd cast off from the mooring rings while she went to the wheelhouse and tried to remember all the things Craig had taught her.

She felt for the spare ignition key under the control panel and found it prudently attached to a piece of cork. Then she took a deep breath. "Turn the key," she murmured. "Power's on! Check the control lever isn't in gear – press the starter button for the engine – push the throttle forward – " A steady throb reassured her. "Now let the engine warm up – "

"Let go forward!" she called, her voice croaky from tension.

The Bluebell began to swing away from the harbour wall so she eased gingerly into gear. "Let go aft!" She felt her heart pounding as the cruiser started to move.

"All clear!" Rupert shouted and somehow they were edging out into the open water of the harbour and towards the mouth of the inlet. She could hardly believe she had done it and felt a great rush of relief and exultation as they approached the River Dart. Only when she was safely out there was she able to relax and pick up speed.

Her father joined her in the wheelhouse. "When did you learn all this, Gabby?" he asked.

"Craig's been teaching me. But I've never taken the boat out on my own before."

"Surprising what you can do in an emergency."

"Yes." She turned to him for reassurance. "Max will be all right, won't he?"

Rupert smiled. "He's a tough old bird. He'll be OK. He'll get to his party, too. You'll see."

But will he? Gabrielle wondered as she pushed the Bluebell on as fast as she dared. They had a long way to go up river and she knew that the stretch around Totnes would be busy. All the way she was imagining Max, cold and wet on the river bank and Craig, having to make the crossing a second time to reach him. Suppose he'd got into difficulties on the way back! She had no way of knowing. Even if he'd made it, he'd be cold and wet, too, and feeling guilty because he'd taken Max fishing against her advice. She wanted to feel angry with him but could only feel anxious and stared fixedly ahead as she pushed the Bluebell on even faster, gripping the wheel until her knuckles shone white.

"Better slow down!" Rupert warned when they were some way on. "The river's getting busy."

They were nearing Totnes and she knew she must slow down, not only because of the increasing traffic but because she had to pass under the town bridge. Craig had said the water would be low enough but she was tense with anxiety as she made her approach.

"We'll never get under that!" Rupert cried.

"We must!"

Instinctively they both ducked as the cruiser scraped through with only inches to spare.

"It'll be worse on the way back," she said, "because the tide's coming in. So we must be quick, Dad."

She picked up speed again, thankful that the newer

Brutus Bridge was higher, as was the one at Staverton when they reached it. The only worry now was whether they could get far enough up river without having to use the dinghy.

"We must be almost there," she said. "Can you see them?"

"Not yet."

"It's getting very shallow." There was an ominous lurch as the Bluebell bumped over a sandbank.

"There they are!" Rupert shouted.

They had rounded a curve and she saw Craig waving at them and her grandfather slumped on the bank at his feet. "Max looks ill," she said and slowed down, trying to make sense of Craig's hand signals and his shouted directions.

"He wants us to use the dinghy," Rupert said. "You stay here! I'll go."

Gabrielle cut the engine and went to hold the dinghy steady while her father clambered into it. She watched fearfully as he chugged towards the river bank and helped Craig haul Max to his feet and half carry him to the dinghy.

"How is he?" she called when they had reached the Bluebell and were heaving her grandfather on board.

"I'm – all right," Max croaked. "Just – a bit cold."

He was looking grey and she feared for him. Once he was on deck she hugged him close, wet as he was. "Oh, Max!" she said. "What have you done now?"

"Been – a bit of an old fool, my darling – "

"There's a flask of brandy in the cabin," Craig said. "Here's the key. Get him down there, Gabrielle! Wrap him in the blankets and give him a drink. I'll take the wheel."

He was looking very pale and his clothes were sodden. "You should get out of those wet things," she said.

"Don't fuss! Look after your grandfather!"

With Rupert's help she got Max down to the cabin, made him as warm as she could and gave him a tot of brandy. Then she left him with her father and took the flask up to Craig.

"Here!" she said. "You need this, too!"

He had managed to turn the cruiser and was already heading back down river. As he took a swig from the brandy flask she asked, "What about the Landrover?"

"That can wait till tomorrow." He looked at her sombrely. "I'm sorry, Gabrielle. It was my fault."

"You couldn't have known."

"I should have known! I took my eyes off him. I ought to have listened to you!"

She sighed. "Well, we all know Max better than you do."

"I said I'd look after him and you trusted me!"

"He's going to be all right, Craig. I'm sure he is."

"But I've ruined his birthday! Ruined it for everybody."

"Not yet. There's still time." She put a hand over his on the wheel. "You're so cold! Let me do this! You go down and find something dry to put on!"

"No. You've done enough already. Just come close and warm me!"

She moved nearer and put her arms around him, then kissed his cold cheek. "I was so afraid," she murmured, "that something dreadful had happened."

"To Max?"

"Or to you."

"Would that have mattered?"

"More than anything." She turned his face to hers and kissed him on the lips. "So never scare me like that again!"

He grinned crookedly and held her close. "Then you'd better always be on hand to rescue me! How was the water at Totnes?"

"Getting higher."

"Then hold tight! We must get a move on if we want to get back tonight!"

He pushed the control lever to full throttle and they raced down river, reminding her of the day they had shared the wheel on their trip to Dartmouth. When they reached Totnes Bridge she covered her eyes and held her breath as the Bluebell slid under it, scraping the awning of the wheelhouse.

He laughed. "No damage done – might need a coat of paint, that's all. I can do anything when you're beside me, Gabrielle, because you're my special crew!"

"Am I?"

"That and much more. Oh, much, much more, my darling!"

Her heart leapt as she saw the ardent expression in his eyes. "Then we'd better do this together," she murmured and put one hand on the wheel to help him as she had done once before.

Twelve

Max's doctor, Molly and all the family wanted to postpone the party but Max would not hear of it. A hot bath was all he needed, he insisted, and if he was a little late getting to the hotel that would be all to the good because he could make a grand entrance.

So Angela, Rupert and Sally were sent on ahead to greet the guests when they arrived. Craig went next door to change out of his wet clothes while Molly and Gabrielle ministered to Max. If anything, the adventure seemed to have exhilarated him for he was full of how he had almost caught an enormous salmon which grew larger at every telling. By the time they were in Craig's Volvo and on their way to Totnes it was a monster which had dragged him down river and almost drowned him.

All his friends were waiting at the hotel and they cheered and clapped him when he entered the dining room. They started singing 'Happy Birthday to you' while he stood there chuckling, his eyes bright and his cheeks pink, dapper in his dinner suit with his white hair and eyebrows bushier than ever after his bath.

Craig took Gabrielle's arm as they moved to find their places at the table. "He's loving it," he whispered. "And we got him here, thanks to you."

"Thanks to you, mostly. He could have drowned, Craig."

"Yes." His face clouded. "It was a close thing. Too close for comfort."

His expression told her he was remembering an earlier, more tragic incident and she felt a rush of tenderness for him. "But it's over now," she murmured. "It's all over, isn't it?"

"Almost."

She saw that he was thinking of Helena but somehow she had ceased to matter. Craig was safe and so was her grandfather and that was all Gabrielle cared about.

Someone had filled their glasses and her father was proposing a toast to Max. They all stood as Rupert raised his glass and said, "I give you Maximilian Broome! Playwright, poet and my very dear father!"

"Maximilian Broome!" they all echoed and Gabrielle felt a catch in her throat as she gazed towards the head of the table where Max sat smiling benignly at them. Her father and mother were at either side of him with Sally and Molly opposite herself and Craig. Angela looked dramatic in a black and white sheath dress, Sally was vivid in yellow and Molly more sombre in brown.

"You're a handsome family," Craig said in her ear. "You look lovely tonight, Gabrielle."

She was wearing a silvery blue, sleeveless dress she had bought specially for the occasion. "It's a wonder I'm dressed at all," she said, "Max kept Molly and me so busy!"

"Well, you'll all look good in the photographs."

Gabrielle had engaged a professional photographer so that the family would have a record of Max's birthday. She saw that the local press was there as well and guessed they had been drawn by the earlier stories. But now there was more drama to interest them as Max related his fishing adventure to his guests. She could imagine the headlines: 'Well-known dramatist nearly drowns on his eightieth birthday' and hoped they might make people forget what had been written about him before.

Max seemed to have forgotten in his enjoyment of the party. The food was good, the wine was excellent and there was a lot of laughter during the meal. When his birthday cake was brought in he cut it with a flourish and then settled down to open all the cards and presents his friends had brought him. Gabrielle made a list so that he would know whom to thank and when that was done she and Sally carried the parcels out to the cars.

"So that's that!" Sally said when they were on their own. "The birthday's over. What will you do now?"

"I'll be around for a while. Term doesn't start for a couple of weeks."

"You're going back to school?"

"Of course!"

"Craig won't want to lose you."

"He'll be off to London once the fishing's over. Anyway, there's nothing decided yet between us."

"Because of Helena?"

Gabrielle shrugged. "She doesn't seem all that important now."

"No?" Sally sighed. "You're in love then, Gabby. Nothing else is important then."

Gabrielle put an arm round her sister's shoulders. "So how are things with you?"

"Oh, I'll survive. I always do."

"It can't be easy seeing Hal so regularly at rehearsals."

"That's work, so we manage. The play's going
well – could be a great success."

"Good." Gabrielle hesitated. "Did you suggest that
Mother should ask Craig about getting a grant from
his consortium?"

"No!" Sally looked startled. "What does she want
it for, this latest scheme of hers? I told her about the
consortium but I didn't think she'd follow it up."

"It's put me in an awkward position."

"I can see that. But don't worry! She's always
coming up with bright ideas and nothing ever comes
of them. Why don't you have a word with Dad?"

Gabrielle approached her father that night before
he and Angela left them for the Angel Arms. Rupert
listened attentively while she tried to explain. Then
he asked, "So what is it bothering you, Gabby – the
fear of more scandal or that you don't want us
presuming on your friendship with Craig Gillard?"

"Both! The family name's been dragged through
the mud already! As for Craig – " She paused, then
stumbled on. "He might think he should help you
because of me and I don't want that. I'd feel indebted.
Don't you see?"

"Of course!" Her father patted her hand. "Your
mother shouldn't have spoken to him. Our plans are
vague, anyway, and you know Angela! If she's offered another good part she'll want to stay on in the
States."

"But what would you want?"

"Oh, I always fall in. If she's happy, then I am."

"Yes." Gabrielle kissed him. "She's lucky to have
you."

He held her close for a moment. "And we're lucky to have you and Sally." A shadow passed over his face. "She's not too happy at the moment, is she?"

"No. But she'll be all right."

"What about you? Are you happy?"

Gabrielle considered. "I think I could be."

"With Craig Gillard?"

"Perhaps."

"Then I'll make sure we don't do anything to embarrass you. We like him – couldn't have chosen better ourselves!"

"I'm glad." She smiled her relief. "I wish you could come back home, all the same."

Her parents were leaving in a couple of days and she wanted to spend as much time with them as she could. When Craig suggested she might go with him on the Monday to see Helena, she excused herself until after their departure.

"Wednesday, then?" he persisted. "I want this settled, Gabrielle. No more secrets! Isn't that what you want, too?"

All I want, she thought, is to have you take me in your arms and tell me that you love me. Because you've never once put that into words! "All right," she said. "Wednesday, if we must. But I'm not all that bothered about Helena now."

"Aren't you?"

"No." She wound her arms around his neck and kissed him.

"But I want you to understand, my darling," he said as he held her close. "When you do, I'll have something to ask you."

So what if I don't understand? she wondered. Will it make a difference? She looked at him uncertainly.

"There's something else," she said. "Mother told me she'd asked you about a grant. I hope you didn't take her seriously."

He looked amused. "My dear Gabrielle, we only take requests seriously when they're presented seriously. It doesn't matter who they come from – Max or your parents – even you!"

"I want no favours!" she flashed back. "Not after what happened with Andy. Have you heard from him – or the press?"

"Not yet. But we'll get our apologies. We've some powerful people in the consortium so the press barons won't want to upset them. As for Andy Doyle, he knows we could hurt him more than he could hurt us."

Gabrielle drew away from Craig uneasily. "You've threatened him?"

"No more than was necessary. Don't look so worried! He deserved it."

But this was the one thing about Craig that did worry her, the power he and his friends had through their wealth to dispense grants just where they thought fit. Well, I shall never ask them for money, she vowed, if my plays ever get to the production stage!

She had shown her script to Max and her father, and Rupert had been so impressed he had begged a copy to take back to the States. Gabrielle handed it over to him the day they all gathered to say goodbye and Craig teased her when her parents had been waved on their way. "So you really are a budding playwright!" he said.

She blushed. "Take no notice! They're biased."

"Well, you know where to turn for support."

"Not with money, Craig!"

He sighed. "You're so independent! Everybody needs help sometimes. Perhaps Helena will make you realize that."

They were going to visit her the next day and Gabrielle was apprehensive. She slept badly that night and when she did drift off slipped into the recurring dream in which she and Craig were cruising out to sea in the Bluebell until they were swamped by the huge wave that crashed over their heads. She always jerked awake at that point with her heart pounding and her ears singing with the noise of the sea. The dream seemed to come to her when she had to make some sort of decision about Craig and she wondered again if it might be a warning.

She was still on edge when he called for her early the next day, looking dashing in his white shirt and slacks with his blazer slung over his shoulder. She had dressed for the occasion, too, and was wearing a full, flowered skirt, tightly belted with a figure hugging top instead of her usual jersey and jeans. So whom are we trying to impress, she wondered, each other or Helena?

"Where exactly are we going?" she asked as she slid into the passenger seat of Craig's Volvo.

He had never told her where Helena lived and even now he answered only obliquely. "Somewhere near Walton-on-Thames. You'll like it. It's near the river."

Before he switched on the ignition he reached behind him for two tabloids which were on the back seat. "Take a look at these!" he said and tossed them on to her lap. "On the front pages, near the bottom."

She discovered their apologies, very brief para-

graphs but to the point. She read them as he started
the engine and drove off. "They don't say much,"
she commented.

"No. But it's enough. Now there are only the Sundays to come up with something similar. At least the
local papers did Max proud after his party."

"He was delighted. Lovely photos of him and they
made a real drama of his fishing episode!"

"Yes." They both laughed and Gabrielle found
herself relaxing as they drove up the hill towards the
main road. Whatever happens today, she thought,
we have this time together so I must make the most
of it.

It was a misty morning with a promise of heat to
come and Craig drove fast once he was out of the
narrow, local lanes and on the main road towards
Exeter and the M5. They talked as they went but
Gabrielle was disappointed when Craig sheered
away from anything that touched on himself. She
had hoped to ask about his wife but sensed she was
a forbidden subject so she made a tentative enquiry
after his mother instead. He told her she had been a
widow for a long time and that he tried to see her as
often as he could as he had no brothers or sisters to
help keep her company.

"You must meet my mother," he said. "I'll take
you to see her once you've spoken to Helena."

It seemed that this was a condition and she
wondered about that. When they stopped for coffee
at a service station he disappeared into the shop and
bought a spray of tight yellow rosebuds for Helena,
making Gabrielle feel a sting of jealousy until he
produced a bottle of perfume for herself.

"This is too expensive!" she protested.

"It's the only thing I've ever bought you!" he said and frowned. "If it's not right you must go in and change it."

"Oh, no!" she said at once. "It's lovely."

But the incident made them awkward with one another and when they drove on again Craig slipped a cassette into his radio recorder, filling the car with music and silencing her unspoken questions.

"We'll have lunch before we call on Helena," he said when they reached the outskirts of Walton-on-Thames. "I don't want her to feel she has to feed us."

He drew up at a hotel overlooking the river but although Gabrielle admired the view from the dining room she found she could eat very little. Craig fixed his intent gaze on her. "No need to feel nervous," he said. "You'll love Helena and she'll love you." He refilled her glass. "Have some more wine. It'll buck you up."

The wine only made Gabrielle light-headed and she walked back to the car in a kind of dream, sitting silently as Craig drove on to Helena's flat. It was on the ground floor in a secluded mews, tucked away and surrounded by trees and he did not ring the bell but walked straight in.

"Helena!" he called. "We're here."

Gabrielle followed him into a pretty sitting room where everything seemed to be painted white. A woman sat waiting for them and Gabrielle realized, with a shock, that she was in a wheel-chair. She was not young but of that indeterminate age which could be anything from thirty-five to fifty and she had a very sweet face with a pale complexion and grey-blue eyes, her mid-brown hair curling to the nape of her neck.

"Come in, darling!" she cried. "So lovely to see you!"

She held out her hands to Craig as he walked over to kiss her. "I've brought you these," he said and gave her the roses. "And Gabrielle's come to see you." He beckoned Gabrielle in as she was still hesitating on the threshold. "Here she is. Gabrielle, meet Helena Fairfax."

Helena reached out a hand to take one of Gabrielle's. "So this is the little girl who looks like me!" She smiled up at Craig. "You're very flattering, darling. It's a long time since I looked anything like that!" She turned to Gabrielle. "I'm so glad you've come. I've heard such a lot about you."

Gabrielle could only murmur her pleasure. She was still stunned that Helena was not what she had expected and that she was the woman Craig thought looked like her.

"Thank you for the roses," Helena said to Craig. "Have you had lunch?"

"Yes. But we could do with coffee. Shall I make it?"

"Please! And could you put these in water?" She handed him the flowers and motioned Gabrielle to a chair beside her. "We two need to get to know one another. I'm a great admirer of your grandfather," she said as Craig moved towards the kitchen. "I've read all his plays. Such an inspiration!"

"Helena's a poet," Craig said over his shoulder. "She's just had a collection published."

"My first," Helena admitted. "It's taken me a long time."

Gabrielle found her voice at last. "I'd love to read it," she said.

"Then I'll give you a copy. Now – tell me what you've been doing in Angel Creek! Looking after your grandfather, Craig tells me. Not an easy task!"

"No!" Gabrielle laughed and soon they were deep in conversation for Helena was easy to talk to. When Craig came in with the coffee his eyes were approving.

"Gabrielle writes, too," he said as he poured for them. "She'll be a successful playwright once she gets round to letting people read what she's written!"

"But I can understand why she holds back!" Helena cried. "I'm just the same with my poetry."

"Like I said," Craig teased. "She's like you! Now, I'm sure you've saved up a few jobs for me to do while I'm here."

There was, Helena told him, a bookcase that needed securing against the wall in her bedroom and a loose tile in the bathroom if he could find the cement to fix it.

When he had finished his coffee he went off obediently and Helena smiled at Gabrielle. "He's so helpful," she said. "So good to me."

Gabrielle realized that Craig's little jobs were a device to leave them on their own. "You've known him a long time," she suggested.

"Yes." Helena looked down at her hands. "You'll have been wondering about me. When Craig told me things were getting serious and that he was in love with you I realized you would have to be told."

"In love with me?" Gabrielle said in wonder.

"He's surely told you so?"

"Not in so many words. I'm afraid I've not been – very cooperative."

"Because of me?"

"Not entirely. I thought I was in love once before but I was badly let down."

Helena nodded. "And now you need to be sure. Well, I can tell you this. If Craig is as much in love as he says he is, you'll never have any reason to doubt him. He'll be entirely faithful. Just as his father was to me."

Gabrielle caught her breath. "His father?"

"We were lovers for years. Of course, I wasn't like this then. We had a wonderful relationship but he was always completely loyal to his wife. It was easier to let people think I was Craig's friend then, so she never knew and she must never find out. Before his father died he made Craig promise to look after me and he's honoured that to the letter. More than that since arthritis struck me down."

"I see. So that's why – ?"

"I wanted to meet you? Yes. Craig's wife knew about me and she kept our secret. I had to be sure that you would, too."

"Of course I would! Craig should have known that!"

"Oh, he did! But I had to be certain. Now that I've met you, I am. Will you forgive me for having doubts?"

"Of course!" Suddenly everything became clear to Gabrielle. "And you'll let me come and see you sometimes?"

"Craig will bring you, my dear."

"Just as he did his wife?" Gabrielle hesitated. "What was she like, Helena? He never speaks of her."

"He will when he's ready. She was a lovely girl and he adored her. But with you – "

"Yes?"

"It's different. Perhaps deeper. I suppose that's because he's suffered and he's grown up. He needs you very badly, Gabrielle, so be kind to him."

"I will. Oh, yes, I will."

Helena smiled. "Then why don't you go and find him? He'll be keeping out of our way until I've told you. Try the bedroom first."

Gabrielle was already moving towards the door. "Thank you," she said. "Oh, thank you for telling me."

She found Craig in the bedroom where he had taken all the books from Helena's bookcase and was surrounded by piles of them. He was struggling with a screwdriver to fasten the staples back to the wall and looked up when she came in. "Good! Have you come to help?"

"If you want me."

He took one look at her shining face and dropped the screwdriver with a clatter. "She's told you!"

"Yes. And I understand. I understand perfectly."

He bounded towards her, spilling a pile of the books as he came. "Then I do want you, Gabrielle! Oh, my darling, I want you so badly!"

"And I want you! Do you really love me, Craig?"

"Ever since that first day when you looked up at me from my garden and I realized that Max's granddaughter had grown into a beauty. I love you so much, Gabrielle, that it hurts. So we needn't wait, need we? We can get married soon?"

He caught her to him and kissed her, at first gently and then with passion, drawing her down on to Helena's bed and holding her so tightly she could feel his heart beating.

"There's school," she murmured as his hands moved over her body. "I'd have to give a term's notice."

"Damn school!" he said roughly as he began loosening her clothes. "We can fix school!"

"And there's Max – and his play – "

"We can fix everything, so long as we're together."

"Yes," she said. "Oh, yes. Because I love you, too, Craig. Oh, so much!"

"We'll honeymoon on the Bluebell – go over to France – anywhere we want – "

And drown! she thought blissfully, drown in our love for one another, understanding at last the meaning of her dream as a great wave of passion swept over them both and carried them away in it together.